SACRED MAGIC

HSA

HARPER SHADOW ACADEMY

LUNA PIERCE

Sacred Magic

HARPER SHADOW ACADEMY: BOOK FIVE

LUNA PIERCE

Alt Book Cover Design by EmCat Designs
Book Cover Design by Mibl Art
Editing by https://studioenp.com
Editing by Cruel Ink Editing
Proofing by Tiffany Hernandez
Formatted by EmCat Designs
First Edition 2021
ISBN 978-1-7332322-7-2 *(paperback)*
ISBN 978-1-957238-16-6 *(alt paperback)*
ASIN B08P3KYN8B *(ebook)*

To nature, for being my inspiration when I needed it the most. To music, for mending the wounds that won't seem to heal. And to heartbreak, for allowing these words to shape past experiences into something beautifully haunting.

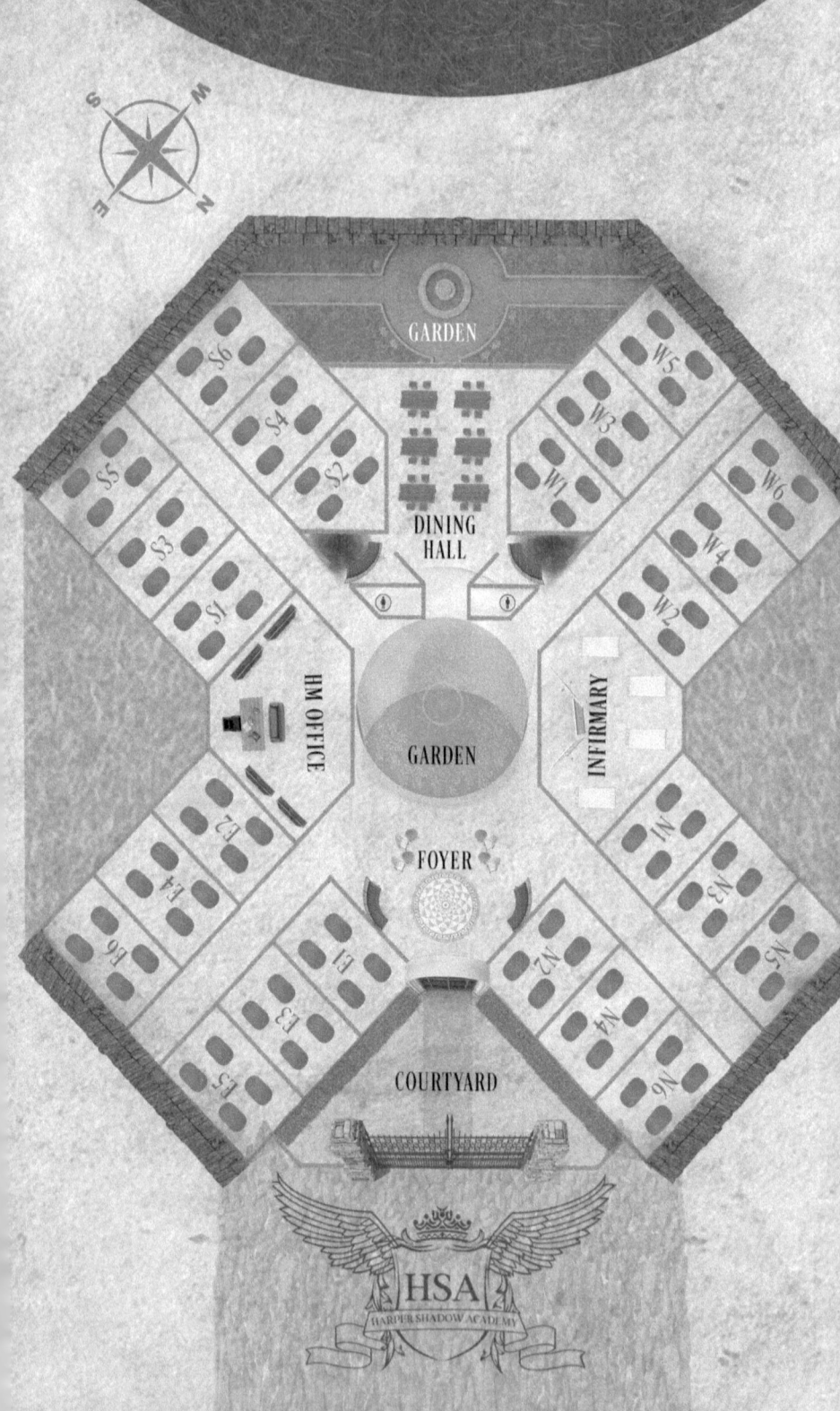

BASEMENT / LIBRARY

PROLOGUE
Silas

I float through an infinite darkness—alone and completely fucking panicked.

A moment prior, Willow's warm hands cupped my face gently. She stared at me with those perfectly bluish-green eyes and whispered that I was going home. Only, the pained expression on her face told me an unspoken story that she wouldn't be joining me.

And there was nothing I could do about it.

I should have acted. Done something. Anything.

I would have been a fool to think I stood any chance against Balial, but I could have tried.

I spent what felt like an eternity in Hell with him, being tortured day in and day out. To be by her side again, to feel her skin against mine, was a shock to my system. Part of me was worried it was another brutal simulation the master of Hell was putting me through. The thing about being completely and permanently in love with someone, though, is that you'll know for sure the second it truly is them standing in front of you. There is a certain familiar comfort in their presence that is so incredibly impossible to mistake.

I ached for that moment to last, for her touch to never leave my pale skin. For her concentration to never be diverted from mine. I longed for a millisecond more.

The truth about reality is, we don't always get what we want.

And watching her body disappear and be replaced by a dim, endless void, I knew I had lost her again.

I land abruptly, face down on a hard surface. Light pools in my eyes, and it takes me a few blinks to adjust.

Hands find my shoulders, and I flinch at the thought of this being another trap.

"Silas," a recognizable voice calls out.

I register where I am. The old sacred building, not too far from Harper Academy.

I breathe in, the scent of sage and pine filling my lungs—a much welcomed aroma compared to what I was forced to endure during my stint in Hell.

The rapid pounding of Sydney's heartbeat thuds loudly in my ears. I tune out the blood rushing through his veins, despite wanting—so fucking badly—to sink my teeth into his jugular and suck every ounce of life out of his body.

Willow may be gone, but I would never risk hurting her like that.

A second pulse registers with me, and it's followed by a musty, dog-like smell. *Deghan.*

Still, it's better than the putrid death and hot burning of flesh I was subjected to.

I tilt my head, finally taking in their long faces.

For me, it was as though years had gone by, but by their

appearances, it may have only been a matter of days, weeks, or maybe months.

I clutch at my empty chest and note the shift in the tether that binds me to Willow. It's faded. Barely hanging on. And that alone fucking kills me.

I'd desperately wished for this moment to come, to be back here, just never did I imagine it would have been without her. I'd trade it all again to make sure she was safe. I'd endure Hell a thousand times over if it meant she never had to experience that kind of torment.

I open my mouth, and my voice cracks.

My fangs ache. They're nearly throbbing with want, with need.

Nothing could ever top the desire I have to get her back.

"Willow," I spit out.

"Silas, where is she?" Sydney plants his hands firmly on my arms and centers me. Tears gather in his frantic eyes.

I flit my gaze to Deghan and am surprised that he's completely silent, except for his pounding heart. Usually, he's the chatty one.

I garner my strength to stand and find that it comes a little easier in this dimension. It was like the gravity was turned way down in Hell and my strength was robbed from me. Slowly but surely, I begin to feel more like myself.

At what cost, though? The woman who shares a part of my soul? I won't accept that.

Sydney tightens his mortal grip and attempts to shake me. "Silas?"

Why is he asking me where she is? There's no way Willow could have done this all on her own. He had to have played a part in her voyage to the underworld. It suddenly dawns on me.

"Open it back up," I demand. This time it's me who clasps on to him.

Probably a little too hard considering the way he winces at my touch.

His green eyes glisten, and he rocks his head back and forth. "I can't."

"What do you mean? You summoned the entrance. Do it again!" I practically yell in his distressed face.

Deghan clutches a stone in his palm and gawks at it idiotically.

I drop Sydney and use what I can of my vamp speed to snatch the rock from Deghan.

He gasps and reaches out to take it back.

"What is this? Did you help, too?" I let out a sigh. "What were you guys thinking?"

Deghan's lip quivers. He snarls at me, and for a second, I'm sure he might shift into his wolf form.

The cold hard thing floats out of my hand with the assistance of a light-emerald stream of power.

"It's not what you think it is." Sydney finishes his task. "Willow gave it to Deghan. They're both connected to it. She has one, too. If he squeezes his, she feels it. And vice versa. She's responded once, before you came back."

I accept his explanation for what it is. Deghan would never have been so foolish to help in this suicide mission. And given what was at stake, I'm surprised Sydney did. "You have to send me in."

"You're not understanding me. I didn't open it. *Willow* did. Even if I wanted to, there's a reset period on this kind of thing. Trust me, I've tried. Plus, there are no guarantees. I'm not entirely sure which Hell realm she went to." Sydney digs his hand through his hair and genuinely looks like fucking shit.

Maybe he's not lying.

We may have our differences, but Willow was always a priority to both of us—to all of us.

I grit my teeth. "There has to be something. You expect me to just do *nothing?*"

"Tell me what happened. Where were you?" Sydney becomes

desperate for any piece of information to guide him toward a solution. *This* is the version of Sydney I don't hate.

"The king of all devils." I internally shudder at the memory. I consider myself a fairly strong man—I was no match to him, though. Neither was my sweet Willow. "I was with Balial."

Sydney flinches, too, only slightly, yet enough for me to note the shift in his features.

Deghan glares at me and holds the stone between his palms, desperately clenching it in hope for some sign of life from the other side.

"I told her not to. I didn't have the strength to act quick enough. She tried to make a deal with him. Her life for mine." The recollection rips my dead and motionless heart in two. "He declined. Said he wanted a *sacrifice*. Balial whispered something into her ear. I couldn't make it out. My powers had been weakened for quite some time. Next thing I know, she's kneeling in front of me with a sad goodbye written across her face. Everything went dark, then I was here."

Sydney nods and absorbs the story, averting his gaze to the wood-planked floor. "Step out of the way." He barrels past me and into a chalk design on the floor. He glimpses over his shoulder at both of us. "I'd back up if I were you."

I disobey and move toward him. "I'm going with you."

"If, and I mean *if* this even works, there's no way you're going. Willow would stop at nothing to save you. It should never have been her." A strange sadness consumes him.

Is he insinuating *he* would have been the one to come rescue me?

His words momentarily stun me.

Sydney hates my guts, why would he risk *everything* for a measly vampire?

That's when I realize, he wasn't doing it for me, he was doing it for Willow.

The same thing any of the rest of us would have done—give up everything for the chance at making her happy. Love brings out a truly selfless nature in people, and in this very instance, for Sydney LeBlanc, I've never met someone so willing to perform a noble act in the name of love.

A new level of respect grows between us.

Sydney mutters incoherently and waves his hands around in his confined area. His power flows from his fingertips and dances in circles.

But that's all that happens. There is nothing else. No magical opening of the dimensions, no portal to Hell. Minutes and minutes go by with Sydney trying with all of his might to break through.

He collapses into a heap on the floor, his face lowered in defeat. A faint whisper leaves his lips, "I can't get to her."

And with that declaration, I nearly lose my goddamn mind.

I see red. Not from Hell, but yet the sheer rage that builds from losing the person I spent my entire existence searching for. How is it possible to have everything and then nothing in the blink of an eye?

CHAPTER 1

The back of my neck drips with sweat from the encroaching heat of the flames surrounding me.

Silas is gone, yet again. And with him, I'm left here alone in Hell, with the Devil himself. I swallow down the fear that threatens to dismantle me.

I can do this; I will do what Balial asks of me.

A wicked grin forms on his flawless face. "Oh, it won't be so bad." He glides closer. "Surely, you can live without it. And that's what you want, isn't it? To live?"

I nod. Not dying is a huge plus, but my main concern was getting Silas out of here safely. "How do I know you fulfilled your end of the deal?"

Balial rushes toward me, nearly throwing me off-balance. He latches on to my wrist and assaults his way into my mind.

A vision appears, clear and concise.

Silas standing above a crouched-on-the-floor Sydney. Deghan tucked in the corner. All of them are perfectly unharmed, considering the circumstances.

"Satisfied?" Balial releases me and stays firmly in place just inches from my body.

I mutter, "That could be fake. A trick."

Balial frowns. "I don't lie."

For some unknown reason, I believe him.

"Now, your end of the bargain. I don't have to say *please*, now do I?" Balial raises his brows, showing even more of his completely black eyeballs.

It's a rather terrifying and mesmerizing sight.

I find myself stalling, despite really not wanting to be here any longer. The thought of following through with his demand is incredibly unsettling.

Ever since I discovered my power, I have fought tooth and nail to protect it.

I thought I could offer him my life in exchange for Silas, but it's not me he desires, it's my magic.

"See, keeping you here is a bit senseless if you ask me. I could have easily taken you up on your offer and traded your life for that pathetic bloodsucker. Why you would risk it all for his kind is beyond me." He shrugs. "But then you could resist and disallow me from channeling your power, which would make this so incredibly daunting. And, the obvious part about the never-ending succession of people who would stop at nothing to come after you. They're actively in the process of it at this very moment. As fun as that sounds, this whole process would be much better for the both of us if you gave it to me willingly."

If they're attempting to summon another portal, I either need to stall more and wait for them, or move quicker so no one else ends up here. And considering Balial seems to be in charge of who leaves this place, the latter is the best and only option. I cannot afford to have anyone else I love put in danger because of me. I won't allow it.

"You'll actually let me go?" The words barely make their way out of my mouth.

He clutches his chest. "I am a man of my word."

For a master of Hell, he sure is polite at times.

I reach out my hand. "Do what you need to do."

"Actually, dear..." Balial grabs on to me and pulls me close. "Relax."

For a second, I'm frightened he's going to kiss me.

His palms encase my cheeks, and his nose rubs gently on mine. His endless pools of black eyes stare deeply at me.

I fight back the urge to panic.

Balial mutters, "Relax," and takes in a breath, creating a siphon to my depth of magic.

With resistance, my powers cling tightly to my being. Eventually, they are no match for his sheer strength.

We stay like this for an uncomfortable minute until every last ounce of my supernatural ability is gone. It's as though someone deflated my entire body, sucked out all the life, and left a strange and empty vessel.

He releases me and yelps. "Whew." He flails his arms to the sides, and a sprinkle of pink spritzes out.

The aching pit that Silas once created with his absence, which was temporarily closed with his return, has been reopened by the loss of my true self.

What have I done?

I stumble and nearly trip over my own feet.

Balial steadies me, snatching me by my waist. "Are you all right?"

I force a nod.

He lets go to test out his new powers by juggling glowing orbs of energy. "Willow Victoria Oliver. It was a pleasure doing business with you." He lets all six spheres land in his left hand. He claps his palms together, creating a massive current, and blacks out my vision.

I reach for something to hold on to as I spin out of control through the newfound abyss.

Moments pass of nothing but an infinite darkness. I'm alone. Completely and utterly by myself swimming in the depths of this void. Not even my magic can keep me company now.

A tear rolls down my cheek, and a bright light appears. I land with a thud onto the same floorboards I had kneeled upon and summoned a gate to Hell.

I blink, hoping with all my might the person in front of me is real.

I stifle in a sob that's forcing its way up my chest. I hold his face in my palms, running my thumb along his cheek, savoring the very realness that he's actually here. I find comfort in his presence, something I had convinced myself I would never feel again. I breathe him in, and somehow, underneath the rotting decay of Hell caked onto his damaged body, he's still there.

My Silas, he's back.

And that's all that matters. He's safe. He's alive. Not even the endless depths that once was the limitless pool of my magic, now gone and forever lost could take me from this moment with him.

Magic is fleeting. It's something that one can live without.

What Silas and I share? That's a sacred bond that has no bounds and cannot be replaced.

And for now, that will have to be enough.

CHAPTER 2

"Are you...are you okay?" Silas anxiously studies my body for any sign of injury.

I bite at my lip to attempt to hide my overwhelming emotions. Does completely giving all of your magic to the Devil count toward being *okay*? "Yeah," I manage to say.

Sydney reaches out to me like I might not be real. A sense of relief washes across his beautiful face. His tense shoulders relax, and a weight that seems heavier than the world falls off him.

The air is cool and filled with various burning scents, but none like the Hell I was just in moments prior. I struggle to register my surroundings and the energy in the room. Along with my power, I must have lost the ability to identify the emotions of others. I'll have to learn how to rely on picking up on body language cues.

Silas gently grabs on to my arm and gasps. "Will…"

I lower my gaze, and like the pain decided to wait until I acknowledged it, the dirty wound sends spikes of agony through my whole side. That must have been where the acid-like saliva from that creature hit me.

I register the memory, and flames form in my vision, reminding me of the burns all up and down my skin. None of it compares to the agony of living the last few weeks without Silas. And if I had to do it all again to come to this same conclusion, I would in a heartbeat. Nothing would stop me from saving Silas, not even the depths of Hell.

Deghan fights his way around Sydney and Silas and into my line of sight. He grips the stone I gave him for his birthday tightly in his hand. "I got so worried when I kept reaching out and you didn't respond."

I rest my palm on top of his. "I'm here now." Instinctually, I try to push my calming energy into him, but nothing comes out. I'm an empty vessel. I do my best to comfort him with my very mundane touch.

"Are you good? Can you walk?" Sydney clutches my elbow to help me from the floor.

I stand with ease although my body feels incredibly heavy without my magic flowing through it. Another thing I'll have to learn how to deal with.

Even prior to recognizing that I had powers, it still ran through my veins. It laid in wait for the opportune safe moment to present itself. Now, there's this vacant nothing inside me. My magic was always rooted so closely to my soul—a permanent part of my very being that is now gone.

If I'm being honest, I'm embarrassed. I feel less of a woman, less of the person I was. Without my abilities, I'm not so sure I even know who I am or what my purpose in life is. To say I'm lost would be an understatement. How will anyone ever see me the same if I don't have it? Will my guys still want to be with me once they find out? It's one thing to be an ordinary human, but to be a witch stripped of her powers, that's something to be ashamed of.

So, for now, I will glue my mouth shut and keep my secret to myself. At least until I can process the majorly violating life change I just experienced.

We walk in silence to the shadowy academy. The fallen leaves crumble beneath us, and the faint crackling of branches sound in the distance with the scurrying of animals from our proximity.

Silas's hand doesn't leave my lower back the entire distance.

We're both covered in dirt and debris with various injuries on our bodies.

His once immaculate leather jacket has burn marks and tears on it.

How he managed to keep it intact during his stay in Hell is a mystery in itself.

"Do you mind if I steal her?" Silas finally breaks through the awkward quiet.

"Sure," Sydney responds. He pulls me into his arms. "You need to tend to those wounds soon. You don't want them to get infected."

I'm well aware there's more he wants to say, like ripping my ass for descending into Hell without him, but thankfully, he keeps it to himself for now.

Deghan doesn't skip a beat—he reels Silas in and hugs him tight. "I missed you, dude. We're all glad to have you home."

Silas hesitates and then slaps Deghan on the back in a reciprocating manly embrace.

The two of them break away and Sydney extends his hand to Silas.

Silas studies the offering suspiciously but ends up gripping it firmly. They nod at one another in some silent agreement.

Deghan and Sydney leave me and Silas behind.

We ignore the passing students and their awkward glances at our disheveled appearances. We make a beeline straight to my dorm room.

Once the door shuts completely, Silas wraps his arms around my waist and lifts me off the floor. He buries his face in my neck and spins me in a circle.

I hook on to him tightly, not daring to ever let go of him ever again.

Touching him, breathing him in—it's more magnificent than I could have imagined.

I didn't realize it was possible to miss someone so fucking much. I thought I would never see him again, that he was dead or simply *lost* forever. Saving him was an impossible feat, and somehow, I was able to pull it off.

I may have had to make a wicked sacrifice, but sometimes life forces you to make bold choices to get the things you truly want.

We stay like this for a little while. Moments tick by, and I couldn't care less about the passing time now that he's back in our lives. Everything else seems totally manageable, and I'm absolutely okay with that.

Finally, Silas speaks low and into my hair. "You have no idea how much I missed you."

I let out a sigh. "I beg to differ."

He lowers me to my feet and stares into my eyes. The color is coming back to his face, and the weakened state of him I had seen in Hell is disappearing. It warms my heart to know he's going to recover from what he went through.

I run my palm along his cheek. "I'm sorry it took me so long."

His brows furrow. "I could die a thousand deaths, and none of them would be as painful or terrifying as thinking I would be forced to live one second without you. It wasn't the fires or the torturous agony, it was the losing you that hurt the most. The only thing that got me through each day was the idea that maybe, just maybe, I could find my way out of it and see you one last time. To hold you in my arms and stare into those beautiful eyes of yours and tell you how my love for you will last until the end of time. I've waged a war that felt like it went on for centuries, but I'd do it all again if it meant I ended up here, right now, with you by my side."

My eyes well, and it's everything I can do to not collapse into him.

He experienced what he did in Hell, and I lived through a torment of my own on Earth. And maybe they're not comparable at all, but if his was anything remotely close to mine, I ache to erase that from his memory.

Never in my wildest dreams would I have guessed that I would fall in love with four completely amazing men, but to have one of them share a connection to my soul the way Silas does, it's unlike anything I could ever put into words. To think that I had lost that forever wrecked me in unspeakable ways.

Silas raises his hands to my face and gently caresses my cheeks. He runs his thumbs along them to wipe away the rogue tears that trickle down. He inches forward and grazes his lips on my skin, leaving the faintest trail until he finally finds a home with my mouth. He kisses me like I'm so fragile I might break in half, like the fate of the entire world depends on him being as delicate as possible. He pulls away just slightly to whisper the words I've waited, what feels like a lifetime to hear, "I love you."

Each movement he makes talks directly to my soul.

I sniffle and find my strength to speak. "I love you, and I will for all of eternity."

He presses himself into me, and I revel in his shape against mine.

He shifts his attention to my shoulder. "We need to treat your wounds, and then, would you do me the honor of letting me hold you until the sun comes up?"

"Nothing would make me happier."

CHAPTER 3

Silas fulfills his promise to stay with me all night. With each passing moment, I beg the universe to slow down and let me savor this time with him.

Although, prior to going to bed, I was a bit worried about tending to my injuries. I thought that if Silas tried to use our Malachi connection to heal me, it wouldn't work and would give away the fact that I've lost my magic.

Luckily, though, our bond has nothing to do with my powers alone, and more of what we share. Within seconds of him pressing his blood-soaked hand to my shoulder, the cut closed, and the pain was erased. He even managed to rid my arms of the burns from the nasty flames that had nipped at me in Hell.

And with Silas back in this dimension and away from Balial's torment, his vampire skills were able to kick in and restore him of his damages, too.

He healed me quickly, and then we spent a while scrubbing the dirt off each other in the shower and followed it up with crawling into bed together to hold each other closer than humanly possible. I had missed his body badly, but sex was the furthest thing from our minds. All we really wanted was to relish in the ability to be near one another.

The door to my dorm creaks open, and a sweet-eyed cutie pops in. Cameron strolls over.

Silas grips me tighter and pulls me to his chest, not for a second caring who it is that entered.

"Morning, Cam," I say from my spot tucked in with Silas.

He kneels next to the bed and shows me his offering. In one hand is a brown paper sack full of something I assume to be delicious, and the other is a drink carrier with two cups. He points to the one with the black lid. "This one is yours."

Silas sniffs like a puppy dog hot on the path of something he's chasing. He sits up and eyes Cameron. "What's in the red one?"

Cam shoves it toward Silas. "*Yours.*"

Silas hesitates but decides to take it anyway. His eyes glow a radiant silver and purple. He breathes in whatever it is and then takes a long swig. "Thanks."

"You can credit Sydney for the idea, and Deghan for the execution. I'm just the delivery boy." Cameron hands me my coffee and shakes his head. "You're something else, you know that, right?"

I tilt my head. "What? Why?"

"Are you kidding? Listen, I haven't gotten the *whole* story, but the Cliffs Notes version that I have, holy shit, Will. You went to freaking *Hell* and back? I'm so fucking proud of you." Cameron's bright-blue eyes stare at me. "A little pissed that you went on a suicide mission, though."

"She would have done the same for you," Silas adds between sips.

Cameron huffs. "Maybe."

I rest my hand on his forearm, remembering all too late that I have no special juju to offer him. His skin is warm and...different. I can't quite place what it is. Now that I don't have my magic, perhaps things *feel* different to the touch. Another thing I'll have to get used to with this new change.

"You better know that I would," I finally tell him. "I couldn't function without any of you."

Cameron places the bag on my nightstand. "I should probably warn you. Walker and Abigail found out about your little journey to Hell. They're giving you your space for now, but they want to speak with you whenever you're ready. They told me to tell you it's *urgent*, so not to wait too long. Something about reinforcing the realm? Does that sound right? I always mix up my supernatural mumbo-jumbo."

Shit. I hadn't put too much thought into what would happen post-trip to the underworld, considering I didn't imagine I would make it out to divulge the story. I guess it's good news that they haven't kicked me to the curb and banned me from Harper Academy, but if they're expecting me to participate in helping them with the wards and securing our dimension, they're in for a rude awakening. I'm fresh out of magic and have nothing to offer them.

It's not that I don't *want* to help, especially with being the one who caused this shit show to happen, I'm just not exactly in any condition to be of assistance.

I can't lie to them, so what the heck am I going to do to keep up the ruse that I still have my power? I'm not ready to confess that I've lost my magic, not to them, or to anyone for that matter.

"Okay." I sit up and scoot back against the headframe of my bed. "I'll find them soon." I take the hot mug into my hands and breathe in the bitter and sweet scent. Hazelnut latte.

Cameron returns to his feet and points to the bag. "Eat up. I'll see you in a bit?" He leans down and kisses my cheek. "I'm glad you're both okay." He ruffles Silas's hair and grins, knowing damn well Silas hates him doing that.

Silas rolls his eyes. "Thanks, Cam."

Cameron leaves, and it's just the two of us again.

Silas pulls out the muffins and hands me one. "Okay, so...can we skip over the avoidance and just get straight to it?" He eyes me as he peels back the layer of paper lining his breakfast.

It amazes me how someone can do such a simple task and look so damn good. I pick at mine and play dumb. "What do you mean?"

"Something is off. I could sense the moment you came back. I thought maybe it was me, the whole 'being in Hell for a while' thing." He tears off a bite of his food and shares it with me. "You got panicky when he told you about Walker. I don't want to beat around the bush about it. I think it's safe to say you can confide in me about anything. We've been through the worst of the worst. I can handle whatever it is, I promise."

I chew the chunk slowly and bob my head up and down in understanding.

He's definitely right, but there's still the chance that he won't accept me the way that I am now.

"Did something happen? With Balial?" He studies my reaction.

I do my best not to move a muscle.

Silas's jaw clenches, and his voice deepens. "Did he hurt you?"

I shake my head and reach out to him. "No. He didn't. Surprisingly, he was pretty decent."

"I can't handle secrets. Not anymore." His face is nothing but serious.

I sigh heavily and lower my head. After everything he's been through, Silas deserves every bit of the truth he desires.

I barely say the words, "My magic..."

Silas puts his finger under my chin and raises my head. "What?"

Tears are already streaming down my cheeks at the slightest

admission. "He took it. All of it. That's the only way he would let you go. The only way he'd let me go, too."

Realization cascades on his face. He wastes no time processing the information while dragging me into his arms tightly. His way of reassuring me that he's here, that no matter what, he'll always remain.

Anyway, that's what I take from it, because that's exactly what I need right now. For him to hug me and never let me go. To be the glue that keeps me from falling apart. If he does release me, I'm too afraid I'll shatter into a million pieces, never to be put back together again.

"I'm so sorry," he finally whispers into my hair. "This is all my fault."

"Please don't blame yourself. I knew what I was doing. It was my decision."

He breaks away and clenches on to my hand between both of his. He closes his eyes and focuses. Slowly, he grows aware of the truth. "It really is gone."

"Yep," I manage to say.

"Why didn't you tell me?" His expression comes across more as concern than of hurt from not knowing. "Or anyone for that matter?"

I shrug and bite at my lip.

"I love you, so fucking much, all of us do. Nothing is going to change that."

The waterworks continue, and I'm not really sure if it's from the relief of his declaration or the putting it out into the world that I'm completely magicless.

"Willow, I can't imagine what this has felt like for you, to have held on to this secret on your own." He runs his thumbs gently along my cheeks. "I'm here for you. I'm not going anywhere this time, okay? Nothing will stop me from being with you ever again."

His words soothe my aching heart and bring me fragments of hope in this disastrous life of mine. I would choose Silas over my magic any day. I knew that when I agreed to give my power to Balial. That doesn't make the loss any less difficult, though. I had no idea I would feel so *empty* without it. Or that it was such a monumental thing laced into my being.

It will take getting used to, but eventually, I'll learn to live without it. I mean, there aren't any other options. I can't give up now. I will focus on what is left of me and rebuild myself into a new version of Willow Oliver. A magicless one.

A distraction. That's what I need.

In my attempt to dig myself from the trenches of losing Silas, I focused on anything else I could to take my mind off how fucking sad I was. That's exactly what I should do now. There are still a million things that are pressing.

My best friend is still uncovering how to be a witch, and she recently found out she was adopted. Not to mention, we might be somehow related. That situation absolutely demands my attention. Helping her with her magic will be a learning curve, considering I'm lacking in that department, but I'll do what I can to show her the ropes. The least I can do is provide all the moral support in these uncertain times.

Plus, the matter of my own family. I promised my dad I would make an effort to get to know him and, although I made that agreement under the premise that I would be spending the rest of eternity in Hell, a deal is a deal.

Sydney is still reeling from the loss of his parents and the realization that they were *much* more fucked up than he had thought. Cam is having brother issues and probably handling it all on his own because he doesn't want to burden anyone.

The girls will more than likely need to be convinced that Silas is not actually a shitty boyfriend who left me and then all of a sudden came back. I have no idea what story I will feed them, but I don't want Silas to be shamed by them under false narratives. He quite literally has been through Hell and doesn't deserve any grief for it.

Which leads me to Silas, who spent an uncertain amount of

time being tortured by Balial. He's surprisingly holding himself together pretty well, but that kind of thing has to take a toll on a person. It's only a matter of time before he breaks, and I need to be in my right state of mind if that happens. It's unfair of me to focus on something so silly as losing my magic given he has been through so much worse.

Then there is the whole school thing. Magical and regular. I'm still not completely caught up on all of my assignments, and if I want to graduate on my normal schedule, I should get back to studying. Granted, I won't be pursuing any witchy careers, I need to focus on making sure I learn what I can from this college experience. And of course, I'll have to handle breaking the news to Walker and Abigail about not having magic anymore, and figure out how that will impact not only my own studies but the integrity of the shadow realm. It's my understanding that Sydney alone can maintain the seams with his power source, but what happens if that becomes not enough?

Between all of that, and upholding my personal and romantic relationships, I have my work cut out for myself. I honestly don't have time to mope around and be sad about my loss.

"Will?" Silas breaks my train of thought.

I blink back into reality. "Hey."

"Where did you run off to?" He tucks a strand of my hair behind my ear.

"Just thinking."

"Penny for your thoughts?"

I study him over, scanning each perfectly arranged feature on his face. His presence brings me a calm I never knew possible. The world is chaos, and with him by my side silencing the storm, anything is possible. I push the rushing waters of my mind away and appreciate the beauty sitting only inches from me.

The person I never thought I would see again.

"I love you," I say with a sigh.

CHAPTER 4

"D o you want me to go with you?" Silas asks from his spot at my oversized window. He closes the notebook in his hands and focuses his attention on me. An unruly strand of hair flops down across his forehead and barely covers his eye.

I approach him and gently kiss his lips. "I think I should handle this one on my own."

"I won't be far if you need me. I've got my hearing back so just yell my name and I'll be right there."

I leave Silas behind in my room and walk down the long corridor to the girls' supernatural dorms. It's strange to still recognize the buzzing of the power from the magical students, but not having the same vibration within my own body.

My plan is to meet with Walker to discuss what happened and

deal with that situation however it pans out. First, though, as much as I don't want to, I need to find Sydney.

It's not that I don't want to see Syd—because I absolutely do. I miss him, actually. But, regardless of how well Silas took the news of me no longer having my powers, I'm unsure of how Sydney will react. He and I have bonded over our abilities, and now, that connection is no more. What if he doesn't want to be with me because I'm different?

Instinctually, I summon my internal tracker to locate him.

All that comes is absolute crickets. Not like real ones—that would be weird. Rather, a deafening silence where my magic used to lay in wait.

I suppose I'll have to do this the old-fashioned way.

I turn into the upstairs open common area of the academy and head toward the guys' room, making the first of my rounds at the places where Sydney might be.

I raise my hand to knock on his door at the same time it opens.

Sydney's brows are furrowed, and despite my lack of magical energy reading, there is no mistaking the concern lining his face. "Is everything okay?"

I swallow and point behind him. "Can I come in?"

"Yeah." He quickly moves out of my way and shuts the door once I'm on the other side. "What's up?"

I wander near his desk and pace a little, back and forth.

"Willow, spit it out, please. I'm on pins and needles over here. Are you okay?" He approaches me and cautiously trails his fingers along mine.

If I can't say it out loud, the least I can do is show him.

I carefully grab on to his hand like we have done numerous times in the past to secure our connection.

As though he comprehends what I'm doing, he obliges and attempts to hop into my mind.

"I don't understand." He holds on to me tighter. "I...I don't feel anything."

I will not cry; I will not cry.

I take in a deep breath to ground myself.

I force the words out of my mouth, completely terrified of how he's going to react once he fully grasps the new reality. "It was the only way I could get him back."

His gorgeous green eyes widen. "Tell me you're joking."

A million things race through my mind. All of them terrible and threatening to ruin me.

Sydney hates me. He's ashamed of me. He thinks I'm stupid for giving up everything for Silas. That I'm worthless now without my magic. That I have nothing to offer him or anyone else and I'm a waste of space. A pathetic excuse of a witch. That I'm a disgrace to the Oliver name.

"Oh, Willow..." Sydney exhales and drags me into his chest. "I would have done the same thing for you."

A laugh bubbles up and out of my chest. Here I imagined that he would cast me aside for being powerless, but somehow, he completely understands the sacrifice I made.

"Really?" I say into his chest. I take in his lemon-and-sage scent and the warmth of his embrace. "You don't despise me?"

"Are you serious?" He holds me at an arm's length and stares into my eyes. "Don't for a second think that. Am I super pissed at you for being so incredibly reckless? Absolutely. But to think I would ever turn my back on you, that's absurd. You can't get rid of me that easily."

I force a smile and relax my tense shoulders.

"I don't know what I would have done if you hadn't come back." He continues to meet my gaze. "I was already trying to open another portal but, well...you did your research so you get how difficult that would have been. It wasn't supposed to be you. I was going to take care of it all. I never meant for you to be in any danger. I was going to bring him home. To be the one to ease your pain. I'm so sorry I let you down."

I shake my head. "The moment I found out what you were up to, I knew I had to put a stop to it. I couldn't let you risk everything like that. After all, it was my fault he was gone. I had to be the one to get him. I wasn't going to stand by and do nothing once I figured out your plan. You've done so much for me already. Risking your life was not an option I was willing to let you take."

He grazes my cheek with his hand. "You didn't have to do it alone."

I rest my palm against his skin. "You know I did."

Sydney continues to stare at me like I'm not real. "No one. Not a single soul has made it out of there. And here you are, having brought yourself and someone else home. It's incredible, really."

"Yeah..." I only had to leave behind a huge portion of myself.

The recollection of Balial juggling the orbs of my pink power assaults me heavily. The sadistic smile caked across his face turns my stomach and sends a chill dancing over me. I yearn to feel that magic coursing through my veins, endless and potent like once before. The memory seems so distant now.

"This might be the dumbest thing I've ever asked you..." Sydney gently strokes my cheek with the backs of his fingertips. "Are you okay?"

I sigh. How can I possibly answer such a loaded yet simple question? In theory, sure, I'm totally fine. I'm here, alive and breathing, and considering where I was yesterday, I'd say that's a huge improvement from the alternative. I was able to rescue Silas from Hell, and no one else was put in danger. All wonderful things that I am truly grateful for. And then there's the whole being devastated about losing what feels like my true identity. It's strange. I'm not sure how to even process, let alone put into words how I'm doing with everything that has happened.

So, instead, I force a smile and tell him the biggest lie. "Yeah, I'm fine."

Sydney continues to study my face.

I maintain his stare but eventually avert my gaze when I can no longer meet his concerned eyes.

"What can I do?" he asks.

"Nothing. And I'm all right with that. I went my whole life without knowing what I was, I'll get used to this new normal soon."

"Have you told anyone else?" He wraps his arms around my frame and places a soft kiss against my hair.

"Just Silas." I recall my plan. "I was heading to meet with Walker and Abigail, but I wanted to talk to you first. To tell you."

"I can go if you'd like me to."

I shake my head. The guys have fought enough of my battles for me, it's time that I do this on my own. I can't allow any of them to even remotely try to take the blame for the irresponsible things I've done.

"You sure?" His gaze traces along my face.

"I'll be okay. I need to do this one on my own."

"Good, you decided to come." Abigail motions toward the door. "This way." She leads us out of the headmaster's office and through the foyer of the school. She quickly walks across the lavishly decorated area and into the north wing hallway.

Students pass us by, completely unsuspecting of the nature of our soon-to-be conversation.

I follow her into the familiar room we do our shadow realm work in.

Walker is already there, studying an old text at the desk at the front of the class. "Good morning, Willow."

"Morning, sir." I flit my gaze from Abigail to Walker and do my best to prepare for the hell they're about to unleash on me.

"We can discuss details once we're finished." Walker peers around me and toward the door. "No Sydney?"

"I'd prefer to leave him out of this, if that is all right." I swallow down the fear that rises up my throat.

"Very well."

Abigail shuffles through a box and pulls out a pair of over-the-ear headphones, similar to those that Sydney and I used during our realm repair sessions. She holds them out to me.

"I, um. I think we need to have that talk first, actually."

Abigail frowns slightly and doesn't budge.

I clear my throat and raise my voice. "I'm serious." I take a cautious step back like a scared child who is terrified they're about to be in big trouble.

Finally clicking my tone into place, Abigail lowers her arm. "What's wrong?"

Walker gives me his full attention, too.

"I, uh..." I struggle to string the correct words together to tell them what they need to know. "I can't help you."

Abigail studies me curiously. "Okay," she says hesitantly.

"Oh, you're right." Walker nods. "We should have asked. It's just that you had said in the past that you would be willing to make a contribution to the integrity of the realm. We shouldn't have assumed that was still the case. That was foolish of us."

His expression seems kind, but there are layers of hurt hidden underneath.

I have to use extra consideration to figure out the emotions of those around me and hope like heck that I'm assuming correctly.

"It's not that I don't *want* to help you."

Abigail cuts me off. "We understand. Things change." Betrayal lines her voice.

"Abigail, please, let me explain."

She shoves the headphones back into the box and closes the top. "We'll find another way. Don't feel obligated."

"We should allow her to explain if she wants, Ab." Walker's brow softens.

I force away the waterworks that attempt to come to the forefront. I refuse to turn into a blubbering mess every time I have to relive the admission that I've *changed*.

"Fine." Abigail crosses her arms over her chest. "Go ahead."

I swallow and meet her gaze, quickly averting and looking at Walker. "I *can't* help you."

Abigail tenses. She must think I'm being selfish, and unless I say the actual words, she's going to keep that same mindset.

I can't say I blame her one bit, either. "My magic...it's gone." A knife seems to jab its way into my heart.

Walker's mouth drops open. His reaction pretty much matches everyone else's so far. Pure and utter shock. "How could that be?"

Abigail steps forward. "May I?" She points toward my hand.

I place my palm gently into hers and wait for her to confirm or deny my admission.

It only takes a few seconds for her to meet the same surprise Walker is experiencing.

"He took it from you, didn't he? That's how you were able to leave?" Abigail lets go of me and leans up against the desk. "I was wondering how you pulled it off."

"Yes. It was the only thing I had to offer him." Considering he wasn't interested in my actual life.

"You did a very brave and foolish thing, Willow." Walker takes a step away from where he was standing. He reaches out and grabs my shoulder.

I hold my breath in anticipation of where his train of thought is going to lead him. Is this the point where he kicks me out of school? Tells me I'm of no use to him or anyone else here? That my presence has caused more issues than not and I need to leave immediately before anyone else is put in danger. That I should have stayed in Hell instead of coming back here where I'm not wanted or needed anymore.

"It's very difficult to stay mad at you considering all that you've been through in such a short time. You put us and the school at risk by summoning that portal to Hell. It's a miracle you made it out at all if we're being honest. But, with that being said, the past is now the past, and the only thing we can do now is move forward however we can and work on making the most of what we are left with. I foresee the future being no less challenging than what you've already dealt with, but I have faith that you'll persevere the way you always do." He takes in a long breath and exhales. "If I could give you any advice, it would be to focus on the things you can control, and right now, that appears to be your academics and your relationship with your friends and family. Those will help you get through this trying time."

"Wait, I'm allowed to stay?" The words flop out of my mouth.

The corner of Walker's lips turns up. "Yes, Willow. I'm afraid you'll have to do worse than that. It's not like you *meant* any harm. You were only doing what you thought was best, and I applaud you for that. Things could have turned out much differently."

I guess that fear of abandonment I keep struggling with is exactly that, a fear. Something that threatens to break me and somehow keeps being disproved time and time again. I was so sure that my guys wouldn't want me, that I would be expelled from school, but I couldn't have been more wrong. I have a few more people to break the terrible news to, but so far, my odds have been pretty damn good.

Maybe this new me won't be so bad once all is said and done.

CHAPTER 5

Walker and Abigail seem to accept my lack of powers as enough punishment for being so incredibly reckless. They don't push the issue anymore and they basically tell me that we'll catch up once the dust has settled from my journey to Hell.

I recognize they're stressed out, and I wish there was something I could do to help them ease their worries—either by pushing my calming energy into them or offering up whatever magic I could give them to reinforce the realm. But I can't do either of those things, and it makes me incredibly helpless to my core. There has to be *something* I can do.

Maybe focusing on my academics and loved ones will be enough for now. At least that way they won't have to worry about me falling apart and doing something else totally stupid.

I quickly glance at the clock on the far corner of the foyer and do a mental scan for what class Lillian is in right now.

The sooner I let my magical friends in on the secret of my lack of power, the sooner I can get over the awkwardness of the painful conversation and sad stares people give me. Every single time I reopen the wound that so desperately wants to be forgotten and left alone. I can't imagine not having my magic will ever get any easier to stomach, but having to keep talking about it sure isn't helping.

And not just that, I need to check in on Lillian and see how she's doing with *her* newfound powers. I have no freaking idea how I'm going to be able to help her through this transition. Provide moral support? Assist in her lessons?

I guess I can still learn and study, I just won't be actually using any powers.

Leaving the magic world in its entirety doesn't seem like an option, especially considering three of my four boyfriends have supernatural abilities and my best friend is a witch. It's not something I want to rid from my life either. Maybe I don't have my powers, but that doesn't mean magic isn't woven so deeply into my soul now. The thought of leaving it completely behind tears me apart almost as much as being without it.

I turn the corner to walk down the east wing hallway and slam right into a warm body.

I'm instantly reminded of that first day at Harper Academy when I ran into the same person. My heart flutters all the same.

Those golden eyes and broad shoulders welcome me to him.

"Deg," I say breathlessly.

"Princess." A grin consumes his face. He wraps me into his arms without hesitating. "Everything okay?" He squeezes me so tightly I can barely move.

"Mmhm," I mutter. "I was looking for Lills." Now that I've found him, though, I could knock out two awkward conversations in one. And if we're lucky enough to snag Cam, I could break all the news at once. Then, all that's left are people who don't really need to know one way or another, and my parents.

He mumbles something into my hair and holds me snug against his chest. "I missed you."

I relax into him and close my eyes, totally taking in the moment for what it is—pure bliss. Deghan's hugs are a gift from the heavens. It's not often that I stop to smell the figurative roses, and considering everything that has happened lately, I need to spend more time enjoying life's finer pleasures.

"Get a room," a familiar voice teases us from down the hall.

Now I have two of the three people I need to talk to. Just one more, and I can get this madness over with.

Cameron spreads his arms around mine and Deghan's already combined form. A bit of static electricity pops with his touch. "Group hug." He kisses my forehead and presses himself into us.

Cam smells of vanilla and honey with a hint of blueberry. He must be cooking up something delicious to be smelling the way he is.

I pry myself out of their grips. "I actually need to talk to both of you. Do you have a minute?"

The guys side-eye each other in an 'Oh shit, are we in trouble?' kind of way.

They both mutter a nervous confirmation and wait for me to respond.

"If we could grab Lillian, too, that would be great. Have either of you seen her?" I crane my neck to see down the hall in the direction Cameron had just come from.

A millisecond later, her beautiful brunette head pops out of the far class with Ethan at her side. We lock gazes, and she smiles.

She turns to say something to Ethan, resulting in him looking my way then back to her.

He nods and then presses his lips to her cheek before walking into another room without Lillian.

She weaves through Deghan and Cam to get to me. Lillian

eyes me over and then hugs me quickly. "I'm so happy to see you. Are you okay?"

I bite at the corner of my lip to avoid the incessant water display my body likes to default to in these situations. Why can't someone ask me a simple question without my face thinking it's a good idea to leak everywhere? It's freaking embarrassing not being able to control my emotions.

Deghan shifts nervously. "Here she is. What did you want to talk to us about?"

"Maybe somewhere a bit more private." I look around. I could easily take them back to my dorm room, but I don't exactly want this to turn into a big Willow pity party. If I keep it semi-public, they can't react irrationally and make a scene. The initial 'Are they going to accept me?' fear is still there, but not anywhere near what it was the first few times I admitted that my magic was gone. Don't get me wrong, I'm still incredibly uncertain of how they will react—my odds just seem a bit better at this point.

Cameron motions toward a vacant class. "Pretty sure this one is empty next period."

"Perfect," I say on my way toward the door. I poke my head inside and confirm that no one is occupying the space.

My lovers and best friend follow me skeptically.

"What's going on, Wills?" Lillian's face shows concern even though I can no longer sense her energy.

I flit my attention between the three of them and attempt to keep my voice low in case there are any prying ears. I prepare myself to tell my not-so-secret-anymore secret for what will hopefully be the last time for a little while.

"You're kinda freaking me out." Cameron doesn't take his serious baby-blue gaze off me.

"I don't have my magic anymore. It's gone."

They all remain completely quiet like I haven't said a word. It's as though they're processing the information prior to responding.

I continue. "It was the only way I could save Silas, to save myself. I thought you should know. I'm powerless." I fight back the tears and somehow, they still manage to cascade down my cheeks. The anxiety of not knowing how they're going to respond makes each second last for what seems an eternity. I thought that I had built a layer of confidence with this storytelling, but now, I'm not so sure.

Each one of them could turn and walk out that door, and there would be nothing for me to do about it. I shouldn't have expected that they would accept me any more than them disowning me for it. The unknown is certainly the most terrifying thing of all.

Lillian's eyes are broad and show shock—the typical reaction. "Willow, I..."

Deghan blinks a few times and then steps forward to jerk me to him in typical Deghan fashion. His go-to response is to show his love with hugs, and at this moment, that's all the reassurance I need from him. I know for certain that nothing has changed in the way he feels about me.

"I'm so sorry," Lillian finishes saying.

Cameron's arms find their way to my body again, enveloping me in a double layer of a hug outside of Deghan's grasp.

"What can we do?" Deghan chimes in.

I barely shake my head. "There isn't anything anyone can do."

Not even me.

In the past, I've faced numerous challenges, but none of them remotely compare to how insanely impossible this situation is. The Devil has taken my magic. All of it. And considering I've already traveled to Hell and back to rescue someone, something no other known supernatural has done before me, I can't exactly pop over and be like, "Hey, Balial, mind if I get a refund?"

I have nothing to offer him in exchange, and there's no way he'd give it to me for free.

So, unless I find something of greater value than my own power, I'm screwed, and not in a good way. Not to mention, summoning another portal to Hell isn't exactly ideal either. I've already put the academy and the people anywhere near it in great danger, and I would be a completely reckless fool to do it again.

"Whatever you need, we're here for you." Deghan rubs circles along my shoulder blades.

Lillian nods. "Does it..."

I tilt my head and wait for her to finish.

"Hurt?" She seems embarrassed by her question.

"No. Not in the way you think it might." Physically, there is no pain at all. There's only an empty aching lifeforce that's left my body, one I didn't realize was so ingrained in my very being until it was gone. It's a wound that I'm not quite sure I could ever explain to someone who didn't experience it themselves firsthand.

Cameron places his hand on my cheek and gently rests it there. "Guess I'm not the only boring one in the bunch anymore."

I roll my eyes at him and press my palm against his. "You are the furthest thing from *boring*." Our touch tingles in a strange way, something I've noticed more and more recently but haven't been able to pinpoint what the heck it is. It's like we're invisibly joined and becoming an extension of the other.

Maybe this is the way all humans feel when they embrace each other. Cameron *is* the first non-supernatural that I've encountered since I've been back and without my abilities. This could be completely normal. Otherwise, what else would explain the strange sensation?

CHAPTER
6

Telling your loved ones big scary news is incredibly exhausting.

Once I've done exactly that, I break off and head back to my room to get away from the sad looks and helplessness that I'm well aware my friends are undergoing. I understand what they're feeling, but not being able to help them help me is even more mentally draining. There isn't anything any of us can do, and I don't know how many more times I can explain that without breaking down.

I open the door to my dim dorm and quietly close it. I rest my head along its cold wooden exterior and take in a breath while closing my eyes.

"Hey," a familiar voice cracks through the silence.

The sound is a soothing lullaby to my aching soul.

I turn, and he's already there, standing only inches from my face.

"Hi," I whisper. I still haven't quite gotten used to the fact that he really is here, that he's actually back. Safe and sound and right in front of me, completely gorgeous and utterly mine.

Silas's serious silvery gaze studies me over, like he's desperate to memorize my every feature. He cautiously stays in place even though I ache for him to move closer.

I sigh and bridge the gap, pressing my body into his chest and letting him carry the burden of my endlessly heavy form. I would love nothing more than to stay right here forever, in the safety of him.

And in this little moment between the chaos, that's precisely what I'm going to do.

"Do you want to talk about it?" Silas runs his thumb along my cheek.

I angle my head to meet his beautiful gaze. I breathe him in and tug on the collar of his shirt to bring him toward me.

His nose grazes mine, and his lips gently brush the corner of my mouth. "Willow," he mutters.

The single word lights a fire inside me that I once worried was gone forever. The tether that ties us together tugs tightly and reminds me that we are one. Two beings made for each other. I've never cared about free will less in my life—Silas is the other half of my soul, and I am forever thankful for whatever force that bound us to one another.

I'm even more grateful that our bond wasn't severed completely when I lost my powers.

Whatever Silas and I have is more potent than my Oliver magic. Something that will outlive all of time.

Silas kisses me, slow and tenderly, like I might fall apart if he applies the slightest pressure. His tongue trails along my lip, and his hands find their place on the sides of my face.

He's passionate and commanding and everything all at once, and I cannot contain my want for him any longer.

I take the lead and intensify my hold on him. I grip his waist and drag him into me and kiss him like the world could very well be ending, and honestly, I might be okay with that knowing I got to touch him this way one more time.

To feel his warmth, his form, the curves of his muscles, and the broadness of his shoulders. The weight of his firm hands against my skin and the complete softness of his lips. The thick inch-long scar on his lower back that's hidden in a mess of perfectly arranged spools of black ink. The bristle of his just barely stubbly beard as it tickles my chin and the length of his long-on-top and short-on-the-sides hair that suits him so fucking well.

To stare into those silver-ish purple eyes that have an intensity about them that never fails to make my heart skip a beat. To know that regardless of how guarded and misunderstood he is, that he let me in, that he allows me to love him, and that he loves me with an equal force in return, no matter how difficult that is to wrap my head around sometimes.

To be his and for him to be mine. Now and always. Until my heart stops beating, and after I return to stardust.

I ache for him to understand that my love for him will withstand any force that threatens to destroy it.

And with a fierceness in him that tells me he wants me to know the same, he hoists me by the waist and carries me to my bed. He doesn't break us apart as he lowers me onto the mattress and positions himself on top of me. He glides his fingers into my hair and tugs gently.

I let out a sigh against his lips and reach for the hem of his shirt, completely forgetting about his jacket. I readjust my target and yank the thing over his shoulders and somehow manage to wiggle it off of him with his help.

He grins but keeps his mouth on mine.

I hook my legs around his torso, and in one swift move, he raises me into his lap to wrench my shirt over my head.

I take the opportunity to remove his, too.

We stay there, topless, with our bodies pressed together for another few minutes, kissing with a desperate intensity.

Finally, he breaks away and gently pushes me onto my back. He stands at the foot of the bed and slides off the rest of my clothing, leaving me lying there completely exposed.

He exhales. "You're...everything." His lip turns up in the corner into a smile that warms my heart. "There isn't even an appropriate word for you, Willow." He continues to stare. "Perfect is so...outdone. Extraordinary doesn't even come close. Gorgeous could never cut it."

And watching the way he watches me, I suddenly understand completely what he means. There isn't a single term in the English language to describe Silas and the way I feel about him.

His black jeans find their way to the rug at the foot of my bed. Silas places his strong hands around my waist and places me back onto his lap and into the same position we were in just moments prior.

Our bare bodies seem to melt into each other in a beautiful melody of his body and mine becoming one.

Time slows, and all that's left is us.

I wiggle closer to his torso and wrap my legs around his warm and dreamily sculpted frame. I kiss him gently and let my hands roam their way up his chest and onto the sides of his face to grasp him tighter.

Silas streams his fingers along my back and breaks his mouth away to stare into my eyes. He rests his forehead against mine. "I wasn't sure I'd ever see you again."

I graze his nose with my own. "You're here now. That's all that matters."

Our lips find their way to each other again and tangle into a heated mess of hunger.

I adjust my body to give way for Silas while staying in his lap. I bite back a sigh when he enters me. Something that I didn't quite understand how badly I was missing. The sensation is pure fucking bliss.

With our chests pressed together, we ride the wave of each other for what feels like both an eternity and not long enough. We become drunk on the natural ecstasy of our desperate souls trying to savor what we thought was once gone forever.

Silas takes in a breath and in one sudden move picks me up and puts me down on my back on the mattress. He locks both of his hands in mine and holds them over my head while he thrusts from on top of me.

I rock my body to his rhythm and become completely lost in the pleasure. Slow and steady, long and deep movements that inch me closer and closer and closer to the edge.

Silas doesn't take his mouth away from mine; instead, he kisses me fervently like he can't quite get enough.

I match his intensity in an attempt to satiate the hunger I have for him.

His length hardens more so than before, and my body responds to his reaction.

Without my authority, my hands clamp his fiercely, and my back arches—my orgasm funneling in with a sheer force from out of this world.

At the very same moment, almost like our bodies are completely in sync with each other, Silas comes undone with me.

The climax lasts longer than anything I've experienced, and once I'm able to think clearly, it's as though a newfound power seems to be breathed into me.

To say that we needed that would be an understatement.

Silas collapses at my side and rolls me over and onto his chest.

I had no idea that vampires could sweat, but fuck if his scent doesn't immediately make me famished for round two.

I run my index finger down the crease of his endless stomach muscles and study his tattooed skin.

He exhales softly and kisses the top of my head. "Again...no words."

I smile at how relaxed his body becomes, something I haven't seen from Silas in a long time. It warms my heart to give him temporary peace in this time of turmoil.

Although, the faint flicker of a light-purple crackling coming from my own skin instantly forces my thoughts away from his drop-dead-sexy body.

CHAPTER 7

I sit up in a panic. "What the fuck?"

Silas rises onto his elbows and tilts his head in minimal concern. "What's wrong?"

He seems totally drunk and dazed from our sexcapades, and if I weren't freaking out right now, I'd totally savor seeing him be this fucking adorable.

I extend my hand toward him. "Look!"

Silas blinks, clearly confused and unsure what I'm being a weirdo about. He looks from me to my arm, back to me. "What am I missing here?"

"Silas, please. Pay attention. Don't you have vamp vision or something? Come on. Focus." It's then that I notice the faint crackle inside my body that was missing not too long ago. The one that once upon a time was flowing with an infinite supply of powerful magic. Now, it's like a tiny trickle has caressed my drought-filled veins. It's not much, but it's enough to recognize the difference between nothing and something. Even if that something is super small.

Finally, Silas decides to take me seriously and takes my wrist gently. He narrows his gaze and studies my skin. "It's..."

"Fucking magic." I blurt the words out, and somehow, they still don't become any less strange. "How is this possible?"

Silas fully gives me his attention, sitting up on his hind and coming closer to my frantic body. "Willow...this is...*my* magic."

I take a deep breath and summon whatever source is inside me. It definitely feels familiar but slightly foreign. Not like that of my own power. It's shallow, too, and fleeting. A tiny, stolen pool that is disappearing by the second.

I must have taken it from Silas while we were having sex. That must have been what deepened and lengthened our orgasm. He wasn't *just* making me climax, he was fueling my magical reserves, too.

"Here." Silas turns his palm up to me and nods. "See if you can do it again."

I look at him hesitantly, unsure of whether or not we should even try. It could have been a complete fluke for me to have taken some of his magic. I lost my abilities. I gave them to the King of Hell, to Balial. He made sure I'd never feel that recognizable sensation in my body.

Didn't he?

Silas links our hands. "Try it."

I close my eyes and take a breath, totally afraid regardless of which direction this is going. On one side, this could work. I could successfully borrow Silas's power source and temporarily have my magical powers. Or, there's the possibility this will epically fail, and I'd have to stomach the realization that I will forever be without the very core of my existence.

It's not the power I feel first, it's the sensation of Silas's energy —warm and calm and happy and pushing aside a deeper and darker emotion that is fighting to erase the good. I blink back into reality and find Silas grinning at me, our hands enveloped in a floating purple haze.

"Holy shit," I whisper.

"You are fucking incredible." Silas grabs me by the face and kisses me long and hard.

I'm not even sure what the heck to do. Do I use the magic? Do I let it hang out? How long will it last? Can I do everything I had once done but just with limited strength? All of these questions are much better suited for someone with far more knowledge than me.

"I need to tell Sydney."

Silas flops onto his back dramatically and covers his eyes with his forearm. "Uh, you're really going to ruin the moment like that, aren't you?"

I poke him in the side, and a crackle of his own magic zaps him. "Now, now. Unless you can answer the million questions running through my mind, we're going to have to recruit someone who can give us help."

"Seven," is all he mumbles.

"What?"

"You wanted answers."

"Are you really rattling off random numbers?" I reach over and steal the shirt hanging off the edge of the bed. Luckily for me, it's Silas's.

He'll have to opt for one of his spare tees that I keep tucked in my dresser. No way am I giving him this freshly worn piece of heaven that smells of him.

"Maybe. Is it working?" He peeks out from under his arm. "Hey, that's mine." He sits up and tickles my sides.

I fall over and swat him away in the middle of giggling uncontrollably.

It's bizarre to think that just a couple of days ago Silas was in Hell enduring the wrath of Balial, and I was withering away here without him.

"Stop, you're going to make me pee the bed," I struggle to say between laughs.

"Fine..." Silas stands and walks around to the front where the rest of his clothes are.

I watch him intently every step of the way, completely awestruck at his beauty. Something about that ink-stained skin that speaks a sad and lovely story to my soul without saying a word—I'm drawn to him in such an irresistible and otherworldly manner.

I tug on a pair of leggings and tuck a corner of Silas's shirt into the waistband. I slip on the fuzzy slippers near my nightstand and wait for Silas to finish getting dressed.

He manages to find another shirt from my Silas stash and pulls his black leather jacket over to cover his arms. Part of me is glad he's selective with who he shows himself to. It makes it that much more special that I'm allowed in.

Silas whisks the long strands of silver hair out of my face and stares seriously into my eyes.

I'm brought back to that moment months ago in the woods when he inched his way closer, daring to test the restraints of whatever was keeping us apart.

Fate and a curse. That's what we were.

And maybe that's what we always will be.

But at the very minimum, we're here. We've overcome every single obstacle that's come our way, and every time I think it's too much, that we've lost it all, we figure out a way to do the impossible.

His lips gently part, and he whispers the words, "Forever, okay?"

I don't dare look away. "And ever."

That dim and gloomy energy I detected earlier from him lurks to the front, but something stronger holds it back. I'm thankful for its perseverance to overcome the darkness.

Silas presses one delicate kiss on my mouth and then on my nose. "Let's go find Sydney."

I test my abilities and conjure my internal tracker. Something stirs inside me, and I focus on finding the control. My mind is pulled directly across the building and into the supernatural guys' dorms. He's in his room. And I magically figured it out.

Silas's power has run through my veins before, so it's not completely alien, but having not ever used it solely, it will take some getting accustomed to. It was always supplementary to my own magic, not the main attraction.

I weave my hand through Silas's and lead him out of my dorm and down the hallway. I avoid the glares of passing students in the shared common area of the upstairs and do my best to sidestep the clear glass covering of the garden top.

The warmth of Silas's hand is a welcome reminder that no matter what, everything is going to be okay. At the end of the day, my greatest concern is that my loved ones are safe, and Silas being here means exactly that. I can live without my magic. But I can't live without him. And the same goes for Sydney, Deghan, and Cameron, too. I don't know what I would do if I lost any of them.

Maybe losing my magic was a gift from the heavens. There were so many close calls when I was battling the infinite people who wanted to steal my power. Now, I have nothing that anyone would kill for, and that means I won't be putting my friends and lovers in the crossfire while I defend my inheritance.

A knock sends me back to reality. I glance up. Silas and I are standing in front of Sydney's door.

"What's wrong?" Syd says sleepily. He must have been napping. He rubs at his eye and yawns.

Silas pushes into Sydney's room. "Why do you always assume the worst?"

Sydney motions with his arm. "Well, by all means, come on in."

Silas pokes around at a stack of papers on Sydney's desk and picks up a palm-sized orange crystal.

Sydney rushes over and takes it from him. "Leave that alone."

He smacks at Silas's hand. "Stop touching my stuff." Sydney bumps Silas with his hip and tries to shoo him away. "Willow, I'm grateful for your company but I can't imagine the two of you came for a social visit." He stares at me with his serious emerald gaze.

I reach out and weave my fingers through his, tapping into his mind like I had done in the past. There is little resistance—he lets me right in.

"*Whoa. Your magic is back?*" A shocked expression replaces the one of exhaustion on Sydney's handsome face.

I shake my head. "*It's not mine.*"

Sydney turns to Silas and raises his eyebrow.

Silas shrugs and goes back to nosing around.

"*This is incredible. I had forgotten all about your Malachi connection.*"

I wiggle myself free when the supply wanes. I'm already fiending for more, and I'm not sure how long until what I have is gone. I bring my arm close to my chest in a sad attempt to keep the power as long as I can.

Sydney swats at Silas again. "Stop." He snatches the bag of herbs from him. "I never thought to check if you still had access to his magic. I guess I just assumed it was all gone."

Silas exhales. "Willow has questions."

Sydney shifts his focus back on me. "Okay..." His skeptical look is not promising whatsoever.

"How long will it last?"

Sydney puts his soft palm on my shoulder and motions for me to sit. He claims the spot on the bed next to me. "I'm going to be honest, I have probably the same things running through my head that you do. How long? I don't know. If I had to guess, it would depend on how long the siphon transaction lasted and the energy you've already exerted. This kind of thing isn't exactly in the textbooks. It's not common, heck it's completely rare for a witch to not have their powers and rely solely on their Malachi bond. This is completely unheard of. There are limits to the exchange, but I don't think those boundaries have ever been pushed. Usually, the recipient has their own primary source."

I bite at my lip. I was really hoping Sydney would know something, anything. I can't expect him to have all the answers, especially to such uncharted territory.

Sydney lowers his voice. "What does it *feel* like?"

I reposition on the mattress and try to think of some comparison to help him understand. "Imagine borrowing someone's pants that aren't quite your size. It's not that it's too big or too small, it's that they don't *hug* your body the way your own do. The detergent is different, and the way they sit on your hips is a little off. They still fit, and they serve their purpose, but they're not *yours*. I imagine it's something like that. And obviously, it beats being bottomless."

"Interesting."

Silas strolls over and leans against the wall near me. "Feel free to steal my pants whenever you need them."

Sydney rubs at his chin and focuses on Silas. "And what about you? Are you noticing anything?"

"Like what?"

"Side effects, Silas. Come on." Sydney grows irritated. "There has to be something. Exhaustion? Mood changes? How is your energy?"

"I'm fine. My normal peachy self." Silas winks at Sydney in a totally arrogant and adorable way.

Sydney rolls his gorgeous green eyes. "Right. Not like you'd say anything anyway. How long was it before we found out the Reperio stone had control over you?"

"Oh whatever, it wasn't that bad."

"Are you serious? You tried to kill yourself. If you would have *listened* and not broken the circle, that never would have happened."

Silas steps from the wall and toward Sydney. "You want to talk about following orders? How many times have you gotten her in danger?"

Sydney stands, clearly ready to defend his territory. "You forget who's saved your ass on numerous occasions. Stop with your melodramatic..."

I jump between them. "Both of you, cut it out." I put my palms on their chests. "Hello?" I look from Silas to Sydney. "Snap out of it. Please. For me. You're acting like children."

Sydney backs down first. "Willow's right." He slings his backpack over his shoulder. "I'll be in the library. Trying to actually help." He directs his last statement at Silas.

"Whatever," Silas spits out. "You're just jealous it's my magic and not yours."

Sydney clenches his jaw and pauses at the door. "You coming?"

"I'll be right behind you," I tell him.

CHAPTER 8

Sydney and I spend a few hours scouring the supernatural library for anything on the Malachi bond, only to come up empty-handed for the most part. Sure, there are texts to read, but none of them exclusive to what we're going through.

We've pretty much only found what we've already known.

The connection is rare. Not all vampires have one, but when they do, they're unbreakable. The perks are pretty generic and open to interpretation. Healing and transfer of power are noted. Nothing specific on how it actually works. And according to the books, each situation varies. So, what Silas and I have is not interchangeable with another Malachi set. Similar, just not the same.

Sydney lets out an exasperated breath and shoves his stack of old manuscripts to the side. "I feel like I've failed you."

I stand from my seat and go to him. I kneel next to his chair and grip his hand firmly in mine. I don't enter his mind space in fear that I'll use up whatever magic I have remaining. "It's not your responsibility to figure everything out. I appreciate every single thing you do. I hope you know that. This isn't on you to solve." I squeeze him tighter. "And hey, this isn't life or death. If we don't find any answers, it's not a big deal. We've got the rest of our lives. We're not in a rush anymore."

Syd nods slowly and meets my gaze. "I'm so sorry, Willow. I wish I could trade places with you. I'd give anything to make this right, to get you your magic."

I force a smile and surge what's left of my power into him to calm his energy. "I have more than I need." A hollow sensation burns through my veins. A well gone dry. It's strange to feel so... *empty*. But it's something that I will have to get comfortable with. The coming and going of whatever fleeting magic I manage to borrow from Silas.

Without having any real knowledge of the effect it has on him, I'm hesitant to take any more. He claims there were no adverse reactions, but Silas has been known to lie about things in the past to not draw any attention to himself. He's a very self-sacrificing person when it comes to me. I'm going to have to pay extra caution to him to make sure he really is okay.

Nature has its way of balancing things out, so to think I have an endless supply of magic from Silas at my fingertips would be a naïve thought to have. There are consequences to everything, I just have to figure out what they are.

And my biggest concern is keeping those I love safe.

I can live without a single drop of magic if that's how I keep them from harm's way.

But if getting a little taste of his powers here and there doesn't hurt him *and* I'm able to maintain some of my supernatural lessons and help Lillian with her training, I don't see the issue with that.

"You must be starving." Sydney raises my hand to his mouth to kiss.

We go to leave our seemingly forever reserved spot in the enchanted library, and a dusty book catches my eye. I had spotted it in my search but moved it aside. I slip it into my bag and zip it shut. If I can't make any progress on the Malachi research, at least I can read about the man who took all of my power from me.

Remi and Kyra scowl so much at Silas that I'm concerned he's going to expose his fangs in response. The girls are pissed at him, and boy does it show. Neither of them has any clue the literal Hell that he went through in his time away. They're under the impression that he randomly dumped me and left town. That he broke my heart and made me a blubbering mess, only to show up unexpectedly. And it's not exactly like I can be truthful with them.

Until I can come up with some kind of story to get them off his back, the glares and whispers about him will continue.

Silas wipes his mouth with his napkin. "I'll refill your tea." He takes my glass and walks across the dining hall toward the refreshments.

In the past, he usually never ate meals with us, but since he's returned, he spends time with me every chance he can.

Remi speaks first. "It's not like we aren't happy for you. You seem way better off now. It's...I mean, he ghosted you, Willow. How not cool. And he gets to waltz in and pretend nothing happened? Girl code, Wills."

Deghan shoves a handful of French fries in his mouth, and Cameron side-eyes me with those beautiful baby blues of his.

None of them are going to step in, not that they would have any clue what to tell them anyway. We're all at a loss for how to handle the situation.

Lillian takes a sip of her lemonade. "Maybe you're being a little harsh."

Kyra's mouth drops open. "Are you really taking his side?"

"There are no *sides*. Everyone deserves a second chance. She gave him one, so you should, too. It's her relationship, not yours." Lillian looks over her shoulder at Silas.

He winks at her, totally having heard the entire conversation from across the room with his vampire hearing. "Thank you," he mouths.

"Fine," Remi groans.

I have enough drama between Silas and Sydney, I don't need two of my best friends hating on him, too. If I could explain what really happened, the girls would probably feel horrible for how they're treating Silas.

"Thanks," I say to Silas.

"I'll see you later." He tucks my hair behind my ear.

I stare into his wild eyes. "You okay?" I hope what the girls said didn't bother him too much. I ache for him to comprehend I don't have any negative feelings toward him despite them laying it on heavily.

"Yeah. Going to get some fresh air."

Aka, a proper meal.

I should have known Silas would be *hungry*. I can't imagine he's fed enough to replenish the starvation Balial put him through.

I'd give anything to torture that sadistic piece of shit a fraction of what he did to Silas. Maybe if I do enough research I can figure out some way to make him suffer even in the slightest. That man deserves to rot in a worse Hell than the one he calls home.

I won't hold my breath, though. Punishing the Devil doesn't seem like an obtainable goal to have in mind. But, who's to say a girl can't dream? What's that old saying—if there's a will, there's a way. And damn if I'm not one of the most determined powerless witches of all.

"You coming back to class tomorrow?" Remi steals my train of thought.

It takes me a second to regain my surroundings. My head was a mix of visions of a fiery inferno mixed with kicking Balial where it counts.

"That's the plan," I finally tell her.

"Good, because Intro to Management is *so boring* without you."

She's just being nice. It's not like I add anything to the class, or the time spent there. She and Kyra are the life of every gathering. I appreciate the sentiment all the same, though.

Cameron reaches across the table and touches my hand. "Our stats final is Friday."

I peep the clock on the far side of the room. The day has seemed to drag on. Exhaustion rattles my core. In a matter of twelve hours, I've managed to have numerous painful conversations with those closest to me about losing my magic, have mind-blowing sex with Silas, *and* accidentally steal some of his power. If I'm going to make it through the rest of the week, I need to get some rest. Some legitimate sleep and recharging. And there's only one way I'm certain that will happen.

"Meet me at my place?" I nudge Syd and look across the table at Deg and Cam.

A group slumber party is exactly what I need. All of my men in one place. Safe and sound and by my side, lulling me into a deep slumber.

It takes minimal convincing once they're inside my room.

"It's been a long day. I'd feel better if you were all here."

"Say no more." Deghan wraps me into his arms. "Happy to be of assistance."

He and Cameron shove all of the beds together in two-by-two sections. They take one section and leave the other to me, Sydney, and Silas.

Deghan and Cameron both strip down to their boxers while Silas and Sydney stay modestly covered. Syd sports a pair of dark cotton shorts and a white T-shirt. Silas has on a thin long-sleeved shirt and grey sweatpants. Each one of them look sexy in their attire.

Sydney grabs the extra blankets from the closet in the corner and tosses them onto their new homes.

A few moments later, the lights are off, and we're all tucked into our spots.

I turn on my side, and Silas cuddles me from behind, our legs overlapping each other's in a tangled mess of our bodies. He nestles his head into the crook of my neck and kisses my shoulder.

Sydney faces me and takes one of my hands in his and runs the other along my forehead and cheek.

I close my eyes and savor the presence of each of my men. Moments like this don't last, so I say a silent prayer to the angels to slow time and let me enjoy it while I can.

CHAPTER 9

I wake to the aroma of coffee and blueberry muffins.

Silas is still holding me, but now I'm lying with my head on his bare chest.

I blink in confusion at seeing his ink-stained skin so exposed.

"Good morning, love," Silas speaks clearly like he's been awake for a while. He tightens his grip around me and kisses my forehead. "Cam brought breakfast."

I sit up and shove the mess of my hair out of my face. I take in my surroundings, noting that it's only me and Silas left in my dorm. "Where is everyone else?"

"It was pretty early when we went to bed. The guys have been up for a few hours." He hands me my cup. "You were sound asleep, so they snuck out to not disturb you."

I take a sip of the warm and hazelnutty java. "You going to class today?"

He shrugs. "I really only do it to keep up appearances. I have twelve college degrees already. I don't really need another one."

My eyes go wide, and I nearly spit out my drink. "Twelve?"

"I've been around a while, Willow." A grin spreads across his face.

"But you're so...youthful." I graze his wrinkleless skin. "How old were you...?"

"Twenty-two." His expression stiffens.

"Will you ever tell me about it?" I try to remain soft in my acquisition.

"One day."

I don't push any further in fear that he'll retreat into whatever dark corner inside his mind he sometimes becomes lost in. "Okay." I immediately switch gears. "Do we have time to shower?"

The cheer returns to him. "I thought you'd never ask." Silas carefully takes my cup and sets it on the nightstand. He moves quickly and picks me up from the bed and kisses all over my head on our way to the bathroom.

"Let me brush my teeth first," I insist.

It's amazing how quickly we can fall back into our normal routine. A broody and stalking Silas escorting me to and from each class. He even joined me in Speech, but I know it was only to spend more time with me.

I find myself mentally distracted by the overwhelming love I have for him and for each of my men. If it weren't for the occasional reminder that I've lost my magic, I'd think I was finally... happy. I spend most of my lectures forcing away the insistent daydreams so I can focus on soaking up what minimal material I can.

Finals are this week, and this isn't exactly an appropriate time to be distracted.

Prior to summoning a portal to Hell, I had already started most of my major assignments for the end of the term. If I push myself, I can get them done on time and potentially pull off passing this section. Statistics will more than likely be the biggest hurdle, considering it's a massive test that spans the entire depths of our curriculum.

It's possible but will be a challenge. I seem to be the queen of working well under pressure. It's kind of my thing. Doing the impossible on a time restraint.

Only now there is no magic to help me.

I skipped my first section today, given it's my supernatural period. I wasn't sure if I was still supposed to attend and I wasn't quite ready to deal with the disappointment that would follow from not being fully able to do the required work. Not to mention, Silas and I spent a little extra time in the shower, making me late even if I did decide to go.

"What are you doing on break?" Remi asks while stuffing her notebook into her bag.

"Ugh...." I hadn't fully processed that we had next week off between terms. I'd been a little preoccupied with assuming I'd never leave Hell. The thought of doing *anything* seems drab. I'd rather relax and recharge after the insane few months we've all had.

"Ky-bear and I are going with my aunt to her timeshare in Florida. You're more than welcome to come with." The way she says *you're* definitely implies only me.

How could I possibly go a week without my guys?

"I'll probably stay here. Maybe go visit my mom. I have a lot of reading to catch up on." All things that are not a lie. As boring as it may sound, it's what I truly *want* to do.

"Okay. But the offer stands. We leave Friday night if you change your mind. We're driving, and the house is already paid for, so the only thing you'd have to worry about is anything extra you want. She keeps the place fully stocked with food, and it's like two blocks from the ocean." Remi takes hold of my elbow and lowers her voice. "Your men will live without you for eight days."

It's not them I'm worried about. I'm fully capable of being alone, I just don't want to be away from them. Times are strange right now, and there are so many new and uncertain things in my life. Being without them would only make that more difficult to process. And I only just got Silas back.

"I know. I really did promise my parents that I would stop by, though." A deal I'm not ready to follow through with quite yet.

If I go home, I have to have another awkward conversation about losing my magic. I'll have to explain that I activated a portal to Hell and successfully made a passage for me and Silas to return. And in exchange, I had to leave behind my power with the master of the underworld.

I can already sense the disappointment from my mom.

I had fought tirelessly to regain what was taken from the Oliver witches and now I've lost it all. Or at least my portion of it. But if anyone could understand *why* I did what I did, it would be her. She knows firsthand how horribly painful it is to lose love. I'm sure she would have done the same thing if given the opportunity.

"You don't think it's a little creepy?" Remi adds.

Kyra elbows her. "Shut up. It's romantic."

I follow their line of vision, my cheeks warming when I spot Silas waiting near the door to my last class of the day.

Only a week ago I would have died to see him standing there waiting for me. Now, it sends a cooling calm through my body unlike anything I've ever experienced. I pinch myself every so often to make sure I'm not dreaming.

Silas puts his arm around my shoulder. "You hungry? Tired? What do you want to do?"

A few things cross my mind, all of them involving my many men. I push away those thoughts and focus on the here and now. "I need to study."

He takes my bag and leads me through the foyer with his hand gently resting on my lower back.

His attention shifts in the slightest like he's paying attention to something I can't quite make out. I'll wait until we're alone to ask him what it was.

His pace slows slightly, and I match it, letting him take in whatever it is.

Once we're tucked inside my dorm, he speaks first.

"Walker and Abigail were organizing a supernatural meeting to get a proper reading on the power here at the school. Their numbers are off, and they're concerned there might be a breach somewhere." Silas goes to my dresser and takes out a few things and stuffs them into my pack. "We can stay at my place until they figure it out. You'll be safe there, I promise. Nothing will—"

"Silas," I say, cutting him off. I place my hand on his arm to stop him. "That won't be necessary. I know what the discrepancy is."

"You do?" He turns to me.

"Yeah. It's Lillian. We never told them."

"Lillian? What do you mean?"

"Uh, so, when you were gone, Lills became a witch. Well, she was always a witch. But apparently, she came into her magic. My mom told me that's not the only occurrence. Other witches have randomly found their power. Oh, and, um...I have a dad. You already knew that. He's back. At home, with my mom. I guess the moment I sent you and Syd's mom away, it broke whatever block it had on them being able to return."

Silas tosses the bag to the floor and grips my shoulders while staring into my eyes. "I missed a lot, huh? I'm sorry I wasn't here for you."

My mind flashes back to seeing him lying in a heap on the ground in Hell on my bold rescue (suicide) mission. He was covered in dirt and the life drained from him. My heart constricts, and I fight the tears that build—both from sadness and anger.

He drags me into his arms. "I'm here now. I won't leave you again."

"Are you serious?" I muffle my words into his chest. "It was my fault. If anyone is to blame, it's me. I will never forgive myself for what I did to you. It kills me that you went through what you did."

He tilts my head up to meet his gaze. "I refuse to hold you accountable even for one second."

A knock sounds on the solid wood of my dorm room door.

"It's Sydney," Silas whispers.

I turn the handle, and Syd rushes inside.

"Walker is calling an emergency meeting. I have no idea what it's about, but he's making the announcement in a few minutes. Abigail gave me a heads-up." Sydney stops abruptly when he spots the clothes haphazardly packed. "Going somewhere?"

"We were," Silas confirms.

Sydney glances from Silas to me. "Past tense?"

I chime in. "It's about Lillian. That's what they're gathering for. They still haven't figured out where the extra power came from and they're probably on high alert since my little trip to Hell and back."

"And you were going to leave because of that?" Sydney points to the bag.

"Silas was worried. He didn't know about Lillian. He over-heard them talking about a potential threat. But now that we are all on the same page, we really need to get down there before they get the entire student body involved." I make my way toward the exit regardless of what Silas and Sydney plan to do. We've kept this secret long enough—Walker and Abigail deserve to have the truth.

They were skeptical but accepting of my situation, so I'm sure they will be for Lillian, too. Especially considering we have a little reasoning behind why she suddenly has supernatural abilities. With me, it was a surprise to everyone.

I jog down the stairs and rush past the few girls huddled into a gossip group near the dining hall entrance. I should probably find Lillian and bring her along, but if they're going to call this meeting immediately, I'd rather stop them first and *then* locate her.

Walker is just closing his door as I approach.

"Hey," I say, a bit out of breath.

He turns around in surprise. "You okay?"

I nod, probably too aggressively. "Do you have a minute?"

He points generically toward the open area. "Well, I was..."

"Please, I insist."

He studies me for a second and then puts his key back into the lock. "What's this about?"

I wait until we're inside to speak. "I know where the extra power source is coming from. It's not a threat. I should have come to you sooner, but I wasn't sure about all the details. I'm still not. But I needed you to understand the magic isn't a danger to the academy." I blurt the words out in a rush.

He throws up his hands. "Wait. Rewind a bit. What is causing it?"

"Lillian," I say, matter-of-fact.

Walker brings his hand up to his forehead to rub his temple. He furrows his brow. "How is that possible?"

"I'm not completely sure, sir."

"But you're positive it's her? How can you be so certain? There has been an imbalance for a while now."

"Since I sent Silas away."

Walker's eyes go wide. "You've known *that* long?"

"I'm sorry. It was all very sudden, and we weren't sure what to make of it. I didn't want the wrong people finding out if it had something to do with my curse or the LeBlanc's."

Walker lets out a sigh. "Listen, I think I've been incredibly accommodating, but please, for the love of everything holy, you have to talk to me. I can't protect you and the students here if I'm always in the dark about everything that's going on. I assure you that I'm way more patient and accepting of the truth than you apparently make me out to be."

His admission cuts me deep. He's absolutely right. I have shut him out from nearly every single major thing I've done here at the academy. I've been reckless and foolish and done things that he of all people should have been informed of. And every time I've gone behind his back, he's been gracious and understanding. He's proven himself on numerous occasions, and all I do is keep letting him down.

I need to be more grateful for his accepting and supportive nature.

"You're right." I swallow my annoying pride and inability to open up. The time for change is now. "I'm not going to sit here and make excuses for my behavior. I regret not telling you sooner. I won't make that mistake again."

"Thank you. I appreciate that." He leans against his desk. "I'm not mad at you, Willow. I'm just a bit disappointed. I thought by now that you would trust me a little more, but I realize that might take you some time. I do hope that eventually you'll get to that point. I admire you for your ability to overcome everything that you have. And considering all that you've been through this past year, I think it's important that I assure you, I'm with you, not against you."

The overwhelming urge to hug this man who has welcomed me with open arms is strong. Headmaster Walker is more than just a faculty member, he's been the most prominent father figure I've ever known. He's someone I respect and should cherish.

The door creaks open, and Abigail peeks her head inside. "Excuse me, I don't mean to interrupt." She narrows her gaze on Walker. "We were supposed to meet."

Walker waves her in. "No need. We've narrowed down the source. If we can locate her and get a sense of her levels, we can readjust the numbers. If things are still off, we'll call the assembly to evaluate the discrepancy."

Abigail lowers her voice and asks, "You have?"

"Yes." Walker looks at me. "Could you retrieve her, please?"

I nod a confirmation and leave before anything else can be said.

My task of finding Lillian would be a lot easier if I could use my internal tracker. Guess I'll have to get used to doing things the old-fashioned way.

CHAPTER 10

"**I**s he mad?" Lillian asks.

"He specifically said he wasn't," I reassure her.

Sydney stands up straighter. "I'll bring her in. This is on me, too."

Lillian folds her arms over her chest. "What are they going to do to me?"

"They're just going to get a reading of your magic for their records." Syd does his best to keep his voice calm. "Probably ask you some questions."

"And you'll have to sign a supernatural oath," I add.

Lillian's eyes go wide. "A what?"

I shake my head. "It's not a big deal. It's to make sure you don't go blabbing to the humans about the shadow side of the academy. It's how they ensure the two stay separate and the non-supes don't find out."

"I can't tell anyone, ever?" The shocked look doesn't leave her face.

I shoot Sydney a look for some help.

"Students. While you're here. Once you graduate there is a grey area. You're still not supposed to run around telling everyone, but obviously there will be people in your life you'll confide in." Sydney ganders at the clock like he's distracted by something.

"How am I supposed to keep this from Ethan?"

Silas finally breaks his silent streak. "The same way you have been."

"Yeah, you're doing fine, Lillian." Sydney walks to the door. "Let's get this over with and we can get back to studying for finals."

I squeeze Lillian's arm. "You're going to be okay."

The two of them leave me and Silas behind.

"What first?" Silas stands there, leaning against the corner of the wall, appearing delicious like he always does.

It takes all my willpower to shift my train of thought to the most pressing issues at hand.

"Marketing."

He meets my gaze and strolls over, stopping right in front of me. He trails his thumb down my cheek and along my lips. Silas presses his mouth gently onto mine. "Okay," he breathes against me.

"You're going to have to cut that out...otherwise I'm going to fail out of college, and with nothing else going for me, I kind of need my degree."

We decide to take up residency in our normal spot in the supernatural section of the library.

Silas mentioned he had some research he wanted to do, and

given the secluded location, I'm bound to have minimal distractions from getting my work done.

That is, if I force myself to stop gawking at Silas every two seconds.

Between him being so fucking breathtaking and being back in this universe, it's hard to keep my eyes off him. It's a soul-soothing thing to see him simply existing near me.

The first half hour while we were here, I made the decision to map out what I needed to accomplish before the week's end. With some kind of big assignment in each of my classes, I needed to strategize the best way to get things done.

Considering statistics will be the most difficult of them all, I need to spend a portion of each day going over the material if I plan on covering it all. Everything is due on Friday, including the comprehensive exam. All of our teachers are allowing their lecture times the rest of the week to be dedicated to the completion of our work.

In theory, between my evenings and in-class hours, I should be able to make this work. Today and tomorrow will be focused on Marketing and Intro to Management, with Supplementary Statistics. Then that leaves Thursday and part of the day Friday to finish Speech and cram for Stats.

As long as nothing massive goes wrong, I can do this.

If only I could borrow Silas's extensive brainpower along with his magic, I'd be a lot more capable of getting this done. *Twelve degrees?*

"It's almost time for dinner," Silas tells me. "Try to find a good stopping point to take a break."

"Okay." I skim the last section of the text and shut the book. I've made an appropriate amount of progress, but meals are going to have to be cut shorter if I'm going to pull all of this off. I can't exactly skimp on sleep since my brain pretty much requires it to function properly. I'll have to budget everything where I can.

I'm close to finishing my Marketing project and if I can keep up this rate, I should be completing it tonight and making a dent on my Management one.

I scarf down the chicken tenders that Cameron had a hand in making for dinner.

He paired them with the new recipe of his spin on honey mustard, only this time with no cayenne. Obviously, it was delicious, despite eating so quickly I could barely taste it.

Lillian was grateful to not succumb to her spicy glitch again.

I go down the row kissing my men on their cheeks. "I'll see you guys later." I bolt away to head back to the library to get to work.

They mumble something resembling a confirmation when I jog away, but I'm in such a hurry I barely catch it.

Part of the reason I'm frantic to get all my work done is so I can focus on spending time with all of them next week during our break. I'm sure I could ask all of my instructors for extensions and finish then, but we all deserve this downtime without having anything else going on.

I see lots of relaxing movie nights and fun adventures in our future and I'm not going to be the reason why that doesn't happen. I can't help but feel like I've been neglecting my relationships with them with everything crazy that's happened the past few months.

We've all bonded through the chaos, and without it formally happening, we became this team of best friends and lovers. I want to make sure they know how much I care about them and am thankful for having them in my life.

Those days off will be the perfect chance to do exactly that.

I walk into the library and my vision catches on to the book I had tucked into my backpack earlier. I slide it out and flip it open.

I ate quick enough that I can spare just a few minutes of browsing the text.

Balial, master of all demons. King of Hell.

A chill creeps across my spine.

...represents the punisher of evil...cruel and ruthless...strikes fear in all...rumored that Balial is a fallen angel but it could never be confirmed...he is a wandering tortured soul...little is actually known of him...

I let out an annoyed sigh. Everything I've read seems to be wild guesses about him and nothing concrete. How am I supposed to plan my revenge when no one knows a damn thing about him?

There's nothing in here about his excessive good looks or the oddly weird energy he exudes. Nothing about his age or how he came to find a home within the farthest fold in Hell. No family history or relationship status or favorite food. I can't find his weakness, if there is jack shit on him.

"What are you reading?" Silas comes around the table and moves my hand to get a better look. "I'm going to have to have a word with your instructors if that's the kind of reading material they're giving out."

I shove it aside. "I'm sorry. I..." Was trying to find a way to punish Balial for hurting you because it eats me alive to know that you suffered in any capacity. But instead of saying that, I blank.

He leans against my table. "I get it."

"You do?" I blink up at him.

"You're trying to find a way to get your magic back." Silas takes the book and thumbs through it. "Right?" His gaze melts into mine.

I'd been focused on revenge so heavily that I hadn't even considered the possibility I could ever get my powers from Balial. I didn't think it was an option. I gave him the only thing I had worth bargaining with, I have nothing left that he would trade me for.

If I tell Silas the truth, that I want to hurt the man who hurt him, he'll try to talk me out of it. He'll tell me it's okay and he's fine and I shouldn't concern myself with Balial on his behalf. And until I find a lead on how I can follow through with my plan, I should keep it to myself to disallow him the opportunity to deter me.

"Yeah," I finally lie.

He tosses the thin text on the table beside him. "Don't." Silas reaches out to take my hand. "Let me worry about that. You have enough going on."

"Wait, that's what you've been researching?" I suck at hiding the surprise in my voice.

"You really think I'm going to let that bastard get away with what he did to you?"

My thoughts exactly.

"I'm serious. Your job is school." Silas shoves my Statistics notes toward me.

My curiosity piques. "Have you found anything?" A strange sense of hope blossoms in my chest.

"Not yet. But I will. If it's the last thing I do, I'll get you your magic." He hops down from the table and kisses my forehead. "Now, get busy. You're never going to catch up if you can't even get your first degree." He winks at me and strolls across the room to browse the far shelf.

Maybe I'm not doomed after all.

CHAPTER
11

I manage to pull it off by Thursday evening.

Well, most of it.

Now it's me and Cameron on my dorm room floor with a Statistics book between us and notes sprawled around messily.

My projects are ready to turn in, and all that's left is the massive exam that Cam and I are incredibly stressed about. We've crammed every second we could, but we're not sure if it will be enough.

"I'm so fucking glad we're allowed to bring a notecard to the test." Cameron doesn't look up from the page.

"Double-sided, too," I add. "Shame she specified the size, otherwise we could have gotten one of those extra-large ones to fit everything on it."

"Right? I have no idea how I'm going to read my own hand-writing." He holds the thing close to his face and squints. "It's *so small.*"

"It'll be fine. We just have to make sure to cover the basics. If we get all the core formulas, we should be able to put it all togeth-er." My confidence is fake, but it helps boost morale.

"In theory."

My mind switches gears. "You have plans for break?"

Cameron's body tenses. "Does murdering my brother count?"

"I'm available if you need help hiding the body."

He nudges me with his elbow and smiles. "What would I do without you?"

"For starters, you'd have to take care of a corpse by yourself." I lean into him. "I'm sure Deghan would lend a hand, too."

Cam sighs. "Probably."

"You want to talk about it?" I glance up and lock my gaze onto his sky-blue eyes.

"Pretty sure he's been drinking again. It's not a big deal. But with the booze comes the not working...the not paying any bills." He pauses for a second. "I assume the house is trashed."

The thought of someone causing any of my guys to feel nega-tively sends a fiery rage coursing through me. They're all great men, and treating them any less than what they deserve is a big fat no-no.

I'm well aware they're capable of fixing their own issues, but I can't help the possessive protective instinct that kicks in the moment they are treated unfairly.

"It's not much, you know? But it's home. And it's like he doesn't care one bit. About it, about me, about anything. Can you believe I used to look up to him?" He shakes his head. "When I was a kid, I thought he was cool. I admired him. He had a job and played baseball. He had a bunch of friends, and everyone got along with him. He balanced it so well. It's like he peaked in high school, though, and never grew up. It took me a while to realize it, though. The first few times I had to pick his drunk ass up, I chalked it up to being a phase. A bad breakup maybe. Boy was I wrong. He spiraled out of control and hasn't managed to find his way out. He can't keep a job. He spends all his money on alcohol. He's wrecked his truck three times while under the influence. I'm honestly surprised he hasn't lost his license. The system is flawed..."

I watch him carefully as he spills what he needs to. It's only when he doesn't continue that I decide to speak. "Sounds like you both grew up too quick." A situation I'm all too familiar with.

Cam nods slowly. "Yeah. I mean, he took care of stuff at the house for a while. Until he didn't. Then it was all dumped on me. I figured it out, though. I didn't throw my life away just because it got hard. Sure, he had to do it first, but I didn't have it any easier. Why is giving up an option for him?"

I place my hand gently on his shoulder and remember I don't have any magic to calm him. Now would be a great time to have borrowed some from Silas. "Not everyone handles things the same. If anything, it should show you how strong you are. How resilient you can be. I'm proud of you for the path you took in life. And maybe I'm a little selfish, because it brought us together." I shrug. "I think you're capable of doing anything you set your mind to."

"How can you be so sure?" His thoughtful gaze locks on to mine.

I let out a little chuckle. "Is that a serious question? You mean other than the fact that you're incredibly smart, probably the kindest and most genuine person I've ever met, you're *stupid* attractive, and by far the greatest chef in all food history? With that stuff aside, let's just say it's intuition. My gut is telling me you'll do great things, and she's not usually wrong about matters like that."

Cameron blushes and observes our pile of papers all over the place. "I think we've earned a break."

I grin at him and climb over the book between us. I position myself in his lap and lower my lips to his.

He grabs me by the waist and drags me into him, kissing me deeper with each passing moment. His tongue dances with mine, and his arousal grows against me.

I grind my body along him and rake my fingers through his golden hair. I run my mouth away from his and make my way along the base of his neck and down his jawline.

Cam clutches my hips and grinds me into him while moaning and tilting his head to grant me further access. His thumbs hook under the waistband of my leggings.

I stand to allow him to drag them the rest of the way off me.

He tosses them into a heap on our study papers. Still in his seated position, he inches my body forward to straddle his face.

The second he makes contact, my knees threaten to buckle from the pleasure. I do my best to stay in position and enjoy the attention he's so graciously paying me.

Cameron swirls circles up and down my most sensitive area and digs his fingers into my waist to drag me closer.

When I can't take any more of his beautiful torture, I kneel and unbutton his jeans, freeing him in the process. I climb back on top of him and slide him into place.

We stay like that for a while, rocking up and down in a heated motion until he locks his arm around me and lifts me from our spot on the floor.

With our bodies still together, he carries me to the closest bed.

I release from him and turn onto my stomach, positioning myself to let him enter me from behind.

He glides in easily and holds on to my hips to move me as he pleases.

I grip the sheets firmly and match his rhythm. My face is smashed against the bedding, but my mind is focused on the mountain of pleasure I'm climbing with Cameron.

Cam slows his pace and extends his thrusts, sending me that

much closer to the edge. He reaches a hand under and gently rubs in exactly the right spot.

I clench around him and fall into a magnificent whirlwind of gratification. I pulse uncontrollably while he continues to lengthen my climax.

The moment I'm done completely, Cameron pulls himself out and finishes onto my back. He breathily collapses next to me with a huge grin on his face.

With a stifled breath, I say, "That was…"

"Incredible," he adds.

"Mmhm," I mumble into the sheets in a post-orgasm daze.

"Pass me the fries?" Deghan asks.

I reach across my bed and get them for him. "You want the onion rings, too?"

"Yes, please."

"Your room is going to smell like fried food for a week." Cameron takes a bite of his burger.

"If that's the price I pay for some alone time with my guys, I'll gladly take it." Well, some of my men.

Silas took the opportunity to tend to his special dietary needs, and Sydney said he had to finish up some things in the library prior to joining us.

"This is nice. We should do it more often," Deghan says in between bites.

"The eating?" I smile at him.

"That, too."

I swallow the last of my chicken sandwich. "I'll be so relieved once tomorrow is over."

"I think we all will." Cam wipes his mouth with his napkin. "That exam is going to be brutal."

It's so great to be here with them, like a normal college student, eating food and hanging out and complaining about how difficult finals are going to be. It's a pleasant shift in the dynamic considering how hectic life has been lately. It warms my heart to share such a simple yet meaningful experience with them.

A loud thud rumbles against my door.

I quickly look from Deghan to Cameron.

I can't imagine any of us were expecting company, other than Silas and Syd, but neither of them would knock, they would just come inside the way they always do.

"Willow," a voice calls out.

Immediately, I hop from my place at my impromptu dinner and rush to the door.

The second I turn the knob, a frantic person meets my gaze.

"Could we have a word, it's urgent?"

I step back to give Headmaster Walker the space he needs to enter my room.

He nods at the guys and focuses back on me. "I need your absolute honesty."

My heart picks up its pace, and I have to fight the bubbling anxiety that forms from the tone he uses. "Okay."

"You were hesitant to divulge your knowledge of Lillian gaining her powers, but I have to ask, are you aware of any other new magical source at the academy?" Walker stares at me intensely while he awaits my answer.

I shake my head quickly, not fully processing the severity of his question. "No. I promise. Only Lills." It suddenly dawns on me that he's so panicked. "Why?"

Walker clenches his jaw. "I don't want to cause any alarm, but it's possible that we may have been breached. I caution you to stay put until we figure things out further." He moves to grab on to the handle.

"Wait, what? Are you serious? What can I do to help?"

"It would be best for everyone if you remain in your room for now." He turns toward the guys. "All of you. That's an order."

Walker leaves before we can protest.

I stare blankly at the door while an endless supply of questions racks my brain.

What is happening?

Are Silas and Sydney and the girls okay?

Who could have broken into the school?

How can I possibly do anything when I'm completely powerless?

CHAPTER 12

"How are neither of you freaking out right now?" I gush to Cam and Deghan.

"It's safe to say you've got it covered for all of us." Deghan plants his hands on my shoulders and stops me from the pacing I've been doing back and forth across my dorm.

"We can't just sit here like freaking ducks." There has to be something, *anything* I can do.

"I'm with Deghan, Will. Why don't you come sit?" Cameron motions to the spot next to him on my bed. "We can study while we wait?"

A scraping sound sets me on high alert. I nearly jump out of my skin when a familiar face appears outside my window.

I run over and unlock the latch, opening the big pane wide to let him in.

Silas jumps onto the floor and wraps his arms around me. "Are you okay?"

I sigh and hold on to him tight, breathing deeply as a bit of relief washes over me. But it's short-lived, Sydney and the girls are still out there, and I have no idea if they're safe or not.

"Dude, did you seriously scale the side of the building?" Deghan pokes his head out the window and looks down. "That's hardcore."

Silas breaks away and meets my gaze. "Walker has a barrier on the dorm hallways. Nothing in, nothing out. There were no other options to get to you. I had to make sure you were all right."

"Sydney's still out there..." I whisper.

"He's fine," Silas says nonchalantly.

"What? How can you be so sure?"

"He's with Walker. He's the one who suggested my dramatic entrance." Silas makes sure the fastener is secure and pulls the drape to cover the window.

"The girls?" I hesitantly ask.

"Safe and sound."

The river of my relief continues to flood.

"Do you have any idea what's going on?" Cameron hands Silas an extra burger.

Silas eyeballs it for a second and then decides to take it. "Same thing as last time. Unaccounted magic source. Probably another random witch, but they want to make sure."

"How is that even possible? I thought Lillian was an anomaly." But then again, so was I. I guess my mom was telling the truth about the influx of new witches.

Silas shrugs.

"What about the human students? This has to make no sense to them." I decide to finally sit.

"Rogue rodent. That's what they were told. That a skunk is loose in the school and to stay in their rooms until further notice. Pretty sure everyone bought it out of fear of being sprayed." Silas takes a seat next to me and puts his hand on my thigh. "Everything is going to be okay, don't worry."

If only it were that easy, though. Realizing how vulnerable I am without my magic is both humbling and terrifying.

We wait for what feels like forever. And each second that passes only solidifies my feelings of helplessness.

At some point, I fall asleep, only to wake to the steady sound of Deghan lightly snoring.

I rub my eyes and blink through the darkness at my surroundings. I'm lying on Silas's solid chest, his arms wrapped around me.

He loosens his grip and tucks my hair behind my ear. "Go back to sleep, love."

"What time is it?" I ask, and my voice cracks.

"Five something."

"Have you slept at all?" I run my thumb over his brow and along his cheek.

"I'm not tired." His serious gaze melts into me.

"Any word on what's going on?"

He rocks his head slightly from side to side. "Nope." Silas averts his eyes and focuses on the door. "People are coming." He shuffles out from under me and vamp speeds to press his back against the wall.

I clutch at the blanket that's still covering me like it will somehow protect me from the intruders.

Deghan and Cameron are passed out next to each other on the bed opposite mine.

I should wake them, but my mind won't let my body act. I'm seemingly frozen in a daze of tiredness and shock.

Silas suddenly moves from his spot and turns the handle, letting the figures in.

Sydney rushes past him and to me. He kneels next to the bed and cups his hands in mine.

"Wh—what's going on?" a sleepy Deghan calls out while stretching wide.

The sound of the latch clicking shut sends my attention away from my guys.

Headmaster Walker clears his throat. "We've secured the perimeter. You are safe to carry on within the confines of the academy."

I finally gain control of my motor skills and stand, throwing on one of Deghan's sweatshirts in the process. "What happened?"

Walker rubs at his temple and then meets my gaze. "We aren't certain, but we think it was Tremont."

My heart seems to beat ten times harder, and my jaw drops open. I thought that sadistic creep was gone for good.

What a freaking time to not have any of my magic. I would have loved to destroy him for the part he played in getting Silas sent away. Granted, it was ultimately my fault Tremont's actions brought us to that horrible day.

Sydney places his hand on my lower back but remains silent.

"Holy shit, really?" Cameron chimes in.

Walker shifts uncomfortably. "I'm afraid so. His desk was ransacked. It's possible that he broke in to retrieve something he had stashed away. As of this time, there has been nothing brought to our attention to allude that he did anything other than that. We've since confirmed the integrity of our barrier and have put up added protection. We will continue to do so until we can locate and apprehend him. I've sent out our best scouts to follow the trail."

"You're sure it was him?" I ask.

"Unfortunately, no. But we feel confident it was him or someone helping him."

I can't help but feel like Walker is withholding information. Or maybe it's just the way he reacts to these kinds of situations. Not being able to read his energy the way I normally do is definitely a curveball in figuring out what he's really thinking.

"I encourage all of you to try to get some rest. Finals will go on as scheduled." Walker turns to leave but then stops. "If any of you intend on staying through the break, please let me or Abigail know so we can get a proper headcount."

"I am," I say without skipping a beat. "No sense in waiting to tell you. I'll be here."

"Same," Cameron adds.

Walker scans his gaze around the room and collects nods from the rest of the guys. "Very well." His attention lands on Sydney. "Shall we?"

"I'll be right there," Syd responds.

Once Walker is gone, it's like the whole room lets out a sigh.

"What the fuck?" I say to Sydney.

"I'm shocked, too, trust me." He takes my hand and leads me to the bed. "You sure you're okay?" Sydney glides palms toward me and scans my body. His green ripple of energy flickers during his exam.

I shake him off. "I'm fine. Nothing happened."

Sydney turns to Silas. "You."

Silas narrows his gaze at him. "What?"

"Give her some of your magic." Sydney stands and waits.

Silas stares at him and then at me.

"She can't be left completely defenseless. Even if it's just to keep in her reserves. Something is better than nothing." Sydney's insistence grows.

"I was here," Silas says, his voice deepening.

Cam and Deg seem hurt but keep their mouths shut. Clearly, this is between Silas and Sydney.

"Only because I told you how to get to her. Why do you always have to argue with me?"

Silas's body stiffens. "You act like you're the only one with her best interests in mind." He points to the guys. "I don't see you insulting their ability to protect her."

"This is different, and you know it." Sydney seems more tense than usual.

I hold my hands out in both of their directions. "Can you two stop already? We're supposed to be a team." I look to Silas. "If you don't want to give me your magic, you don't have to. No one is going to make you." I shift to Sydney. "I'm safe here. I only have one actual class today and then I have to turn in my assignments. I'll stay with one of the guys, I promise. Walker is expecting you; you better go."

Sydney runs his hand through his hair. "Fine." He turns to the guys. "Please take care of her." He briefly kisses my cheek and leaves my room.

Once he's gone, Silas rushes over and grabs my hand. "Take all you need."

I roll my eyes at him. "You are so difficult."

"Explain to me how this works?" Deghan strolls over toward us with Cam on his heel.

"It's a Malachi thing. Apparently, I can borrow Silas's power. Well, it's not really borrowing because I don't give it back, but I can siphon his magic to use." I anchor on to Silas and initiate the connection.

The bubble of energy funnels into me immediately and sends a euphoric sensation cascading through my entire being. Like a flat tire being inflated, I'm brought back to life. Although, the slow leak will eventually catch up and deflate me again.

"What about mine?" Deghan says.

"It doesn't work that way." Even though I wish it did.

Deghan clutches Cameron's shoulder. "Man, now I know how you feel. Sorry, buddy."

"Join the club. I never get to help this pretty one." Cameron cups my face with his hand, sending a jolt of unexpected power through me.

I jump away from all of them, wide-eyed and heart racing. "What was..."

Cameron flips his hand over in front of him and studies it. His eyes are as big as mine.

Silas grips my arms. "Are you hurt?"

I take in a breath, tasting the sweet sensation of a secondary power source running through my veins. It's faint, but there. And I have no idea what the hell it means.

CHAPTER 13

I study my fingers like they're foreign to my body. They glitter with Silas's purple magic and a faint shimmering of gold. I slowly turn to Deghan.

"Is that my...?" His mouth hangs open in surprise.

"Wait. Did I?" Cameron clutches his chest.

"Everyone, calm down," Silas urges.

I thought the shock of using Silas's magic was overwhelming, but it was something I was always capable of doing. This? I have no idea what to think about what is happening.

I have Deghan's magic running through my veins alongside Silas's. And the most shocking thing of all, it came from *Cameron*.

Cameron is some kind of transporter of power.

Silas snaps his fingers together like he's suddenly remembering something important. He points to Cam. "You're a conduit."

"A what?" the rest of us say at once.

Silas shakes his head. "Can life get any weirder for you?"

"Tell me, please." I try to keep my voice neutral despite the uncertainty surrounding me.

"I've never known one firsthand. They're *super* rare and only occur in even more uncommon situations. Kind of like our Malachi connection. I'm not sure how it works if I'm being honest. But that has to be what it is." Silas rubs his perfectly sculpted chin.

"That literally explains nothing." I glance at Cameron.

He's still holding his arm to him. "Did I hurt you?" he finally blubbers. "I'm so sorry. I...I didn't mean to."

"Cam, no. You did nothing wrong. It was just unexpected." And completely freaking bizarre.

Deghan steps forward. "Are you saying that Cameron is a means to carry magic from one person to another?"

"In theory, yeah," Silas confirms. "But only to her."

"Wow." Cameron sits on the edge of my bed. "I thought..."

"Guess you're not ordinary after all." Silas slaps him on the back.

This makes sense of those moments between me and Cameron when I've felt *something* but haven't been able to put my finger on what it was. I probably didn't grow hyperaware of it until my magic had been lost, and now my being is on high alert to that kind of thing.

I thought Balial had taken these abilities away from me, but in reality, he opened my world to a whole new life force I was completely oblivious of. If it weren't for him, I might never have found out about Cameron's gift. I may have missed this possibility at a deeper connection with one of the men I love dearly.

If anything, I should be thanking him for this opportunity.

But there is nothing positive he could do to ever erase the torture he put Silas through, and for that, I won't stop until I figure a way out to repay him for his cruelness. Plus, it's not like he did this on purpose, it was only a side effect of him taking my magic. A silver lining on my end, not his.

I always knew Cameron was special, but I never expected it to be in this form.

"Dude, this is rad." Deghan sits next to Cam and throws his arm around his shoulder.

"I could use some coffee," Cameron murmurs.

Deghan jumps to his feet. "On it."

Cameron blinks into reality. "I'll go with you." He looks at me with a hopeful stare. "Any special requests?"

I shake my head and offer a weak smile. "Surprise me."

"Your usual?" Cam asks Silas.

Silas nods stiffly. "Thanks."

I try to process what went down with Cameron, but my brain doesn't want to cooperate. How is it possible that I share such a rare and unique connection with Silas and Cam?

"Why don't you go ahead and shower while you're waiting?" Silas offers gently. "I'll get your water started."

I watch him stroll to the bathroom with such an elegant ease. He's a mix of grace and swagger and he pulls it off so well.

A moment later, he's at my dresser rummaging through the contents to find me something to wear. "Is this okay?" Somehow, he chose what I already had in mind—a dark pair of jeggings and a black fitted T-shirt.

"Are you a mind reader now, too?" I say to him.

He grins. "I just pay attention to what you like."

I walk across the space and take the items from him. "Thank you." I press my lips to his cheek. "Would you like to join me?"

Silas tilts my face up toward his. "Rain check," he whispers and kisses me sweetly.

Butterflies flutter in my belly at his touch, and my body seems to ignite with an undeniable passion for him.

I'll never quite get used to feeling his skin on mine. After the many hurdles we've gone through to get to this moment, I never want to take for granted a second with him. I'll cherish each one like it's the first and last.

Heck, there was once a time that he was forbidden from laying a hand on me in any way. The very act caused him unbearable pain.

"Penny for your thoughts?" His radiant greyish eyes stare at me intensely.

"This." I graze my fingertips along his pale cheek. "Remember when it was impossible." I swallow and take in his immense beauty. "And now here we are."

"I was worried I'd lost you forever." Sadness takes over him.

"Not even the gates of Hell could keep me from you, Silas."

"I have no doubts that you're capable of doing anything you set your mind to." He nudges me to the steam-filled room. "I'll be out here waiting."

"And we're supposed to go on with the day and pretend like someone didn't break into the academy?" The more I think about it, the more I realize how insane that is.

"I'm not letting you out of my sight," Silas reassures me.

"What if something happens to you?" I can't stomach the thought of something bad happening to any of my guys. "We need a buddy system."

Silas blankly stares at me. "Willow. I'll be fine. You're the one I'm worried about."

"Has anyone talked to Syd?" I look from Silas to Cam to Deghan in search of an answer.

"Walker's got him busy." Deghan pulls a muffin from the brown paper sack sitting on the small table in my bedroom. "I wouldn't stress, princess." He holds out his hand. "Here, eat."

"Do I need to like...I don't know...do something official?" Cameron plops onto my bed and takes a bite of his pastry.

"I doubt it," Silas responds. "You don't actually have any

magical powers; you can only transfer them. I'd wait until things die down before we make a big deal about it."

"Right." Cam frowns. "Yeah."

I roll my eyes at Silas and go to Cam's side. "Listen, I think what you can do is freaking incredible and I can't wait to see what we can learn about your new abilities." It's then that it dawns on me. "Wait, has anyone checked on Lillian?"

"Saw her on the way over here." Deghan fumbles through the selection of breakfast food. "She was heading to take a final."

I let out a breath of sweet relief. I guess everything really is fine for now and I should focus on getting through this school day. At the very least, if I get my stats test over with, I can concentrate on all the other crazy shit going on in our lives.

"You about ready?" Cameron asks me.

I snatch the postcard cheat sheet off my dresser. "Here goes nothing."

Cam and I stand and, like a shadow, Silas follows us to the door.

"I'm going with you." Silas fixes the collar of his leather jacket.

I pull my knitted sweater off the back of the chair. "It's a two-hour test."

"And?" Silas meets my gaze. "You act as though a couple hours is anything in the grand scheme of things. I already told you, I'm not letting you out of my sight. This isn't up for discussion." He guides me out of the room.

"Just admit it," Cam teases him. "You're concerned about my safety, too."

Silas barely grins. "Whatever you say, bud."

Cameron's eyes go wide. "Wow. I'm surprised. I expected some backhanded insult."

"Don't push it." Silas narrows his eyes at him.

Cam throws his hands in the air. "Okay, okay."

I can't help but smile at the thought of all of us getting along. Silas and Sydney have a long way to go, but in the short amount of time they've shared, there have been drastic improvements and moments of great breakthrough with them.

"I'll catch you cool kids later." Deghan tugs me into his side and kisses my forehead. "Knock 'em dead." He pauses and then continues. "Maybe that's a bad expression to use." He ruffles Cameron's golden hair. "Good luck."

Deghan cuts left and we turn right. We walk the rest of the way to Statistics in silence, dodging the random students going to and from their last moments of this school term.

Each body we pass makes me wonder who's staying behind during break and who's leaving to go home and visit their families or perhaps travel, like the girls are doing.

They're probably still hoping I'll change my mind and go with them on their vacation. Even if I had wanted to, last night's events absolutely ruled out any chance that I would go. Between the evil and fucked-up Tremont potentially breaking in here and Cameron having some random magical thing, there's too much at risk if I leave.

Plus, I'm absolutely looking forward to getting to spend quality time with my loves. To have an entire week of low-stress, no-pressure hangs is going to be freaking amazing.

The stress factor is still up in the air, but not having to worry about school or another daunting Oliver curse will be such a breath of fresh air.

I follow the short line of people into the class and wait for my turn. One by one we show our cards to the teacher for her inspection, and she hands us the thick test. We each take a calculator from the stack and settle into our seats.

Without seeing him, I sense Silas's presence. It's calming and reassuring to have him nearby. There's something about his proximity that sets my soul at ease.

I glance out the door and locate Silas. Taking in a deep breath, I flip open the packet to the first question.

CHAPTER 14

"Are you sure you don't want to come with us?" Remi pleads with her hand clenched tightly around the handle of her overpacked suitcase. "It'll be fun. Just us girls. We can lie out on the beach and sip daiquiris. Virgin, obviously."

Kyra elbows her. "Give it a break. If she wanted to come, she would. She's got four hot dudes; I don't blame her for staying." She winks at me and nudges Remi again. "We're going to be late, come on."

"Uh. Fine." Remi pulls me in for a hug. "Try to have some fun. It won't hurt, you know."

I give her a gentle squeeze. "I will. Don't worry. I'll see you in a week. Be safe, okay?"

"Yes, Mom." Remi slings one of her bags over her shoulder

and rolls the other behind her. She heads toward the door, leaving behind another set of students who are going elsewhere.

I stand there, watching the two of them exit through the massive front entrance.

"Would you have rather gone?" Silas says under his breath next to me.

I don't hesitate in my response. "No."

"Willow..."

I wait until the girls are fully loaded and driving away until I respond. "I promise. I want to be here. But for them, I'd rather they get out of here. It's much safer than them staying. This place can be dangerous in times like this."

Ruby waves a passing goodbye on her way out, subtracting her from the list of attendees.

I pivot and look around. There aren't many people left, and most of them have bags attached to them, telling me that they'll be gone soon, too.

"You hungry?" Silas extends his arm for me to loop mine through.

With no great urgency, I pause and savor not having any immediate pressure on us to be somewhere specific. "Can we catch the sunset first?"

He cups my hand with his and leads me through the dining hall and to the patio doors. "Your wish is my command."

We get out there and Deghan is already sitting on the step to the patio, his head tilted to the beautiful orange-and-crimson sky.

"Mind if we join you?" I ask him.

A huge smile breaks across Deghan's face. He scoots over to give us room. "It would be my honor."

I sit next to him and after I tug at Silas's hand, he takes the spot beside me. I weave my fingers through Silas's and lean my head on Deghan's shoulder.

We stay that way for a little while, gawking at the changing horizon. I let all of my worries fade away with the day and focus on breathing in a new life with the coming darkness. What a wonder the sun is—no matter what kind of weather it experiences, it's always back to show us that despite any storm, we can shine bright again.

My gaze falls to the forest behind the school. What remains of the leaves are all shades of brown and reddish. A slight breeze rolls by, and I take my hand from Silas's to hug my arms to my chest. The air is crisp and cool with winter pushing its way in.

An unsettling feeling trickles along my body at the depths and uncertainty that lie in those woods. Could Tremont somehow be in hiding right outside of eyesight range? Could something else be lurking and waiting to pounce when the timing is right?

Silas grips my hand. "It's getting chilly. Better get you inside."

"Good idea," Deghan answers. "I'm starving."

***

"One more, I'll get it, I promise." Cameron steadies his aim and sends his projectile flying toward the intended target.

Deghan opens wide and catches the tater tot in his mouth.

They both clap their hands together and shout and laugh, and it's probably the most wholesome thing I have ever witnessed in my entire life.

"Your turn," Cam tells me. He grabs another puffy potato from his plate and sizes up his mark.

I shake my head. "I am not catching that."

He pouts and drops his shoulders. "Aw, come on." Cameron points toward Silas. "What about you?"

Luckily for everyone involved, the food flinging abruptly halts when Sydney arrives into the room.

I didn't exactly want to be embarrassed by my lack of hand-eye coordination and I wasn't sure how Silas would react to Cameron's childish antics. He's Mister Serious and sometimes he can be an ass with the other guys.

I jump from my spot at the table and rush over to Syd. I throw my arms around him. "Is everything okay?"

He acts surprised by my embrace but ends up pulling me into him. "Yeah. It's been a long day."

I break away and hold him at an arm's length. "You're sure? You were gone forever. Did they find him? You must be starving. Here, sit down." I lead him to where the rest of us are sitting in the big empty dining hall.

Everyone else is either tucked away in their rooms or has gone home for break.

It's a bit eerie being in such a big place alone, but with my men, I nearly forget there is a world that exists at all outside of them. And I wouldn't change a damn thing about that.

They're my home—my safety and my constants.

Sydney plops into his seat. "No word on his whereabouts yet. Don't worry, though. He'll be found." He rubs at his forehead. "We spent most of the day going over the barrier. I'm freaking spent."

Deghan arrives from the kitchen area and brings a tray full of food and sets it in front of Sydney. "Here, bud. Eat up."

"Thanks." Sydney sighs and rests his elbow on the table. He leans his head on it and uses his other hand to shove a few fries in his mouth.

A few minutes pass, and Sydney seems to gain a bit of life back into his body.

We all watch and wait for him to come around.

Some, more impatient than the rest.

"So, what's the plan?" Silas finally says when he's had enough of the silence.

Sydney shifts his focus from the cheeseburger to the touchy vampire. He chews his bite much slower than his normal pace and dramatically swallows before he speaks. "It's under control."

I sense the sudden shift in Silas's mood. I find his hand under the table and shove the little bit of magic still pulsing through my system into his body to calm him. It works, barely taking the edge off enough to relax his reaction.

Sydney turns to glance around the vast space. "Abigail went

with the scouting team. She's an amazing tracker. I'm working with Walker to help in any way I can, but honestly, it really is taken care of. We're all here and that's what matters. We're safe." He looks directly at me. "That you're safe."

"Oh, speaking of me. There's something we need to tell you." I figure, what better time than now?

"What happened?" Sydney moves his tray out of his way and turns to face me completely. He studies me over, intensely. "Are you...?"

"Syd. I'm fine. Everything is fine. We've just..." I flit my gaze to the anxiously awaiting Cam. "Had a new development."

Sydney follows my attention, and his eyes widen. "Cam's a witch, too?"

"No, he's not." I seem to get Syd's focus back on me. "Well, I'm not sure." I tilt my head in Silas's direction. "Is he?"

Silas stands. "You." He points to Cameron. "Over here."

Cam does what he says and plants his feet between me and Sydney.

"One hand here." Silas motions to Sydney, then to me.

Cam closes his eyes and takes in a breath.

Almost immediately I sense the familiar and decadent magic that can only belong to one person—Sydney.

I tilt my palm up and study the faint glittering of green on my skin. It's beautiful and magnificent and tastes so sweet in my veins.

"Try me, try me." Deghan comes around the table and latches on to Cam's exposed forearm.

Another power source funnels in and sends waves of heaven raining down me.

It's like I'm high on the magic of my men.

Wild-eyed and curious, Sydney breaks contact. "How is that possible?"

I rub my fingertips together. "Pretty incredible, right?"

Silas crosses his arms over his chest. "He's a conduit."

Sydney nods as though he's putting it all together. "That

would make sense." He smooths his hair out of his face and seems to get lost in thought while he processes the information.

I allow the power to dance through my being and I revel in the bliss of feeling the well of my magic being temporarily replenished again. It's nowhere close to my full capacity, but being starved for so long, even the smallest amount is enough to satisfy your needs.

"How is your system handling all of this?" Sydney examines me for any sign of distress.

"I'm great." I really am. What more could a girl ask for?

"And you?" He concentrates on Cameron.

"Uh." Cam averts his eyes and shrugs. "Fine? How should *my system* be?"

"I don't know. This is new to me, too. Tired? Lethargic in any way? Do you have any headaches or nausea? You're just totally normal?" When Cam doesn't have anything to add, he shifts to Silas. "Have you dealt with this kind of thing?"

"Nope. I wasn't sure it existed. Kind of like the fae. It's something you hear about but have to see it for yourself to believe it." Silas rubs the spot between my shoulders.

"Interesting. I'll have to do some research on this. I'll talk to Walker in the morning to gather any information I can, and I'll fill you all in." Sydney suppresses a yawn. "I would probably hold off on utilizing Cam's new skill until we've learned more about it. With how crazy things go for you, Will, I think we should play this one safe."

I'd been so excited with Cam's discovery that I hadn't thought through that there could potentially be consequences and side effects to using it. "You're right."

Cameron exhales dramatically. "Man, I finally become of some use and I'm benched."

"It's okay." Deghan wraps his arm around Cam. "In due time."

Silas trails his hand down my back and snakes his way under

the hem of my sweatshirt. His touch is electric on my bare skin. "You must be exhausted."

"I think we all are." I glance around the table at my sleepy guys. "Let's call it a night."

And so, we do exactly that. Once we've cleaned up our mess from dinner, we make our way toward the stairs to the upper level of the academy.

My head and heart swim with happiness, and I can't help but wonder, is this the calm before the storm?

CHAPTER 15

The academy is different when classes aren't in session and everyone is mostly gone.

It's pleasant, really. The lack of pressure that awkward small talk and forced friendly smiles brings. It's not that I don't enjoy the company of outsiders, it's just that this whole experience is new—the college thing and the supernatural world —so it's a bit overwhelming at times. Having the place to ourselves is a lovely and welcomed change.

Although, the looming thought that Tremont is still out there, and the variables of Cam's new ability, add an interesting edge to the situation.

"Good morning," a chipper voice calls out.

My heart nearly beams at the sound. In the chaos of everything, I completely lost track of what Lillian would be doing during break.

I jump from my spot at the dining hall table and rush over to scoop her up into a hug.

"It's nice to see you, too, Wills." Lillian lets out a little laugh.

"Where's Ethan?"

"Obligatory family thing. He couldn't get out of it."

"I didn't know you were staying. I'm so happy you're here." I grab her hand and pull her toward the rest of the group. "Are you hungry? Cam made pancakes. They're freaking delicious. Do you want coffee?"

I can't help but bubble at having her around. Things have been so strange lately, and I haven't gotten much one-on-one time with her. This week is shaping up to be exactly what I needed.

"Mind if I join you?" Walker comes through the large entrance and waves at us.

"The more the merrier." Deghan shoves another piece of bacon in his mouth.

Walker claims a seat at our table, and Cameron passes him a plate.

"This smells heavenly." Walker pours an unhealthy amount of syrup on his flapjacks.

The rest of us settle into our spots and finish off our breakfasts.

Silas keeps his hand on my thigh the entire time and remains stiff in his place next to me. His energy is restless and dark—not totally uncommon for him but enough to tell me something is bothering him.

It could be the Tremont situation.

I weave my fingers through his and rub the spot between his thumb and index finger to loosen the tenseness.

The next opportunity I get to be alone with him, I'll see if I can figure out what's troubling him. After everything we've been through, I don't want anything to drive a wedge between us or risk him pulling back or pushing me away.

"Great job, Cameron," Walker says between bites. "You're really onto something with this whole cooking thing. You've got a natural talent."

Sydney clears his throat. "Speaking of..."

I flip my attention at the beautiful green-eyed boy sitting across from me. I tighten my hand around Silas's and hold my breath.

"Yes?" Walker seems curious.

"There's been a new development." Sydney shifts his gaze around the vast yet empty room. "Is this an appropriate place to speak?"

Walker nods. "This is it. The last of them cleared out this morning. Unless anyone comes back, we're it for the next week."

My eyes widen. I thought we might be the few that stayed behind but I didn't realize we would be the only ones.

"Very well." Sydney glances at Cam and then at the slightly grey-haired man sitting with us. "It's come to our attention that Cameron is potentially a conduit."

Lillian pauses mid lifting her cup to her mouth and tilts her head to the side.

Walker takes a careful sip of his coffee. "Interesting." He turns his sights to me. "You're full of surprises, aren't you?"

"What did I do?"

He laughs. "If this is true, and Cameron is, in fact, a conduit, it's only possible by having a strong bond. These instances are incredibly rare and can only happen when there is a mutual connection. A *loving* one."

My cheeks flush, and upon looking at Cam, I realize his match mine.

"Let's back up, though." Walker studies me intently. "You're capable of carrying magic?"

I nod. "It's fleeting, but yes." I pause. "And my Malachi thing is still intact."

Walker smiles. "Leave it to you to find the loopholes."

"Wills, that's great," Lillian adds. "I'm happy for you."

Silas decides to speak up. "What else do you know of Cameron's ability? Are there any risks? Anything we should be concerned about?"

"Well." Walker wipes his mouth. "With magic, there are always concerns. The universe demands a balance. I'm not completely familiar with the skill but I assume there are limits and a toll that must be paid for the usage. I can imagine the transfer of power would be exhausting for everyone involved. Those giving their energy would be depleted, and the one exchanging it would experience some sort of drain. I definitely suggest it be done in a controlled environment in an attempt to monitor how each person reacts." He runs his index finger along his cheekbone like he's thinking something through. "This situation might be completely unique. It's incredibly uncommon for a witch not to have access to their magic in some capacity. Usually, it's a supplementary source, not one entirely on its own."

"That's what I had thought, too." Sydney nods in agreement. "I'm not sure we'll find much in the history books to help us with this."

"You're not wrong. The Malachi connection alone is a mystery, given that the circumstances change case by case. And to have that along with a conduit—I'd say it's unheard of." Walker looks at me again. "Fascinating, really. Pair that with your heritage and..." He seems to get lost in his mind again. "The possibilities are endless."

And somewhat terrifying. The fact that I'm a witch at all, and the supernatural world exists is mind-blowing. But to throw in the fact that I'm descended from the angels, was cursed, and have incredibly rare magical connections with two of the men I love—it's a bit of a shock.

Not to mention, my best friend just found out she's a witch and there are more random people finding their powers. Then there's the whole 'conquering the impossible' time and time again.

"I'll see what I can find." Walker stands from the table. "I'd tread lightly in the meantime." He places his hand gently, yet firmly, on my shoulder. "You have immense potential, Willow. Don't take that for granted."

With that, he makes his way from the room, leaving my mind reeling in his wake.

"What do you say we hit the library?" Sydney asks.

A chance to leisurely peruse the expansive supernatural section of texts stored beneath the academy? Heck yeah!

"I'd love that."

Silas takes my tray to dispose of, and a second later, he's back in front of me. "Will you be okay for a little while? I won't be long." His voice is gentle and somehow a comfort to my aching nerves.

"I'll be fine."

He tightens his grip on my hand. "Here." A rushing current of his magic comes coursing into my body. "Just in case."

I lower my voice so only he can hear. "Are you all right?"

Silas grazes my cheek with his lips and whispers into my ear. "I'll be better once I'm back by your side."

I want to ask him what's wrong, to figure out whatever it is that's bothering him, but I know now isn't exactly the time or place. Silas is a secretive person, and I'm lucky he lets *me* in— there's no way he's going to want to open up in a room full of other people. Even if it's our closest friends.

"You two lovebirds coming?" Deghan approaches us with a grin spread across his gorgeous face.

He's in a good mood, and I love it.

"I'm afraid I need to step out. Take care of her while I'm gone?" Silas nudges me toward Deghan who's already waiting with arms wide open.

I look over my shoulder on our way out of the dining hall and catch sight of Silas standing in place, watching us leave.

There's a sadness in his expression that pains me in an unspeakable way.

I ache for the moments to pass quickly so I can be near him again.

"Holy shit, this place is incredible." Cameron gawks at the endless rooms full of books that seem to go on and on. "Does it ever end? Where did they come from? Who do they belong to? How are they organized?"

I weave my arm through his and tug him toward the private reserved section I have spent so much time in since I've been at the academy. "I've found that I always have more questions than I'll ever get answers. And I've grown to be somewhat okay with that."

The hallway hums with energy and reminds me of all the power I'm missing.

At least now I can get my supply from more than just Silas. Not that his isn't enough, but if there are downfalls to this, it would be better to have more than one option if it's needed.

All of us, minus Silas, funnel into the space and look around.

Sydney goes directly to a stack of things he had piled up on the table he frequents, whereas Deghan scans the far wall for something specific. Lillian chooses a book at random and plops into a seat to dive in.

Cam, still wild-eyed and full of excitement, can't seem to decide where to go. "What are you working on, Will?"

I locate the few old manuscripts I had left behind and take the top two off. I hand him one. "Just a little light reading."

Cameron examines cover. "*The Illusions of Evil?*"

I shrug. "Can't hurt, right?"

We settle into the oversized sofa chair in the corner, and Cameron slides my legs on top of his lap.

"This is nice." I relax into the old worn-out cushion and let the weight of my bottom half fall onto Cam. Flipping to the last page I had last studied, I scan for where I left off.

Minutes go by filled with the quiet shuffling of pages and discreet breathing.

Every so often I glance up and smile at the sight around me. The only thing missing is Silas. I check the clock on the wall periodically to see how much time has passed since he's been gone and wish like hell he'd finish whatever it is that has him occupied.

He's probably feeding. It would make sense that he's still attempting to replenish his reserves after being starved by Balial. I'm not sure how all of that works, but it's the most logical explanation for his absence. Unless it has something to do with Tremont. I hadn't considered that until now, and the thought alone sends an uneasy chill down my back.

Cam rubs at my shin. "You cold?" His blue eyes melt my heart.

"No, I'm okay."

He smiles and goes back to the book in his hand. "Have you heard about the Faustian bargain?"

"The what?" I sit up to focus my attention on him. I catch Sydney in my peripheral centering in, too.

"It's essentially a deal with the Devil." Cam points at the page he's on. "According to this, people can offer the dude something in exchange for something else. Usually fame or fortune, cliché shit like that. But, here's the interesting part, say you don't have anything to offer him, you can challenge him." Cam seems really excited about his newfound knowledge. "There's this elaborate battle, and if you beat him, you get whatever it is you ask for. This says it's pretty much impossible, but the option is there. Quite a few people have tried it and failed. Did you know Marilyn Monroe was a witch?"

I allow his words to sink in and weigh the magnitude of them.

Sydney rushes over and plucks the book from Cameron's hands. "Nope. Don't even think about it. Not happening."

I jump up and try to stop him from taking it. "It could work."

"You are the queen of suicide missions, and for once, I am putting a stop to it. This is too much. It's too far. You think *trav-*

eling to Hell was hard? Battling the Devil himself without having your magic? No. I mean it. Absolutely no." Sydney tucks the text under his arm and refuses to let me have it.

"Please. Can't I just *read* it?" I look to Cam for a little help.

He throws up his hands. "I'm out of this one."

I shift to Deghan, who's sitting across from Lillian, both of them looking completely bewildered. "Uh, come on. This isn't fair."

"What isn't fair?" Silas strolls into the room like a seductive model, or maybe he just has that effect on me.

Sydney doesn't break his grasp on the book. "Your girl. She's out of control."

"I like how she's mine when she's causing trouble." Silas leans against the wall and waits for further explanation.

Sydney turns open to the page Cam was on and shows it to Silas while holding on to it tightly.

Silas scans the tattered paper and then pivots his gaze onto me. "Not happening."

Internally, I chuckle—like their disapproval has ever stopped me in the past.

CHAPTER 16

"I can't believe you're really on his side for this."

Silas stares at me. "And I can't believe you're surprised."

I pace back and forth in my bedroom, huffing and puffing about being shot down. "I'll say it again, this isn't fair."

"What's that saying about life?"

I stop and pivot abruptly toward him. "Don't mock me."

Silas rolls his eyes and sighs. "I'm not, but you have to take a breath for a second. Think this through. It's dangerous. More so than anything else you've done." His shirt hugs his chest in the most distracting way.

I force myself to focus. "And every single time I've pulled it off. I've done the impossible. You said it yourself that I'm capable of doing anything I set my mind to." I run my hand through my wild silver hair to drag it off my face.

"Yeah. I did. This is different. There's too much at stake."

"This is an opportunity of a lifetime. Quite literally the *only* chance I have at getting back at...I mean, my magic. Getting it back." I quickly try to fix the mistake in my words but I'm too late.

"What is this really about?" Silas sees through my bullshit.

I exhale dramatically and approach him. "I need this, Silas. Please." I meet his serious gaze, and my mind flashes to the memory of him writhing in agony on the ground in Hell. I have to avenge what Balial did to him. I won't let this slip by—I can't.

"I'm sorry, Willow. My decision is final. I won't stand by and watch you risk it all."

His energy bubbles with that familiar sadness and despair. It reminds me of when I was without him and could barely function. There was this empty pit in my chest that felt endless, like it was swallowing me whole from the inside.

"If you won't say yes, then will you tell me what's wrong?"

He averts his attention to anything but my face, letting me know that I'm on the right path with thinking something is bothering him.

I place my hand gently on his chin and tilt his head toward me. "Please. I can *feel* it."

"I don't want to burden you."

"We're in this together."

Silas bites at the inside of his lip before he decides to speak. "It's difficult to explain."

"Try." I take his hand and pull him to my messy bed. I sit and drag him down beside me. "I'm here for you. No matter what. You don't have to go through anything alone anymore."

Silas exhales in such a human fashion. "There's this darkness... it's heavy." He rubs his temple. "I'm sure it's part of the process. The being back from Hell, it's just a lot. I was there so long. I know it didn't seem like it here, but for me, it was years. There were moments..." He pauses and stares blankly at the ruffled comforter.

I wait patiently for him to continue. It's not often that he opens up to me, I don't want to rush and ruin what I've managed to get started, no matter how difficult it is to hear.

"I became familiar with the screaming. And the moment I did, there was nothing but silence. My shadow became my friend, the only thing to distract me from the torture, until he took it from me. Every single time I found something to cling to, he ripped it away. The one thing he never managed to steal from me was you. I clung to the thought that maybe I'd see you again. You were this vision...this angel through the inferno. My bright light that kept me from giving up when that's all I wanted to do." He lets out a sigh. "You can't imagine how badly I wanted to at times. But you were always there, guiding me and telling me to hold on for just a little longer."

It pains me to watch Silas suffer with the demons Balial snaked into his mind. He was already such a broken man, and now this. I'm afraid it may be his undoing. The thing that finally sends him over the edge.

What could I possibly do to save him from himself? To ease this inner turmoil that threatens to ruin him?

I take his hand in mine. "I'll always be here for you. Please don't ever doubt that. No matter what storms we face, we will make it through this together. You and me."

"I used to worry about whether or not you actually wanted to be with me. Which is funny, considering how there isn't much in this universe I care about. But with you, it's something entirely different. I can't imagine a world without you. It's suffocating to even imagine it. I exist for you. And I will spend all of my days keeping you safe from harm." He pauses. "That's why I can't let you challenge Balial. It would go against everything I believe in to allow you to do something so incredibly dangerous."

I want to protest, to demand that he reconsider, but for once, I absolutely understand where he's coming from. I would feel the same if the roles were reversed. There would be no way that I'd stand back and consent to such a battle. If anything, I'd want to step forward and take the burden onto my own shoulders and do it for him. That's what love is all about, right? Self-sacrifice and grand gestures?

"It's not that I doubt you." He shakes his head. "You really are a force to be reckoned with. It's that there is no winning with him. He's a twisted man. He'd find some loophole, some escape route or technicality that would ensure his victory. Balial is the epitome of narcissism, and he's a master manipulator. The game is rigged, it's unwinnable. I can't let you fall victim to his sick ways."

I divert the conversation. "Do you still question the way I feel?"

The tension in his face releases, and the corner of his lip turns up slightly. "You went to Hell and back for me. It was probably the stupidest thing anyone has ever done, but if that doesn't profess love, I'm not sure what does."

My cheeks blush. "I could scream it from the rooftops if you prefer?"

"Too dangerous." He winks at me.

It's everything I can do to not melt into a puddle on the floor.

How I got so lucky, I'll never know.

His expression is one of happiness, but his sorrow is still seeping from his pores.

I lower my voice. "What can I do to ease your aching heart? There has to be something."

Silas tucks a lock of my hair behind my ear. "Stay alive."

"I have that one covered for now. What about in the meantime?"

He nods toward the pillows haphazardly thrown at the top of my bed. "Let me hold you for a little while?"

I sigh and kick my shoes off. "Try to think of something more difficult next time."

He tosses his jacket onto the floor and climbs in after me, settling in next to me with his arm outstretched for my taking.

I nuzzle myself onto his chest and throw my arm around his torso. I breathe in his crisp scent and savor the sensation of our bodies fitting so perfectly side by side.

Silas and I end up falling asleep.

Somehow, I wake prior to him, which is one of the most amazing things that has ever happened. I take the wonderful opportunity to study the relaxed features of his existence that I rarely get to witness.

He's usually tense and hardened, but in this moment he's peaceful and angelic. It's a beautiful sight that I wish I had a more photographic memory for.

The door to my dorm creaks open and Silas stirs. I curse whatever it is that brought upon the disturbance.

"Willow," Cameron whispers.

Silas takes in a breath and opens his eyes. Shock and alarm wreck him from his serene slumber. "What's wrong?"

"Nothing," Cameron says a bit louder. "Will has a phone call. It's her mother."

Surprise and concern register throughout me. Why could she possibly be phoning me? Perhaps something is wrong. Did Tremont attack the house? Could my father be missing again? She never reaches out. What if Danny had an accident?

I swing my legs over the edge of the bed and slide them into my solid-black Vans. I hop down and make a beeline for the door without looking back.

Silas makes it there before me and has it opened a millisecond later. He must sense my urgency to figure out what it is that could possibly have happened.

"She doesn't call. She's not *that* kind of mom," I mumble to anyone who might listen.

"You might be overreacting," Cameron blurts out from behind me. "Walker didn't make it seem pressing."

"You don't know, Cam. She's a strange woman, but this is a new level of weird for her." I rush down the stairs and across the foyer in record speed.

Silas matches my pace, staying at my side the entire way. It's like he's a buffer for anything that might get in my path.

I beam into Walker's open office.

"Willow, whoa. What's the hurry?" His dark eyes meet mine.

I point to the phone on his cluttered desk with the blinking light, indicating someone is waiting on the line. "May I?"

"Yeah, absolutely." Walker takes his leave. "I'll be out here."

I suck in a breath in an attempt to calm myself. I pluck the thing from the receiver and push the glowing button. "Mom?"

"Sweet pea, how are you doing?" Her voice is cool and calm, nothing like what I expected.

"Um, fine. Is everything okay?" I glance to Silas, knowing damn well that his vamp hearing can pick up on the conversation.

"Well, yes, honey. Although, I was a bit surprised to hear the news."

I clutch the cool hard plastic against my ear. "What do you mean?"

"That you were staying at school during your break, what else? I thought sure enough that you'd want to come home for the week. Your headmaster filled me in briefly that there were some pressing issues and you felt best to stay put for the time being. And while I'm glad you're safe and sound, I was hoping that your father and I would get some time with you is all." Something clangs in the background. "Sorry about that. The oven door keeps sticking."

I can't help but worry there's something I'm missing despite her assurance. "You're certain nothing is wrong? You and Dad and Danny are all okay?"

She lets out a chuckle. "Yes, Willow. We're all fine. Can't your mother call and check in on you?"

A wave of guilt flows through me. Of course, she can, but the fact that it's unfamiliar territory is what sets me off. I've been the one to look after her, and it's been that way for so long that I've forgotten what it's like to have the roles reversed.

"You're right. I'm sorry. You know how I worry." I try to relax into these new positions, but it's going to take more than one minute to adjust to this foreign thing.

"Oh, how I do." A bit of static comes through the line. "So, tell me, what's new?"

Other than the fact that I went on a suicide mission to Hell, lost my magic to bring back my fated lover, found out that my other mate has a rare connection with me that can allow me to have magic from others, my best friend is a newbie witch, and an evil man broke into the academy and stole some of his own things? And how I'm trying to figure out how to go through with challenging the master of Hell to win back my power and punish him in the process for what he did to Silas? Besides all that, not much.

I scratch my forehead. "A lot, really. But I'd rather not get into it all right now, if that's okay."

"I see," she says seriously. "Okay. I respect that. I'm here, though, Will. If you ever need to chat, I'm happy to listen. This *world* we live in is a very strange place, and it can be difficult to deal with it at times."

"Yeah..." I'm taken back by her openness. Her willingness to be someone I can lean on if needed. It's something I always hoped she was capable of but eventually grew to handle things on my own because it was easier that way. She had never been stable enough to be the one to guide me through hardships. I never blamed her for it, but eventually, a subconscious resentment formed. I'm not unhappy with how I turned out, I just feel like part of my life was robbed from me when I was forced to grow up at such a young age.

"Listen, dear. I know you don't want to get into anything

heavy right now." The tone of her voice shifts to something much more serious.

I prepare for what's to come; I knew this conversation would turn into *something*. I meet Silas's gaze again and brace myself in his steel-grey eyes. "What is it, Mom?" I try to knock the edge off my words, but my attempt falls short.

"Things are changing." The phone rustles like she's switching to the other ear. "Largely. There's been an influx in the witch community. More and more are coming out of the woodwork with powers. The covens are trying to get a grip on it all. So far, they've had it under control. I've loosely been following along, trying to make sense of what I can. They're going to be meeting soon, and I've heard it's going to be monumental. I'm not sure what it's about, but rumor has it they're going to be looking for a new leader."

"That's common, though, right?" I say, not having a clue what any of this means.

"Sweet girl, how you have so much to learn. I'm referring to all of us. Now that the LeBlanc's have lost their reign and hold on our kind, there's room for a major shift in the balance. Reform. We've been suppressed far too long. It's time for the light to outshine the darkness."

I'm still not sure how to process any of this information. Isn't this a good thing?

Sydney's family were terrible people, and it's about damn time they were stopped.

"Anyway, they're coming together soon. If the news is traveling through the grapevine correctly, they're going to be performing an angelic calling ceremony."

My mind pings with the unknown. "Mom, English, please."

"They'll call upon the angels to appoint a leader. It's an old sacred ritual. The way it should have been from the start, before the demonic witches took control. I just thought you should know. It probably won't have any effect on you, but we may be under new management soon." Muffling fills the phone, and her voice comes through choppy. "I'm finishing up, I'll be right there." She returns loud and clear. "That's your father. He's home from work. Did I tell you he got a job at Bryon's hardware? He's doing sales and some odd jobs that are needed around town." She seems genuinely happy.

"That's great," is all I can manage to spit out. My head is reeling with the details of our conversation.

"I agree. Listen, it was great to chat with you. We should do this more often. Promise me you'll come visit as soon as the opportunity presents itself. I miss you around the house, Will."

"Sure, yeah. Sounds good."

"Love you, sweetheart."

"Love you, too, Mom."

The line disconnects, and I'm left listening to the clamoring dial tone that fills my ear and the endless questions that invade my mind.

CHAPTER 17

"What do you know about this?"

Walker rubs his chin like he does when he's thinking intensely. "I've been so concerned with what's happened at the academy that I haven't been paying attention to much else. I'll put out some feelers and see what I can gather."

"I wouldn't worry too much. I mean, my parents are gone." Sydney leans against the large glass encasing the indoor garden. "They're the Voldemorts of our world. All of their followers have more than likely crawled back into whatever hole they came from or have reverted to the light. Without them, I doubt there's anything bad that could happen. The ceremony is meant to be divine. Whoever gets chosen is who the angels see fit. They wouldn't steer us wrong—it's not in their nature."

Walker lifts his shoulder and nods. "You're definitely correct. My understanding is the person would have to pass a purity test. Only the truest and most pure of hearts can withstand the trial. I'm sure whoever is picked will be more than worthy of the position."

"Tremont is still out there, though. That has to mean something. Sure, your mom and dad are gone, but *he* could do something." The thought of him returning gives me the creeps. I can't believe I was foolish enough to let him take advantage of me. To dupe me into trusting him.

"He's going to wish he'd never come out of hiding." Silas stands firmly in his place by my side.

Walker puts his hands up like he's trying to calm us. "He'll be dealt with. Rest assured, he won't get away this time."

It suddenly dawns on me how strange it is that Walker is here, conversing with us and spending his break at the academy. Didn't he have family to visit or some kind of vacation plans during his time off? I always kind of assumed that he and Abigail had something *else* going on between them, but I never thought to ask him about his personal life. And maybe that's normal, not discussing those kinds of things with your headmaster. He knows so much about me, though, and has proven to be an important part of my life that it doesn't seem completely irrational or out of place to wonder about his life outside of the academic setting.

"Dinner is served!" Cameron calls from the dining hall entrance, distracting us from the serious conversation.

"I was thinking we could have a movie night," Cam suggests. He pushes his plate forward and rests his elbows on the table.

I take the last bite of my lasagna and nod.

"Oh, that sounds fun." Deghan shoves a chunk of bread slathered in Cam's famous honey butter into his mouth.

Sydney moves his food around with his fork and avoids joining in.

"Syd." I gently kick him to get his attention.

He glances up at me like I startled him. He raises his eyebrows in question.

"What's wrong?" I mouth to him.

"Nothing."

I narrow my gaze and tilt my head.

"Just a lot on my mind."

"Well, maybe you could take a break from it for the rest of the day and watch a show with us."

"I don't know...I have work to do. I need to run the numbers on the barrier and make sure we're still good."

Walker interjects. "Sydney. Have a moment to yourself. The defense is secure. You can take the night off."

"Then there's the..." Sydney tries to speak, but he's cut off.

"Whatever you're about to say can wait until tomorrow. You're only young once, don't waste these opportunities to enjoy yourself a little. I insist." Walker takes a drink of his extra-sweet tea.

The man likes his coffee black and his tea so sugared up it will rot your teeth with one sip. The mystery makes no sense to me, but I don't bother trying to figure it out. Not everyone prefers the dirty sock water the way I do.

"Okay," Sydney finally says.

I clap my hands together and bust into a smile. "Really? Yay!" I turn to Cameron. "What did you have in mind?"

"I was thinking something funny. *Wedding Crashers* or maybe *The Hangover*. Or we could do *Risky Business*, *The Great Gatsby*?" Cam looks around. "Someone please have some input."

"I choose the first one." We could all use a little humor in our lives right about now.

"You don't even remember what it was called." Cam grins at me.

I shrug. "If it was good enough for you to suggest then it works for me."

Lillian chimes in. "I second the vote, it's pretty good."

"I'm down as long as there are snacks." Deghan steals the half-eaten piece of bread off my plate.

"You're an animal." Cam stands and starts to clean off the table. "I already made brownies, and there are plenty of other things for you to choose from. We can make popcorn, too."

Deghan helps him carry the trash away. "You're speaking straight to my heart."

I lean my head on Silas's shoulder. "This okay with you?"

He wraps his arm around me and kisses my forehead. "Nowhere else I'd rather be."

Walker tosses his napkin onto his tray. "Well, kids, I think I'm going to call it a night."

I find myself speaking before I can ask for approval from the rest of the group. "You're more than welcome to join us. There's plenty of room up there."

"I don't want to impose." Walker continues to clear his spot.

Sydney speaks up. "You wouldn't be."

Silas follows suit. "Not one bit."

Lillian joins in, too. "Weren't you the one just preaching about taking time off?"

I guess we were all on the same page after all.

Walker pauses for a second. "It does sound fun...and I could use a little good old-fashioned mundane entertainment in my life."

I go take the dishes from him, and he hands them to me reluctantly.

With everything that he's done for me since I've been at the academy, it's the least I could do. The man has been like a father figure, taking me under his wing and doing his best to teach me the ropes of the supernatural world. He's patient and more than accommodating, even when I've gone behind his back to do shit I probably shouldn't have.

It's like we've all grown into this big, decently-happy family here at the academy.

I made the decision to come to school here but I never imagined it would turn out this way. I thought I would socialize and learn and get a formal education and become a new version of myself. I wanted things to be different, but I just didn't realize my entire world would change. Not like this at least.

Never in my wildest dreams would I have guessed that I'd meet the love of my life, let alone get to experience that four times over. Or form some of the closest friendships I have been lucky enough to have with the girls. I never thought I'd bond with people over shared supernatural traits and study things that are amazingly out of this universe. Finding my magic and growing it to be this unstoppable and powerful force and battling demons and monsters and even petty bitches from next door. And then summoning a portal to Hell and giving up everything I worked so hard for to get one of my guys back.

It's incredible, really. Someone could write a damn book about my life and it still wouldn't be any less bizarre and unreal to me that I got to experience it firsthand.

This journey has been nothing I could have ever dreamt up, and I am so fucking thankful I get to share it with these people.

My men. My best friend. My role model. My people.

Now, if I could only shake that whole *calm before the storm* feeling, life would be fucking grand.

Our movie night turned out better than expected. It wasn't at all awkward with any of us, and at one point, we were laughing so loud and throwing popcorn at each other like totally carefree people.

It was great to temporarily put on our happy faces and enjoy a simple moment.

Looking at us from the outside, you'd never guess the endless issues we have.

Every single one of us is dealing with some shit show in one way or another. Lillian with her new magic and unknown family. Cameron with his deadbeat brother. Deghan with a sadness he keeps hidden from the rest of us. Sydney with the loss of his parents. Silas with the infinite hardships he's experienced over his years. Walker with his seemingly unending role of protecting us and the academy from danger. And me, don't get me started on my problems. The list goes on.

I desperately tried to shut my mind off from it all, but no matter how hard I strained, shit kept coming up and distracting me from our seemingly wonderful get-together.

Walker yawns. "This was a pleasant evening. Thank you for inviting me."

"Anytime." Deghan slides another Twizzler from the bag and gnaws off a bite.

"Absolutely. This was fun," Cameron responds.

"I'll be in my office for an hour or so if anyone needs anything. Otherwise, see you bright and early for breakfast." Walker makes his way toward the stairs.

I stand and head in his direction. "I'll walk you back."

He holds out his hand to stop me. "Not necessary. Get some rest."

"Actually." I find my courage to speak. "I had something I wanted to talk to you about."

The residual magic left in my body alerts me to the shift in mood around the room, specifically coming from the vampire hot on my heels.

I turn to Silas. "I'll only be a few minutes."

He doesn't say a word, but from the look on his face, I can tell he's not okay with me leaving him.

Once Walker and I are on the main level and near the indoor garden, he speaks.

"What's this about, Willow?"

I glance behind me to make sure we're alone and concentrate on Silas's presence. I'm pleased to notice that he remained upstairs, respecting me enough to give me a little privacy. I motion toward the door.

"Sure, of course."

I go inside, and Walker follows me in.

"Is everything okay?" Walker grows concerned.

I take in a breath and decide it's now or never. If I don't spit it out, I never will. "Are you familiar with the Faustian bargain?"

CHAPTER
18

Walker is quiet for an awkward moment, like he's processing the question and figuring out the best response. There is also the possibility that he's contemplating how to restrain me and lock me up until I come to my senses.

I can't say that I blame him. I would probably do the same given the roles were reversed. I'm surprised with myself for bringing it up regardless, but considering literally no one is on my side, I thought that if I could garner the support of the headmaster, my chances of being able to follow through with this would be better.

Walker has always complained that I didn't come to him when I made big and reckless decisions to do risky magical stuff, so maybe this will show him I'm turning a new leaf, trying to be better and more responsible. And perhaps he'll agree to help me, for being upfront with him.

Or, this will blow up in my face and he'll shut me down just like everyone else has and completely ruin any chance I have at getting back at Balial for what he did to Silas.

It's definitely one or the other.

"I know a thing or two," he finally says. "Enough to imagine what it is that you're planning."

A lump forms in my throat, and my mouth goes dry. This is it, the moment he kills this dream without giving it a second thought.

"Is it already set in motion?" Walker studies me seriously.

"What do you mean?"

"Have you already contacted Balial?"

I shake my head rapidly. "No. I've only just discovered this entire thing."

Walker's eyes grow a bit wider. "I have to say, I'm surprised you came to me first. Given your track record for keeping me in the dark."

"I apologize, sir. I've made countless mistakes in my past, some of those even very recently. You've been gracious, and I'm sorry I took that for granted."

He goes behind his desk and flips open a handheld leather-bound book. Walker runs his finger along the page. "Today is Saturday. We have approximately one week from now until students begin arriving at the academy for the next term. The timeline is small, but I can't imagine it's nothing we can't handle. I would suggest that you start your training tomorrow." He glances up from the paper. "I heard about your work with Charles and sanction the use of his services again. Whenever the terms are made, you need to clarify with Balial that this all be completed by Friday. I won't tolerate putting the students and faculty at risk. That will give us a full twenty-four hours to reinstate any breach and be back up and running in time to welcome everyone."

My jaw hangs open, and I find myself speechless.

"What?" he asks. "Did you expect me to say no? Listen." Walker tosses the planner onto his cluttered workspace. "I don't like surprises. Never been fond of them. Not a huge fan of failure either. And, Willow, you have never ceased to amaze me at your willingness to overcome any obstacle that's come your way. If anyone else came to me, I wouldn't consider allowing this for the slightest second. But, I'm well aware you're determined and stubborn enough to go through with this, with or without my approval. I'm relieved you came to me. It gives me the chance to oversee and lend whatever aid I can." He takes a breath. "You've accomplished more than the most advanced witches and warlocks. This will be no easy feat, but it's not outside your wheelhouse to pull it off."

"I...I'm not sure what to say...thank you?" My heart seems to beat out of my chest. It was a long shot to come here, to run this by him. There was always the off chance that he would go along with it, but I thought I'd have to grovel or plead my case. I never imagined it would be quite *this* simple. His reaction makes me wonder what it would have been like if I'd gone to him for all of the other non-academic witchy extracurriculars.

"You ought to get some sleep. You're going to have to cram years' worth of training into a few days if you want to pull this off while you can."

"You mean prior to school resuming?"

"That, yes. But more importantly, if we're going to be under new management soon, there's no saying what type of things will become forbidden again. Making a deal with the Devil seems like one of those off-limits activities. If the angels are going to appoint a light-leader, commencing with the dark won't be allowed. It leaves too much wiggle room for the demonic witches to gain power once more."

I hadn't fully thought about what it would mean after the angelic calling ceremony is said and done. I sort of assumed life would carry on, just without the evil magical beings prevailing and taking control of the vulnerable.

"I'll see what I can come up with to prepare you for what's to come. I'm not completely familiar with the bargain, but there's a pre-test to the big showdown. I'll pull what I can find, and we can go over it in the morning." He makes his way around the table and stands in front of me. Walker places his slightly wrinkly hand on my shoulder. "I believe in you, Willow."

I slowly raise my gaze to lock on to his. Doubt creeps into my core, making me completely question what the hell I'm thinking. This is barbaric—there's no way I can defeat the king of the underworld. But then again, I seem to be the queen of the impossible. What's one more idiotic and completely irrational challenge?

I'm on my way out of his office when he stops me.

"Is that what tonight was about? Everyone buttering me up for this moment?" Walker studies me cautiously.

"Not at all. In fact, the rest of them are totally against this and will probably do what they can to stop me." I guess I failed to mention all of this earlier. I desperately hope it doesn't change his mind.

"It appears you have your work cut out for you then." Walker goes back to his desk, telling me that the conversation is over between us for now.

I walk in a stupor back to my dorm. I arrive upstairs to find the place where we had just watched the movie completely cleaned out and all of the furniture in its normal orderly place. I had expected to see my loved ones still tidying up, but they must have made quick work of it to retire to their rooms. I continue down the hall and approach mine.

The door swings open before I can touch the handle. Silas is there on the other side, worry and fear and uncertainty mixed with longing and desire written heavily across his face.

I step inside and pull my sweater over my head, tossing it onto the chair at the table. The one that has become my catch-all of discarded clothing items. I make a beeline for the bathroom and snatch my dark-purple toothbrush. I sort of feel like a zombie, going through the motions in a daze of my surroundings.

Silas leans against the wall close by. "What is it?"

I spit out a mouthful of foam and rinse it down the sink. How am I going to make him understand what I'm going to do? What Walker has agreed to assist me in doing?

I splash some lukewarm water onto my cheeks and dry myself with the random towel sitting on the counter.

"Talk to me. We agreed. No more secrets." Silas hesitates and then adds, "Please."

"I start training tomorrow." The words fall out of me.

Silas uncrosses his arms and stands firmly on both feet. "For what?"

At first, I want to avoid his deadly stare, but I know damn well that won't go in my favor. I have to approach this head-on, be open, and tell him the truth.

"Walker has agreed to help me. We begin our preparations in the morning." I reach out and touch his shoulder. "I won't let Balial get away with this."

Silas stiffens and flinches at either the mention of that sick bastard's name or my hand on him. He doesn't speak, so I continue.

"I'm going to do this one way or another. You're either on my side or you're against me."

"Please, don't do this. Don't make me choose the impossible." Silas steps forward and grabs on tightly to my arms. "I can't lose you—not again."

"You won't," I lie. Silas is right, there is a significant chance that I will lose this battle, that I will succumb to whatever torture or persecution that Balial sees fit. But the only chance I have at making him pay is by going through with this. And after what I learned from the headmaster, this opportunity could be gone the moment the witches are under new management.

Silas's eyes redden, and fear washes over him. "You don't know that, not for certain."

I push every ounce of magic left in my body into his in a weak attempt to calm him. "I have to try. You understand that, don't you?"

Silas storms out of the bathroom and grunts. "Then let me do it." He turns around abruptly with his hands in his hair, tugging at it. His eyes are wild and glowing. "I'll challenge him. I'll get your magic back. Anyone but you. I am fucking begging you, Willow. I'll never ask you for anything else, just please don't go through with this." He holds out his palms and drops to his knees only inches away from me. "Take mine. Every ounce of it. It's pointless without you. If you need magic, you can have mine. I don't care what it does to me. Aren't we more important to you than this? Choose me, Willow. Choose us. Choose to live."

I stand in front of him and graze my thumb along his broken face. With my voice low, I tell him, "This has nothing to do with my powers and everything to do with you. This was never about the magic he stole from me. I'd give it to him a thousand times over. I can live with that. Him hurting you? That's something I'll never forgive. He has to pay. I will make him sorry he ever laid a finger on you."

He drops his arms to his sides. "This isn't what I want. I didn't ask for this. He's taken enough from me, don't allow him the pleasure of taking you, too."

"He isn't going to. I can do this." I brush his unruly hair off his forehead. "Think of all the times I've done the impossible. What's one more?"

CHAPTER 19

I barely slept.

Between Silas pacing my dorm and then eventually storming out, it was hard to shut my mind off long enough to rest. Plus, the realization that I was *actually* going through with this very insane thing sent a spike of adrenaline through my body, rendering me unable to fall asleep.

"Large mocha." Cameron pushes a steaming to-go cup in my direction.

I take the drink and wait for the rest of the group to arrive.

One by one, they come. Deghan eager to eat some food. Lillian with tired eyes. Sydney looking like he hasn't slept in a week. Silas, brooding in the corner, keeping a little distance but not too much. And finally, Walker, seeming more chipper than usual.

"Now that I have you all in one place, I wanted to make an announcement and give you a choice." My voice cracks, and it's difficult to meet the gaze of my anxiously awaiting friends. I knew this would be hard, but I thought telling them this would be the easiest part. Disappointing and worrying your loved ones is never a simple task, though.

"Okay..." Lillian settles into her seat and leans onto her elbows to give me her full attention.

"After some discussion with Headmaster Walker," I point to him, "I have decided to move forward with the Faustian bargain."

There are a few gasps, and I'm not exactly sure where they came from. If I had to guess, it was Cam, Deghan, and Lillian.

Knowing how determined I am, Sydney must have assumed I would wiggle my way into going through with this, and Silas and Walker were already aware.

"This may come as a shock to some of you, but it's something I feel is necessary. I wanted to voice this sooner rather than later so everyone who wants to be involved can be. I don't want to keep any of this a secret, like I have done in the past. We're a team, and I want this to be a joint effort. With that being said, though, I do not expect any of you to help or be a part of this. I will hold no judgments if you decide this isn't for you. You don't have to make the choice immediately, but it is a rather pressing issue." I nod toward the salt-and-pepper-haired man again. "Walker will be overseeing and lending a ha—"

"Wait," Deghan cuts me off. "You're on board with this?"

Walker politely smiles. "Yes. I think it's safe to say we are all knowledgeable of Miss Willow's power and tenacity. This is something she would have done regardless of our support and considering the risks, I think it's best if I do what I can to make sure she succeeds at this venture."

"Wow," Deghan responds quietly. "Well..." He glances around at us and then settles his sights on me. "I'm in."

Cameron side-eyes Deghan in what I assume to be surprise at how quickly he joined the mission. "That easily?"

Deghan shrugs. "It's Willow, what did you expect?"

I swallow the worry that creeps up my throat. If this is going to work, I need Cameron on our side. And equally important, I need Silas, too. I can't do any of this if either of them doesn't help. Without their magic, I have no chance of defeating Balial.

I'm an empty, powerless shell of a witch by myself.

"I have no freaking clue what I can do, but there's no way I'm letting my bestie go at this alone." Lillian winks at me. "Whatever it takes, I'll be there."

My heart warms to her blind loyalty toward me. But then again, there isn't much I wouldn't do for her either. In a matter of months, we have bonded tremendously. The moment I met her I knew I would cherish her friendship, but I never imagined it to be quite like this.

"And you're sure there's nothing I can do to talk you out of this?" Sydney finally speaks up. His emerald stare bores into me and silently pleads with me to change my mind.

I shake my head slowly. "You know this is something I have to do."

"Okay," is all he says.

Something inside me sparks. A kindling of hope being struck, and with each of their confirmations, the fire of potential growing brighter.

"Really?" I can't hide the surprise in my tone.

Sydney rubs his temple. "Walker was right. You'll do this with or without us. There's no sense in sitting back and doing nothing."

Regardless of not having a single drop of magic coursing through my veins, I can sense Silas's anger increasing by the minute. I assume he was hoping for someone to join him in the rally against me, and with only one person left other than him, his odds aren't great.

But the last remaining soul is one of the determining factors of whether or not I can go through with this entire thing. And maybe Silas is clinging on to the slightest belief that Cameron will choose his side.

"What do you think?" Deghan slaps Cam on the shoulder, seemingly knocking Cameron out of a serious train of thought.

Cam blinks himself back to life. "I...uh..."

I promised myself and them that I wouldn't harbor any ill feelings if any of them decided they didn't want to be a part of this. It isn't fair of me to expect anything from them, and I am thoroughly aware that this is *my* battle. They don't even know what they're signing up for, so of course, that would give someone reservations. If Cameron and Silas don't want to offer their support, I'll find another way to beat Balial because that's what I do—conquer the impossible.

I decide to speak up. "I understand if you need time. This is no small thing to ask of you. Why don't you take the day? Think it over." I tuck my hair behind my ear as the uncertainty creeps through me. If I push him too much, he'll say no immediately. Maybe if I take the pressure off him, he'll be more willing to consider joining the rest of us.

"Willow..." Cameron's blue eyes meet mine.

I hold my breath in anticipation of his next words.

He motions around the room. "Everyone else is on board. Did you really have any doubts that I would be, too?"

I nearly jump out of my own skin as I process exactly the weight of what he just said. I rush across the table and throw my arms around him.

He laughs and hugs me back. "If I knew I'd get this kind of response, I would have signed up earlier."

I settle my sights a few feet away at the man who has direct ties to my soul. I watch him lower his head and walk out of the dining hall, disappearing around the corner and out of my line of vision. I ache to make him understand that I'm doing this all for him.

I won't rest until I make Balial pay for what he did. When this is all said and done, Silas will understand the sacrifice I made for him. Or, I'll go down in history as another one of the many pathetic creatures who tried and lost against the master of Hell.

"Where do we start?" Lillian chimes in.

Headmaster Walker pulls a notepad out of his briefcase. "I came prepared, assuming Willow would convince *everyone* to do their part." He glances over his shoulder to the empty place where Silas was a moment prior. "With the change of plans, I'll adjust to have Lillian, Deghan, and Cameron on research duty. Sydney, Willow, and I will meet with our trainer to discuss a plan of action moving forward." Walker concentrates on Cameron. "Well, given you don't mind supplying Willow with some power to get her started."

Cam stares blankly for a second and then snaps out of it, almost like he's realizing, *oh shit, that's my job*. "Yeah, absolutely."

"But, first things first. Breakfast. Feed those bodies and magical reserves. We'll commence in an hour." Walker locks his gaze on mine. "I'll be back. I'll see if I can do any convincing."

My mind processes what he means too late because, by the time I decide to stop him, he's already gone, following the trail of the grumpy vampire.

CHAPTER 20

I have no fucking idea how he does it, but Walker manages to get Silas to come back with him.

I'm in the middle of taking a drink of my coffee when they both come in, not saying a word. Their body language doesn't give away what's going on either.

Somehow, I feel calm despite the storm waging war in my chest, the loud and quick thumping of my heart going out of control at the sight of our new arrivals.

Silas might be pissed at me, but having him close by is exactly what I need in these times of such uncertainty. I'm not sure I can do this without him, and seeing him walk out those doors made me aware I don't want to. He's the piece of this broken puzzle I can't live without. And the fact that I traveled to Hell to rescue him, it's pretty clear I'd do anything for him. If giving up on my chance to avenge him is the only thing I could do to keep him, I'd have to make that sacrifice.

Luckily, he gave in before I did. And now with him at the very least sitting in the same room with the group of us who intend on challenging Balial, it's the push I need to make this happen.

Silas comes around the table and sits in the spot next to me. He stiffly whisks the hair from behind my ear and whispers quietly so only I can hear. "Don't make me regret this." He pulls away, and his metallic-silver gaze glimmers into mine.

"Thank you," I mutter in response.

He turns and faces forward, a clear indication that he doesn't want to talk anymore.

I inch my tray over to him. "Eat something."

Walker waits until we're nearly done with breakfast to clear his throat. "Now that we have a full house, I'll revert to the previous plan. Willow, Silas, and I will be meeting with the trainer, the rest of you will be on research duty. Sydney, you're in charge of delegating." He holds out a different pad of paper for Syd. "I've jotted down what I think might be useful. Feel free to use your own judgment."

Sydney reluctantly takes the assignment. "I could assist with summoning Charles?"

"That won't be necessary. Although, I will let you know if we need the help."

I study Sydney's face and do my best to gauge his reaction. I've been an empath my entire life, but not having my magical reserves makes it more of a challenge to determine what it is that people are feeling. And if I didn't know any better, I'd say Sydney was disappointed.

I'd be lying if I said I wasn't, too.

Syd and I have been through a lot together, including the Charles thing, so not having him around for these kinds of tasks is a bit strange. Sydney always provided this sense of security and comfort—like having your childhood blankie with you at all times to soothe any nerves that may arise. He has been my guiding light and compass through the uncharted terrain of being a newbie witch.

On the other hand, Sydney is potentially the most qualified to handle heading the research part of our project. He's incredibly intelligent and capable of solving damn near any problem. He's always my go-to for advice or pointing in the right direction. This will be no exception—Sydney will do wonders at uncovering the details we need to win this battle.

We all say our goodbyes and head off in different directions. The four of them toward the library and the three of us down the hallway and into that all too familiar classroom where so many things have happened.

I'm not really sure why, but it's proven to be the ideal location for accessing the shadow realm and performing various magical tasks.

We pause once inside.

"Silas, if you wouldn't mind." Walker motions to me.

I wait for Silas to make his move.

Slowly, he extends his hand, leaving it hanging in the balance between us.

"Are you sure?" I whisper. Magic aside, I'd give anything to feel his skin against mine.

Silas reaches down and grabs on to me gently. "Yes."

I allow the connection to assemble and revel at the flow of power that drifts through our joined bodies. It's pure relief to sense the renewed energy expanding my veins and bringing on a fresh life within my core. I take in a deep breath and let the wave of indulgence crash over me.

It's like I'm seeing out of different, more detailed eyes. The air is crisper, the room is electric.

Silas tries to hide it, but he grins in the slightest. Perhaps he's satisfied with bringing me this very welcomed rejuvenation.

An eager headmaster breaks my concentration by handing us slips of paper. "This is what we will be reciting."

I study it over and recall the incantation to summon Charles. "Okay."

"Whenever you're ready." Walker puts his palms up in our direction.

A few words later and a swirling of wind around the room, the memorable grey-haired man appears. He's smiling from ear to ear, his excitement barely contained.

"Well, well, well. What do we have here? The infamous Willow Oliver." Charles keeps his eyes trained on me. "Wasn't sure I'd ever hear from you again. I'm always happy to be proven wrong, though."

Walker clears his throat. "Hello, I'm Headmaster Walker. I don't think I've had the privilege."

Charles casually looks at Walker. "Charles Cutwright." He nods toward Silas. "And you must be Silas Harlow, the reason for Willow's foolishness."

"Now, now. Play nice," I interject. "I take all the credit for my stupidity."

"As you should. Along with everything else. You've caused quite a ruckus if I may add. You're the talk of the other side. And considering I was the one to train you, I've had loads of attention thrown my way. At this point, I'm not sure if I should thank you for that or not. I haven't caught a break. My existence was rather dull in retrospect, so I guess a little spice won't hurt anyone." Charles hovers near the desk in the center of the room. "I don't imagine you called me here to thank me for my service."

"No," the rest of us say in unison.

Wanting to be the one in charge here, I take the lead on the conversation. This is *my* dumb decision, they're just the unfortunate enablers. "I'd like to ask for your help again, if you'll have me."

Charles crosses his greyish see-through arms over his chest. He narrows his gaze at me and sighs. "This smells of trouble."

"You know me all too well."

Charles stares at me, not seeming to be bothered by anyone else in the room. "What's the damage? I can't imagine what could be worse than what you've already been through. Speaking of which, there's a running bet between us trainers...how'd you pull it off? No one makes it there and back alive, especially two of you."

"I had something he wanted. I gave it to him in exchange for our lives."

Charles raises his eyebrows and smirks. "Oh, did you now?"

"Not that, you perv." I shake my head and let out a laugh. "My magic. He took my powers."

Charles's expression shifts immediately. "Oh. I see." He rubs his chin. "But you're here?"

I point to Silas, who's standing firmly in place next to me with Walker on the other side. They're both being patient and allowing me this chat with Charles. I can only imagine how they're both bursting at the seams to gain control over the situation.

"Silas and I share a Malachi connection. We realized it's still intact, even with Balial taking my resources." I graze Silas's shoulder. "And the reason I've called upon you today is because I'll be activating the Faustian bargain."

Surprisingly, Charles doesn't react to my last few words. I assumed with the way he responded to everything else I've said he would be stunned, but he's just hovering there like I told him the weather forecast for the day.

"Do you know what you're signing yourself up for?" Charles's tone is serious and calm.

"Yes. Well, as much as I've gathered. I understand the dangers." Pretty much that if I don't beat him, I'll be stripped from the world and tortured until the end of time. No big deal.

"This will be no easy feat, but I'm sure you're aware of that." Charles rubs his sheer forehead. "You never cease to amaze me, kiddo."

"So, will you help us?"

"You think I'm going to leave you hanging?" Charles stares off past me and accesses his mental database. "I'll have to readjust my programming since you no longer have your powers. What kind of magic are we working with here?"

"Vampire," Silas speaks up.

"It's worth mentioning..." Walker adds.

Charles blinks into the room and to Walker. "Yes?"

"She has a conduit source, too."

A grin spreads across Charles's face. He slowly turns to me. "And that will be your secret weapon. But I must warn you, you need to stop the use of this connection immediately. Drain every ounce of it from your veins and do not speak a word of it. Do you hear me?"

His stare bores into me, and if I wasn't already familiar with Charles, I would be frightened. He's proven to be a good man, and if he's telling me to do this, he must have a good reason.

CHAPTER 21

Silas somehow stiffens his stance next to me, slightly stepping up and in front of me like he's going to block an incoming attack. His protectiveness is sweet and thoughtful but not necessary. Charles is only offering his advice, not planning an attack on me.

"Okay..." I mutter.

"Do you mind elaborating?" Walker says studiously.

Charles floats a little closer and lowers his voice. "Balial is no fool. I'm almost certain he'll anticipate the Malachi connection. But if I were you, I'd play dumb and make him think you didn't see that coming. Let him assume he has the upper hand on you. When you initiate the contact to him to commence all of this, he'll summon you for a pre-battle. A trial of sorts to see if you're worthy of such an encounter. It's my understanding that if you don't approach him with a good enough deal, he won't allow you to pass through to the next phase. Or, like he's done time and time again, he'll offer you unbeatable terms and take whatever you have.

"This conduit situation, though, they're nearly untraceable bonds. Often the active members aren't even aware it's there until they stumble upon it. If Balial accepts, he'll do so under the impression that Silas's magic is all you have. He'll never anticipate you have a gateway to more. This could be the very edge you need to beat him at his sick and twisted game. But, if he senses any other sources during that initial meeting other than the vampire's, you'll lose your advantage."

I hadn't thought about it this way, but it makes total sense. Balial will have no clue that I can tap into Deghan's and Sydney's magic, so why would I let him in on that secret? If I can prolong using Cameron's ability, I might be able to sneak it past Balial. But that also means I won't be using any of their powers during my initial training, making the utilization of the sources a bit of a challenge.

Now is the time for being adaptable and figuring shit out on the fly.

"That makes sense," Walker chimes in. "Good thinking."

"You need to purge your system, rid yourself of any excess magic from anyone other than Silas." Charles stares at me. "You can't take any chances."

I nod. "I'm clean. I emptied my reserves and have only since used his." But what if I'm wrong? What if there are lingering flickers of emerald or gold energy floating through my body?

"How many additional sources have you gained access to?"

"Two. Deghan and Sydney. Although we haven't tried with anyone else."

"Ah, your mates. I'm pleased to hear the LeBlanc boy is on the list. I imagine his aid will prove to be quite helpful. He's a power-house, that chap."

I glance at Silas out of the corner of my eye. His jaw tenses at the talk of Sydney. I wiggle my fingers around his and pump a little of my calming energy into him. It's a bit different than usual, considering it's his own magic, but the flare I add to it seems to do the trick.

He relaxes slightly, but it's enough to lighten the heavy mood he's throwing off.

"Are you at all familiar with conduits or the springs from which they can pull from?" Charles switches into teacher mode.

"Not really, no." I turn to Walker to see if he has anything to add.

"Just that it requires a specific *loving* connection." Walker waits for Charles to elaborate.

"Yes," the youthful old man confirms. "Although it's not the lone stipulation. It requires trust and devotion, too. A strong bond that goes all directions. The conduit itself must have this, but so does the giver. Only those who truly care for Willow and have an openness in their heart for her will be capable of giving her their magic. Basically, it's a safeguard to eliminate the receiver from taking from those who are not willing." Charles winks at me. "It's a good thing you have multiple mates. This will be a great advantage in overcoming Balial."

"Now that we've squared that away. How should we move forward?" Walker seems to grow anxious of the chitchat.

"Very, well. Shall we establish a timeline? What are we working with...a few months? Years? When will you trigger the encounter? The main battle typically takes place around forty-eight to seventy-two hours your time after the initial meeting with Balial, so make sure you're prepared to move forward once you call upon him." Charles blinks stiffly, clearly running through his mental database for a detailed program.

I do the math in my head. If Balial makes us wait for three days, that would push the limits on being finished by Friday and wreck any chances we have of getting the school back in shape for returning students on Saturday. The only way to make sure we have enough of a buffer is to act swiftly. And that's assuming the battle takes no longer than a day. What if this ends up being much lengthier than that? Given the difference between Balial's world and mine is separated by years, and I'm guessing we will battle there, that should work out, right? Even if it's six months in his dimension, it would only be a few hours in mine.

"Tomorrow," I blurt out.

Charles returns to gawk at me. "I'd ask if you're joking but I'm afraid I already know the answer."

"Are you up for the challenge?"

"I should be the one asking you the same thing." Charles goes back to his processing of information for a moment. "Okay. I may have found something that will work. Given there are no hard or fast study aids for this type of battle, I have to make do with the available options. Balial is a man of great power and wit. Do not underestimate his ability to get into your head, to trick you, to make you confident that you have him figured out, only to pull the rug out from under you. He will do everything he can to confuse you and get under your skin. There isn't any level he won't stoop to. Always be prepared for the worst."

Finally, an instance where my constant negative and over-thinking mind will actually prove to be useful. I may do some incredibly dangerous and reckless stuff, but I'm continuously running a risk analysis in my head of what could possibly go wrong and how to avoid it. I learned at an early age that if you're aware of what kind of bad shit can happen, you're much more capable of figuring out how to fix problems that arise.

Don't let me fool you, there are plenty of times I haven't seen stuff coming, but more times than not I've had a backup plan in place when crap hit the fan.

I guess it's one of the perks of being forced to grow up at an early age. I learned to count on me, myself, and I. I found comfort in my ability to figure out how to overcome obstacles that came my way. I stopped allowing other people to disappoint me when I eliminated the expectations I had for them. Humans are unreli-able, or at least I have had a history of unpredictable ones in my past. It's wired my thought process to do everything it can to protect me from harm. But it's also made trusting others quite difficult.

Since I've been at Harper Shadow Academy, I've given in to the uncomfortableness of letting people in. Because at the end of the day, what's life without a little vulnerability? And with that openness, I've paved the path for some of the greatest love I've ever known. Both from incredible friendships and romantic relationships.

Now, I just have to find a balance between this new me and the old one who doesn't want to completely go away.

I will take the strong and honorable pieces of each version of myself and mold together a Willow Victoria Oliver who can do anything she sets her mind to.

Even if it may appear to be impossible.

Balial might think he's won, but he has no idea what's coming for him.

Charles moves closer to me. "We shall commence training immediately if we want to utilize all available time. I have prepared a few various simulations ranging from easy to incredibly difficult. Although they will not be in order, so don't expect the first to be the simplest, nor will you be aware of the hardest. I will also be stacking them together, so unlike in the past upon each completion where you were brought back to this room, you will remain until an unspecified time. I should reiterate in the case that you have forgotten—these are not real but come across as very genuine. Be vigilant and mindful of the damage you undertake. Your injuries will not remain once you return, but you must trick yourself into assuming them for what they are if you want to prepare yourself appropriately." He holds his hand up and waits. "Are you ready?"

I shift my gaze to Walker and then Silas. They both nod in approval.

I take in a deep breath. "Yes."

CHAPTER 22

For a moment, everything is pure fucking black, until it's not, and the sun is shining and I'm alone in the forest behind the school.

The air is warm, nothing resembling the cool fall breeze I've grown accustomed to. It reminds me that no matter how *real* this seems, this is a made-up world I'm currently in, it isn't reality. Regardless, though, I have to be serious and put my game face on.

I look over my shoulder to find that I'm not wearing the same clothes I was a second ago. These are tighter and appear to be made out of some kind of stretchy spandex material. They're black, which is totally fine by me, and they offer a great deal of support while being comfortable and airy. I trail my gaze down my body and spot a holster around my ankle with small knives tucked into the elastic. My boots are lined with little shiny crystals around the edge of the inside.

A branch cracks in the distance, alerting me that there are more important things than my outfit and its many intriguing details.

The sound is followed by a whimper.

Whatever is causing this noise is potentially injured. Maybe the demon I'll be facing has already hurt its first target.

Carefully, I tiptoe my way in the direction of the whining. I pause and lean against a tall tree and peer over some shrubs to try to get a better visual of what it could be.

I come unglued the second my gaze lands on a petite and crumbled form lying on the dirt-covered ground. I rush over, skidding to a halt in front of the child who appears to be no older than ten years.

Her hair is matted to the side of her cheeks with a mixture of sweat and tears and her plain brown dress is in tatters where something clearly clawed at her.

"Are you all right?" I whisper in an attempt to not draw attention to us.

The little girl tilts her head slowly in my direction. Her pale-blue eyes are rimmed with red. "Help me...." Her voice is even smaller than she is.

My heart aches at the thought of someone having the audacity to lay a hand on this poor defenseless human.

I extend my hand. "Here. Let's get you out of here. Can you walk?"

The girl reaches toward me, and the sudden shift in energy dawns on me entirely too late.

Charles's previous words float through my head, *"Balial is a man of great power and wit."*

And when the girl's face contorts and transforms into a fanged half-human, half-demon, I know I underestimated Charles's warning that Balial would trick me.

I go to slide out one of my daggers, but I don't move quick

enough. The *thing* jumps on top of me and pins me to the ground.

With my hands restrained above my head and my torso held in place by the insane strength of the beast, I struggle to gain an inch.

I twist and turn and try to buck the disgusting abomination off me but end up no closer to being free.

The creature exposes its large gangly mouth and snaps it toward my face. Spit lands on my cheeks, and the gas-like stench alone is enough to make me want to vomit. It lets out a loud growl, and the second it goes in for the kill, I react.

I narrow my gaze and focus with all my fucking might, summoning the purple power flowing through my veins. The delay is a bit frustrating, but once I've engaged contact with Silas's magic, I blast a seething death ray straight through the little girl's demon body.

Black goo and a nasty tar substance explode and fall to the earth.

I scrape the gross mixture off my forehead and toss it aside. "Thanks, Charles," I say to seemingly no one. But I know all too well that he, Walker, and Silas are watching this unfold like a creepy big-brother reality TV show.

I stand with caution, making sure to note any other sounds that might arise from the forest around me. I have to be more prepared for my next challenge and not miscalculate the unknowingly simple or complex encounter I will face. I've already proven to be easily duped and I won't make that mistake again. Or at the very minimum, I'll try my fucking best.

I'm only a few steps away from the massacre when a strange exhaustion settling over my body and a fog-like haze forms in my head. If I had to guess, I've been poisoned. And at further muddied thought, I assume it was probably a result of ingesting some of that goop that flung out of the girly demon thing.

Great, I'm barely in this first simulation and now I'm going to die from a weird gunk overdose.

I shake my head and smile, suddenly realizing exactly what's happening.

I may have figured out what's wrong with me, but I have no clue how to remedy the situation. These types of things require another witch and some magical crystals.

I fall to the ground and dig my finger around the inside of my boot, desperately trying to locate something to help me get myself out of this stupid predicament. With my eyes shut from exhaustion, a faint buzzing alerts me that I've landed on the exact thing I need. I wiggle the stone out of its encasement, lie on my back on the hard ground, and set it on my chest.

I mumble a few words and drift off into the darkness. I've done all that I can do, it's up to the universe to guide me from here. Either I fail this simulation and Charles rips me a new one, or I somehow pull off a Hail Mary.

A light wind caresses my cheeks, and a calming presence envelops me. I must be back in the real world, with Silas nearby. But if that's the case, why won't my body let me open my eyes? And why do I still feel so *bad?*

Slowly, the remnants of my glitch reverse, like someone is sucking it out of me.

I blink to life and focus in on the glowing and fluttering fairies hovering near my chest.

There are four of them, each a different and beautiful color. Cobalt blue, neon pink, yellow, and light lilac.

"Thank you." My voice cracks and ends up scaring the pink one slightly.

The rest of the fae continue fluttering their wings and ridding me of my hindrance.

I think back to my encounter with the demon child and put two and two together. That gross smell wasn't just its nasty breath, it was the alcohol lining its insides. The very thing that incapacitates me quicker than anything else.

I'll have to consider this as a possible route Balial will take. It's a low blow but it's highly effective and would render me completely helpless if I can't reach out to the universe and get any help.

I wonder if there is some kind of glitch antidote I can take or a barrier to protect myself from that style of attack. Being in the Hell realm, I doubt the fae will be able to reach me. I'll be on my own there without any chance of assistance. If I succumb to my glitch, Balial would be the only one to bring me back to life. And knowing him, he'd leave me that way just to get his sick and twisted rocks off.

"We must go now," a sweet voice says gently. "Be well."

I open my mouth to thank them, to tell them how grateful I am for their services, but my vocal cords fail me, along with my vision. My entire world goes black, and a moment later, I'm standing firmly on both feet with Silas, Walker, and Charles staring at me.

"Welcome back, Ms. Oliver." Charles grins and blinks through his programming.

Silas jumps toward me. "Are you okay? Angels, that was fucking dreadful to watch." He glides his hands up my arms. "You're really not hurt?"

Charles chuckles. "I told him it was part of the simulation. The realness of it all."

"I'm fine, I promise." Aside from the massive wake-up call that I have my work cut out for me in this upcoming battle with Balial. Doubts creep into my mind at whether or not I'll be able to pull this off. There are moments I feel confident and others when I wonder what the fuck I'm thinking trying to do this.

"That was impressive, Willow." Walker pats me on the back.

"I should have seen the first one coming. I have the ability to read energy, I should have used that. I let my emotions lead me right into that trap. I didn't recognize the shift until it was too late." I turn to face Charles. "The glitch thing was clever, too. That nearly sealed my fate."

He smiles triumphantly. "But it didn't, and that's what

matters. Timing could have been better." Charles shrugs. "It could have been worse, too."

Eager to get back to work, I ask, "What's next?"

"Believe it or not, you need a break." Charles floats in place. "I want you to get something to eat, take a quick nap, and meet me in a couple hours. If we are going to get the most effective use of our time, we have to be smart about how to allocate it. Rest is equally important to training."

Although I'd rather do anything other than take time off, what he's saying makes sense. Witches are finicky about the way their bodies react to this kind of pressure, and considering I don't even have my own source of power, I have to be extra cautious with recovery. Not to mention, I'm unfamiliar with the way Silas's magic will respond to my system.

Charles clears his ghostly throat. "Could we have a moment alone?"

I nod to Walker and look to Silas. "I'll only be a minute."

Silas clenches his jaw and glares at Charles. "Fine."

"He's an intense one," Charles says while watching Silas close the door behind him.

"Yeah, he is." I smile at the sight of my grumpy and protective vampire.

"I wanted to touch base with you. I'm well aware that I might as well be a stranger to you, but I feel the need to at the very least confirm that you're really sure this is what you want to do. You're incredibly powerful, even without having a drop of your own magic. And you're quite brilliant, too. It would be a shame to see that go to waste if something were to go wrong." Charles's serious gaze meets mine.

He might be a strange spirit, but I'm still able to decipher that his energy is genuine. He's actually apprehensive about my decision to challenge Balial. He cares.

"I appreciate your concern, I really do." I glance at my shoes and then back to his dim eyes. "I have to do this."

"You're not doing this for you." Understanding washes over his face.

"He has to pay." A silent rage builds inside me at the anger I have for the King of Hell.

"Fair enough." Charles exhales and seems to grasp my stubbornness. "I'll provide whatever assistance I can. In the meantime, go relax. I don't intend on going easy on you next time."

And here I was thinking that was the difficult level.

CHAPTER 23

By the time I finish with my second round of Charles training, I nearly have to drag myself back to my room. Luckily, Silas is there to lean on and essentially guide me the entire way. He offered to carry me, but I humbly declined. I will permit myself to appear exhausted, but not so weak that I have to be treated like a baby.

Babies don't win against Balial.

Strong women do.

And that's what I intend on being.

"Dude, you kinda look like shit." Lillian comes across the common room and into the hallway of my dorm. "I take it training was brutal?" She rushes in front of us and opens my door.

Immediately, the smell of warm comfort food caresses me.

Cameron and Deghan are already inside, divvying up the grub onto plates.

My belly growls in anticipation. I hadn't known how hungry I was until I stepped foot in here. Now it's all I can think about. That probably explains why I'm dead-ass tired.

I plop into one of the seats at the small table and allow my body the pleasure of relaxing into the stiff wooden chair.

Cameron pushes a full plate toward me. "Chicken and noodles, and mashed potatoes. Thought you could use it after the day you had."

I take a massive bite of the steaming deliciousness. "Are these homemade?" I point to the squiggly things.

"Yep." Cam smiles. "I made you brownies, too."

I scarf down half the contents of my dish in a totally animalistic manner. I worry if I slow my pace, I might fall asleep and land face-down in my dinner.

"Damn, Will. You're eating at my speed." Deghan winks at me.

Silas comes up from behind me and plants his hand on my shoulder gently. "Shower is running whenever you're ready."

"Don't throw this out." I point to what's left and make my way to the bathroom with Silas.

A fresh set of clothes are on the counter along with all of my beauty supplies laid out neatly. His thoughtfulness warms my heart.

I reach out to stop him from leaving. "Will you stay?"

"Sure." He comes toward me but hesitates.

"Come here." I drag him to me and wiggle my arms under his jacket and around his torso. I revel in the comfort of our bodies being this close. I melt into him and close my eyes. Letting the stress of the day float away, I become one with him.

Silas tightens himself around me and kisses the side of my face. "You okay?" Concern pulses through him at a steady rhythm.

"Mmhm. Just tired," I mumble into his tee. "Are you?" I pull back and stare into his beautiful greyish-purple eyes. I'd been so wrapped up in training that I hadn't considered if he had any side effects to giving me his magic. Not to mention, the very clear PTSD he has from his stint in Hell.

"Yeah." He tucks my hair behind my ear.

Sometimes I wish I could enter Silas's mind the way Sydney and I can with each other. Silas is such a complex and shut-off person that it's often difficult to truly pinpoint what he's thinking or feeling. I don't want him to have to suffer through anything alone, but it's hard to get him to open up when he's so used to blocking everyone out.

I run my thumb along his cheek. "This is all going to be over soon."

"That's what worries me."

"Silas. That's not what I meant."

"It's a possibility."

I shake my head. "No."

Steam continues to fill the bathroom and fog up the mirror.

"You'll see. Have a little faith in me." I stand up taller to reach my lips to his.

He kisses me back, slow and steady at first, and then grips my face in his hands and deepens the embrace. "I have more than you know."

I wake up the next morning ready to face the world, or, well, the King of Hell. I still have a few hours until I astral project to Balial, but I feel strangely *ready* to see him. To get this show on the road. This really dangerous and potentially life-threatening show that could either end tragically or triumphantly. You know, just another case of the Mondays.

"Here, eat this." Sydney holds out a small container filled with various nuts and berries.

My eyes widen at the contents.

"Don't worry, I had Cam handle them. No glitch exposure for me today."

"What's it for?" I poke around at the contents.

"Healing, recovering, rejuvenation, protection. They're magically infused, so I'm curious to see if they help at all." Sydney seems equal parts excited and anxious about his concoction.

"Hey...speaking of glitch." I meet his emerald gaze.

Sydney leans against the table. "I heard about what happened during the sim. That was good thinking on your part. It's definitely something to consider going into all of this."

"Well, that's what I was wondering. Is there an antidote or maybe some kind of barrier I can put into place to prevent him from using that against me?" It's a long shot, but it's worth bringing up.

Sydney rubs his chin. "I'd have to do some research. I can't say I've ever heard of such a thing, but that doesn't mean it doesn't exist. It's just never been on my radar until now."

I reach out and touch his forearm. "Thank you for checking." I point to the Tupperware. "And for this."

He sighs and shakes his head. "I can't believe my girlfriend is going to challenge the master of the underworld and I'm over here figuring out which antioxidants are the most powerful."

I take his hand in mine. "Hey now." I push myself into his mind with what bit of magic I have left over from yesterday's siphoning from Silas. *Every single thing you do is incredibly important, no matter how small you think it is. I couldn't do this without you. I hope you know that.*

"It's hard to sit back and watch you risk so much. I wish I could trade places with you."

"I know you do. But listen, in a week, all of this will be behind us. We'll finally be free of him. Classes will be starting up, and we will get the chance to be normal. To have fun and laugh and not worry about curses or revenge or Hell. We will get the opportunity to live the lives that we deserve. That each one of us has fought so fucking hard for." I study his intensely green eyes.

"I hope you're right."

And so do I. Because if I consider for a second that I might fail, I will lose any momentum I have of actually making it through this. I have to be strong—not only for myself, but for the many people that are counting on me and putting their trust in me to defeat this potentially winless battle.

"Are you ready?" Headmaster Walker stands at the end of the table with a bag slung over his shoulder.

I swallow down my fear and let go of Sydney to collect my things. I don't answer Walker, but instead follow him through the school and out onto the back patio where not too long ago, I was a naïve girl completely unaware of the supernatural world.

Silas and Sydney trail behind me on our trip to the sacred run-down witch house located in the forest near the academy.

The air is cold and smells of dirt and the remnants of the fallen leaves. I focus on my breathing to steady my mind. In and out, slow and steady. Attentive lungfuls that will ground me from allowing my thoughts to wander and lead me into freaking out.

I pause at the entrance. "Wait."

Silas is the first to speak. "What's wrong?"

"I should do this alone." I don't know why this didn't dawn on me sooner.

"No way," Sydney chimes in.

"Hear her out," Walker adds.

"If he thinks no one is helping me, he'll assume I'm an easier target. I have to take any advantage I can, and this seems like a no-brainer." I step closer to the door. "This isn't up for discussion." I have to be stern otherwise I'll allow them to talk me out of this. I'm fully capable of handling this on my own, but I'd be lying if I said I didn't want their moral support.

They'll be nearby, though, and that will have to be enough.

Silas's energy shifts from his normal concern to something deeper, like genuine fear.

"This is the trial run," I assure him. "Nothing bad will happen. I'll be right back."

He grips my hands in his and links our connection. "Take all you need."

I siphon his power and revel in the strength it gives me. Having him with me like this is a blessing more than he realizes. To feel *him* coursing through my body, through my veins, is a level of intimacy I never imagined possible. "Thank you."

"Here's this." Walker hands me a notepad. He points to the words at the top of the page. 'Incantation.' Then at the bottom: 'How you get out.'

I study it over and recall not too long ago when Sydney and I astral projected to try to find Silas. We weren't successful with our search, landing in Mammon's Hell. But we were able to locate Sydney's parents—who are now more than likely rotting away to nothing.

It pains me, for Syd, that he lost his family this way, despite them being some of the evilest people to ever exist. He didn't deserve to suffer through being raised by them. And no matter how strong he appears, I know losing them bothered him. Maybe not because of who they were, but for the potential they had. For the people we always hoped our parents would have been but weren't.

I guess I wasn't the only one with a fucked-up childhood.

"There's chalk inside. And you'll want to light the candles and sage." Sydney rattles off the things that I need to do.

I'm well aware of having to do all that, but I let him finish anyway. I don't want him to feel like his presence here is anything less than necessary.

"Okay." I let out a breath and look at each one of them. "I'll see you soon."

"Good luck," Walker says while I back into the cabin.

Once I'm inside, I shut the door. I rest my head on the cold wooden thing.

"I can do this," I tell myself.

The quicker I get this started, the sooner I can be back in the company of those who care about me.

I make quick work of illuminating the room with lit candles of various sizes and wafting the sage to rid any negative energy left stagnant and trapped inside. I pry the window open and let the bad vibes flow out into the wilderness and away from me. Locating the chalk, I go to the center of the room and find the spot where Sydney and I had drawn outlines around each other on this very floor.

I trace my finger along the faded edge and drag the piece of chalk along the smaller of the two to freshen it up—only this time, I don't connect them together with a spot for joined hands. I'd have loved to bring Sydney with me, but if Balial knew he was in on this, he might decide to make things more difficult for me.

I lie back on the hard, dusty floor and take one last look at the spell before recalling it to memory.

"Bronta bur tey magna plak fie..." The words roll off my tongue with ease. Even with someone else's magic flowing through me, witchcraft comes naturally to me.

It feels comfortable, familiar—like home.

Closing my eyes, I allow my mind to be free of nothing but the task at hand. I become one with the universe, with the powers surrounding me, with the divine being that is the cosmos.

Wind rushes around the room, and I have to force myself to stay focused, to stick to the plan. Usually, at this point, I'd have the reassuring company of Sydney, but it's only me now, and I have to find consolation in myself for a change.

My skin warms, and a blaring heat flickers on my cheeks. It's not the inferno that gives away my location change, though, it's the putrid smell of death and rotten flesh.

I open my eyes to find my semi-translucent body lying on the filthy ground. I jump to my feet and wipe the dirt off my legs.

"Well, well, well. What do we have here?" The sound of his voice circles around me. "Did you miss me already?"

CHAPTER 24

My gaze slowly raises as I gain my composure and look at the evil man I came here for.

"Balial."

A sly grin spreads across his eerily attractive face. "Ms. Oliver."

I study the way he glides across the floor with such grace despite being the master of Hell.

He towers over me with his broad shoulders and endlessly black eyes. Balial keeps his distance, though, not seeming to come any closer than a designated ring about five feet from me.

I remain calm regardless of the rage building inside. I'd give anything to rip him apart and leave nothing to be salvaged.

"Did you come to get a refund? I'm afraid the return policy has expired." Balial winks.

Come on, Willow. You can do this. It's only the Devil incarnate.

"Actually, Balial. I have something to say to you."

He raises his eyebrows and cocks his head to the side. "Now that you mention it, I have a confession, too. But, by all means, ladies first." He motions for me to go on. The sleeve of his tailored suit slides up his wrist to expose ink-stained skin.

What could he possibly need to tell me that I don't already know? He's probably just trying to get in my head and throw me off from the reason I came here.

I clear my throat to make sure I don't fuck this up. "Forne lotum Faustian barge." A bit of purple magic flows out of my mouth and through the stagnant air toward him, initiating the deal I just commenced with him.

Balial laughs loudly for entirely too long. A smile envelops his evilness, and for the slightest moment, he looks not so fucking terrifying.

But that's all part of his game. His ability to lure you in and snap your neck without the tiniest clue of what went wrong. I refuse to fall for his tricks.

He regains his composure. "And you're sure?"

Since when did the Devil become so concerned with consent?

"Yes. Why else would I have come here?" I grow irritated with him and find it difficult to hide my emotions. I need to work on my poker face otherwise I'm going to give away my advantages.

"You've come for your magic, then?" Balial slithers a little closer and turns his hand up between us. He pulls my pink power to the surface.

It dances gently on the edge of his skin with a faint glitter of black accompanying it.

The sight is breathtaking—beautiful, really. There is no denying that the two complement each other well.

I pull my gaze away from the light show and up toward him. I swallow the fear threatening to wreak havoc on my being. "There was one other thing, too."

He lets the magic fizzle out and focuses intently on me. "Yes?" Balial glides within two feet from where I stand.

The space around us becomes silent, and the fire seems to dim out in the slightest like he's preparing for whatever it is that I'm about to say next. He doesn't want to miss this.

"Quia oculo ad oculum." Eye for an eye.

His expression darkens and tells me he wasn't expecting that.

Finally, I'm the one with the surprises.

I don't dare break eye contact with him, even though every fiber in my body screams at me to run. I'm not really sure how, but I'm certain he won't hurt me—not now. And if my Spidey-senses alert me to an actual danger, all I have to do is say the magic words to teleport me back into my living body in my home dimension.

Balial's lips part slowly. "Oh." He seems disappointed.

Something that makes no fucking sense to me.

"I'm sure you have something specific in mind?" Balial glares at me.

"I want you to suffer the same torment you put Silas through. And I want to oversee it." My pulse picks up its pace with each spoken word. "I want to guarantee that you experience the pain you inflicted on him."

Balial scratches at his human-sized ear. "This that vampire fellow you're referring to?"

His playing dumb only continues to nurture my anger.

"You know who I'm talking about." I narrow my eyes at him.

He sighs. "Very well. I accept your terms."

My heart skips a beat, and I become confused at his easy acceptance without even attempting to negotiate. If I would have known how carefree he'd be I would have asked for him to pay with his life. I just sort of assumed he wouldn't go for that. Who in their right mind would?

"You do?" I fail at hiding the surprise in my voice.

"I'm not an unreasonable man, Ms. Oliver." Balial adjusts the large onyx ring on his finger.

Is he fidgeting? I can't quite read his energy, but something is definitely *off*. Am I about to fall into some secret trap and be locked here forever without even getting a chance at challenging him for my sweet revenge?

My palms sweat despite my actual flesh not being in this dimension.

"That's awful sweet of your boyfriend to lend you his magic to come here and fight his battles for him. What a gentleman." His tone is condescending.

"That's not what this is."

"It's not? Why didn't he challenge me then?"

I put on a straight face. "He doesn't know I'm here."

Balial nods and grins. "Right...you have more than a normal dose of magic running through your veins. Don't pretend like that's a coincidence."

"How did you even find out?" I attempt to avert the conversation in a different direction.

"Oh, you really thought I wasn't aware of the Malachi connection? Don't insult me like that, Ms. Oliver. I can practically smell the bloodsucker's energy from over here." His voice is thick and deep, and to any other person, I'm sure it would come across as intimidating.

But to me, he's the man I want to ruin, so my drive to destroy him supersedes the nature of his dominating presence and my ability to actually think rationally. It's a foolish process, but it serves me well...for now.

I have to shift this exchange to another topic, otherwise I'm going to give too much away. I need to avoid the issue of Silas and the source of my power.

Balial glances over his shoulder. He flicks his wrist and blasts off a large burst of black toward a random corridor in the distance. The darkness floats away and out of sight. It never once dims, regardless of the fires lapping it up along the way.

My mind reverts back to the deal we need to finalize. "And if I lose, what do you want?" I suddenly become aware of the missing link to this entire agreement.

"Hmm, internal damnation perhaps. I'm sure your soul tastes

delicious." He raises his long fingers to his hauntingly beautiful face. "Although, I have something else in mind."

I grow increasingly irritated with him. "Stop beating about the bush."

He hovers closer and looks me dead in the eyes with those solid black orbs of his. If he's trying to intimidate me, it doesn't work. "You."

But with one single word, I nearly come unglued.

I swallow down the fear that rises. "Me?"

"I've grown quite fond of you, Willow." Balial smirks and then continues. "And having your magic...I feel like we've...what's the word for it...bonded."

"I don't understand." I can't help but meet his obscure gaze.

"Having your power is one thing, but having you here to use it, that's something entirely different. I want *you*. To live here. To stay with me. To be mine. My Queen of Hell." He motions all around us.

Well, that sure escalated quickly.

I gawk at the supposedly terrifying man in front of me. He can't be serious. Can he?

How is it possible that the king of the underworld is proposing such a thing?

This has to be a joke.

A sick and cruel prank by this evil and sadistic monster.

"You aren't..." I shake my head to rid myself of this foolishness. "Is this one of your games?"

I was warned that Balial was clever, but I never imagined him to get in my head this way. How could I have ever anticipated *this* to happen?

Balial kneels to the ground and lowers his head. "On my honor." Even stooping, he's taller than me. He slowly stands back up and extends his hand. "What do you say?" A kind of innocence lingers on his otherwise hardened exterior. "Either way, we get to spend some time together."

I came here to bring honor to Silas by avenging him, not to be asked to spend eternity with the man who carelessly tortured him.

But the only way I can follow through with my plan is to agree to Balial's very insane terms. I knew he would want *something* from me, but I had no idea it would be this. My first-born child, a human sacrifice, or a kidney maybe. Not an offer of marriage.

I take a deep breath and consider my options. I'm here in Hell, and he's already agreed to my end of the bargain. I have to provide some kind of value otherwise this won't be worth it to him. And if this is what will get him to go through with the battle, I have to accept the terms, too.

If anything, maybe him asking me for such a crazy exchange was a good thing—it got us both distracted from everything else I'm trying to avoid being brought up.

He can't find out, especially now that I slide my hand into his and firmly grip the warm and surprisingly soft skin.

There is no backing out at this point.

"You have a deal." I let the words fall out of my mouth and watch the smile meet his dark and endless eyes.

Balial continues to hold on to me. "Now, let's talk details."

CHAPTER 25

"And he's agreed to having this all completed on our timeline?" Walker exudes nervous energy.

But it's nothing like the bubbling anxiety foaming out of Silas and Sydney.

Silas's is mixed with fear and Sydney's more with concern and helplessness.

They both want to trade places with me, but that just isn't an option. Not if we want to win this war.

"Yes. He didn't quite understand why it mattered but he agreed that we would be done by Friday our time." Honestly, Balial was rather accommodating of my requests. It's like he's trying to butter me up in case he actually succeeds in beating me. That way I won't be defiant against claiming my spot at the throne next to him in Hell.

"That's great." Walker goes over and blows out the various candles on the altar.

"Did he question your magic source?" Sydney runs his hand through his shaggy hair.

"He didn't suspect a thing. He thinks it's all coming from Silas." Luckily, I didn't completely crack under pressure and give away my one saving grace. The upper hand I am desperately clinging to in hopes that it will help me beat this evil man.

I peek out of the corner of my eye at Silas leaning against the wall.

He hasn't said much since I've been back, and I find myself internally freaking out about his lack of input. He's normally pretty reserved, but in situations like this, I expect him to have *something* to say.

I'm not even finished with my thought when he clears his throat.

"What does he want?" He continues to gaze at his shoes.

"What?" I fully turn toward him.

Silas sighs. "What did you agree to give him?"

My heart aches with him, and it's like he already knows without me actually saying it out loud. Our sacred bond gives more away than we think it does.

Walker extinguishes another candle.

"Please." Silas finally looks up and at my face.

"Me."

"You." It's more of a statement than a question. A confirmation of what he was already afraid of.

"He..." I find the courage to spit it out. "If he wins. He has asked that I be his bride."

A flame of anger consumes the room as Silas's energy shifts to a version I have never felt from him. He's been mad in the past, but nothing like the level of pissed off he is right now. His eyes glow, and his jaw clenches so hard I think for a second he might shatter his own teeth.

"Silas..." But it doesn't matter what I have to say.

He's out the door before I have time to take a step toward him.

"I'm sorry," I whisper into the room.

A hand rests on my shoulder, and when I turn, I find Sydney offering a sympathetic look.

"Well..." Walker exhales dramatically. "Guess we have our work cut out for us if you're going to kick Balial's ass."

Sydney is upset about my deal with the Devil, but he's more understanding than Silas will ever be. "I believe in you."

And for a second I pretend that he doesn't have to say that just because the alternative is a reality that none of us are willing to stomach.

A measly three days stand between me and the greatest battle I may ever be involved with, and if I want any chance of pulling this off, I need to focus on doing whatever I can to better my odds. And right now, that's getting my ass some more coffee, a quick snack, and summoning my ghostly trainer.

Silas will come to me once he cools off—I can't afford to waste any time moping around while he fumes about the possibility of me spending forever in Hell with another man.

I'm not fucking thrilled about it either, but the only thing I can do is try with all my might to make sure it doesn't happen.

The bargain has been secured, and there is no backing out now. I have to do everything I can to make sure when it's all said and done, I'm *here* in this dimension, not stuck there with Balial.

This time, Cameron and Deghan accompany me and Walker to the room where we will summon Charles.

Silas is nowhere to be found, but I still sense his energy *somewhere* nearby, which tells me he's mad but not enough to completely leave me high and dry. It's not much, but it's reassuring all the same. If he had left entirely, I'm not sure I'd have the courage to go through with this. I'm honestly unclear what would happen if I did cancel the challenge—would I automatically forfeit and have to follow through with Balial's terms? Or would there be some kind of worse punishment for wasting the master of Hell's time?

Fortunately, I don't have to find out, because Silas is close, just keeping his distance. And for the time being, that will have to be okay.

"Are you sure I can be in here?" Cameron nervously gazes around the space.

It dawns on me that this was where he was tricked into that trap not too long ago and nearly killed when the shadow realm was breached and demons attacked the academy.

I reach out to caress his forearm and simultaneously push a little calming energy into him with the magic of Silas's that's still coursing through me.

"Yes. Everything is secure and the perimeter is fortified." Walker clasps Cam's shoulder. "You're part of this world. Officially."

Deghan winks at Cam and slaps him on the back. "You're one of us now. Well, I guess you always were, but you know what I mean."

Walker gets right to business. "All right, everyone ready?" He glances around. "Join hands and repeat after me."

We do what he says, and only a few seconds later the wind stirs around us and comes to a sudden stop.

"Good day," Charles beams. "I see we have a new face among us."

Cameron skeptically looks to me and then at the ghost-like man floating a few feet away.

I guess we could have been a little more detailed with our description of Charles.

"This is Cameron." Walker points to Cam. "He's the conduit we mentioned."

Charles studies Cam up and down. "I see." He focuses on me. "Shall I assume you've met with Balial then?"

I nod. "Yes. Everything is a go. We are scheduled for battle on Thursday."

Charles rubs his see-through chin. "You have your work cut out for you then. He didn't suspect you had other assistance?"

"No." Unless Balial has a perfectly crafted poker face, I truly don't believe he had any idea about mine and Cam's connection. And I'm not sure how he would. Without him having secret spies lurking in the shadows here or the ability to read minds, I didn't give away any other clues as to what I was hiding.

"Very well." Charles loses himself in thought for a moment and then returns. "You'll have to perform a joining if you want to utilize this for the match. In some instances, they're said to only work for up to forty-eight hours, so you'll want to wait until the very last minute to guarantee it's in place for the duration of the battle. I'm sure the LeBlanc boy can assist with this."

"A what?" I say the moment he stops speaking.

Charles hovers in place. "Essentially a unification between you and Cameron, that way his conduit powers will reach to you remotely while you're in Balial's territory. Cameron won't have to directly come into contact with you but can continue to channel your magic from here in this dimension. Obviously, you can't take him with you. That would be too dangerous, not to mention, he wouldn't have access to any sources there."

"Right. Yeah. That makes sense." I turn to Cameron. "You still okay with all of this?"

Cameron nervously rocks his head up and down. "Yes."

"I'll be right there with you, buddy." Deghan elbows Cam.

"We all will be," Walker adds.

"How cute," Charles says pompously. "Now that we have that out of the way. I suggest we get started." He motions to my guys. "Do your thing."

Deghan takes Cameron's hand, and I take Cam's. Together, we ignite a flowing of power that bubbles into me.

It's sweet and earthy and fiercely strong. It's undeniably Deghan.

It mixes with the remnants of Silas to create an even more commanding energy within me. It's fucking glorious to sense them dancing through my veins in a beautiful symphony.

"Let's begin." Charles breaks through our moment.

I find myself reeling with a new sense of life and confidence that I can take on the world. Or in this case, whatever Charles throws at me today. It won't be easy, but with the help of my men, anything is possible.

"I'm ready."

Closing my eyes, I take in a breath and prepare for the shift in terrain. The smell is the first thing that alerts me to the change, followed by the temperature increase. It's nothing like that of Hell, but it's definitely warmer than a normal summer day in Harper County.

Is this what Dorothy felt like when she wasn't in Kansas anymore?

Although, I'm sure she didn't anticipate a demon to jump out of the woods and maul her to death or something.

I assess my surroundings and try to figure out the angle Charles is taking for this simulation. The air is thick and hot. There is silence other than the creaking of the trees surrounding me. I'm in some kind of forest area but not like that behind the academy.

Back home it's dense and full of greenery. Here it's patches of gangly overgrown branches that actually look like demons themselves. I didn't realize I could be intimidated by twigs sprouting from long and tall trunks.

I let my gaze trail over my body and onto the ground near me. Those same daggers are tucked neatly into the band around my ankle. Anticipating the worst, I go ahead and unsheathe one.

The moment my sights raise from the short and dangerously sharp object, I spot a seemingly soundless many-legged creature barreling toward me at an uncomfortable speed.

And when I say that, I mean for me, not the demon.

I never was fond of spiders, and considering this thing resembles exactly that, I waste no time lining up my sights and sending the knife flying into the beast's chest.

The thing falls to the ground and skids closer like it's trying to slide into home base before it gets called out.

For safe measure, I toss another blade and land it between the many glowing eyes layering its massive dome.

Once the twitching and flailing stop, I walk over and remove my weapons. I sling the goo onto the earth and wipe them on a neighboring plant. I won't take any chances of getting that gunk on me and succumbing to yet another glitch situation.

I stand and pivot at the waist, glancing all around me to locate my next task.

I'm not sure who or what it is, but I will be ready for it when it comes.

CHAPTER 26

"Has anyone seen Silas?" I'm so fucking exhausted from the hardcore all-day training session with Charles but there is no way I'm going to go to bed without seeing him with my own eyes.

"Nope." Lillian takes a bite of her cheeseburger.

Sydney adds, "Me neither, but I'm sure he's around here somewhere."

I drink the rest of my tea and place the glass gently on the table. I go within my body and measure the remaining magic in my system. The well is nearly empty. I bite at the inside of my lip and consider my options.

I don't have enough power to use it to locate Silas's whereabouts, and considering he isn't here to borrow from, Cameron is the only other way to gain some strength.

But Cameron has been my go-to lately, and Deghan is more than likely drained, too.

Sydney could always funnel me some through Cam. However, that doesn't fix the *Cam being overused and fatigued* part of this dilemma.

I guess I'll have to do this old-school and find Silas without my powers.

I'll channel my inner Silas, put myself in his shoes, and think of where he might be hiding out.

I doubt it's anywhere far from campus, because he would anticipate me coming to find him and wouldn't want to put me in any danger by venturing too far. It's also probably not in any usual spots—my dorm, his, any of the guys', the reserved library room. He's undoubtedly close enough to keep an eye on me but far enough to stay out of the way. He's pensive like that.

An idea strikes me out of nowhere.

"I'll see you guys later." I make quick work of tossing everything onto my tray and disposing of my trash. The moment I'm done, I head out the back door and onto the patio.

My arms instinctually cross and cover my chest to brace myself from the cold.

I start to doubt the intruding thought that Silas might be out here.

I round the corner and deny my suspicions. It wasn't magic that brought this on, it was something deeper—love.

Silas is in the exact spot I had envisioned. With his back against the brick of the building, he sits directly under the window of my old dorm. The one where he rescued my phone from its untimely death and had placed it safely on the ledge for me to find.

I stumbled upon it those many months ago and couldn't believe my eyes at it resting there completely unharmed. I had sensed him then, watching me. It wasn't at all unsettling, but actually completely comforting. Like my soul had finally found a calm in the chaos of life. He was a total stranger, and yet I felt this sense of familiarity with him that was just *right*.

I knew I needed him—I just never anticipated the depth of what was to come.

And watching him, *feeling him*, hurt like this, it's nearly unbearable.

I approach him cautiously in fear that he might jump up and leave at any moment. For some reason, I'm dumb enough to think treading lightly will cause him not to start. He's a person, not a freaking stray animal.

When he doesn't bolt away from me, I lower myself to the ground next to him.

Everything in my body screams at me to grab on to him and hold tight and never let him go but I'm careful not to encroach too much.

The thought of losing Silas is one that shatters me into a million pieces. I nearly lost him to the pits of Hell, I won't let that happen again.

"Is this okay? That I'm here?" I hesitantly rest my back onto the hard stone building and pull my knees toward my chest. I fight with all my might to not shiver. I don't want him to tell me to go because of the cold.

He avoids looking at me. "Yeah."

It doesn't take him long to figure it out, though.

"You must be freezing." Silas goes to stand.

I put my arm on his and attempt to stop him. "No. I'm fine." I internally plead for him not to leave. "Just stay with me." The crappy weather and my exhaustion are no match to how badly I yearn for him.

He pulls away and rises to his feet.

Such a simple act unravels me, sending a rogue tear rolling down my cheek.

He turns and extends his hand to me. "Come on."

I blink through the liquid and confusion of his gesture.

"You should rest." His voice is gentle but still commanding.

I let him help me to my feet while I try to silence the sadness spilling out of me.

Silas rubs at my shoulders in an attempt to warm me. "Why are you crying?"

Is that a serious question? Where do I even start?

I'm overwhelmed. I'm scared. I'm unsure of literally everything going on. I'm terrified I might actually lose this battle. That I might be taken from this world all too soon. I'm in a constant internal war with myself on whether or not I'm making the right decision. The last thing I want to do is hurt anyone else but how can I possibly go through life without attempting to make amends for what Balial has done? Why should he get to flourish when he's done such terrible things? And most of all, I'm frightened that I might push Silas away, that he will succumb to the darkness in his mind, that he will decide all at once that I am too much and not enough.

That alone might be my biggest fear of all.

Without him, everything else seems to fall apart. He is the glue that keeps me together and makes everything else possible.

"Willow." He wipes a tear from my cheek. "You're trembling."

I lean forward and rest my head on his chest. I let the weight of my body press into him.

"What's wrong?" Silas tilts my face up toward his. He stares into my eyes with genuine concern.

"I don't want you to leave me again." Between my fatigue and overwhelming emotions, I barely get the words out.

"I'm right here," he murmurs.

"And if I go back inside? Then what? Where will you go then?" I hate how pathetic I sound.

"I'm going with you. To bed." He runs his fingers along my neck, up into my hair, and tenderly embraces me. "You really do need to get to sleep."

"Wait." I burn my gaze into him. "You are?"

Silas presses his lips on my nose softly. "Yes."

"I thought you hated me."

"You'll never quite understand it, will you? I could never." Silas exhales. "You've made it clear I can't stop you from going through with this. But that doesn't mean I have to be okay with it. And that surely doesn't mean I *hate* you. You've proven time and time again that you are not a woman to be controlled. It's an incredibly difficult pill to swallow given the one you love literally does everything in her power to risk her safety when it's ingrained in your DNA to protect her from harm. That's why..."

He doesn't continue so I speak up. "What?"

He continues to pause for entirely too long. "I made the decision that if things don't go accordingly..."

My mind goes a million different places, and they all lead to a terrible outcome. Vampires are quick by nature, why does he have to make this so excruciatingly slow?

"I will pledge my service to Balial."

I gasp and hold him at arm's length. "No." I violently shake my head back and forth.

"Willow." Silas grabs on to me. "I will not be without you. Not now, not ever. If this is the path you choose to take, I go, too. We're a package deal. I can't talk you out of your choice and neither can you with mine."

It's one thing to risk the rest of my life, but for Silas to toss his around so freely, it's unspeakable. If I had known he would resort to such extreme measures, I would have highly considered not challenging Balial. But now I have no other option than to follow through. The deal has been set in motion, and if I back out now, I can't imagine the price I will have to pay.

"Forever, okay?" Silas rubs my cheek with his thumb.

"And ever."

If I thought I had a lot to lose ten minutes ago, I was hugely wrong compared to the stakes now. If anything, this will only motivate me more to ensure that I put everything I have into winning this impossible competition. I could never live with myself if I was the reason Silas ended back up in that Hell with

Balial. There's no telling the level of torment he would subject Silas to, regardless of whether or not I'm his wife. I'd rather die than let that happen.

"You two okay?" a person calls out from around the corner.

It interrupts me from my train of thought—the one that was becoming derailed by the minute.

"Yeah," Silas responds. He lowers his head to me. "Come on."

I should be sleeping, but it's fucking impossible.

Thankfully, Sydney gave me some magical snooze aid that kept me out most of the night, so I was able to get the rest that I *needed*.

Now, though, it's five in the morning and my body and mind have had enough of this restless shit. I have work to do and I can't exactly do it while I'm lying here wide awake doing nothing.

"You have another two hours." Silas pulls me to his chest and hugs me tight.

"I'm not tired anymore," I mumble into his bare chest. I kiss the spot near where his heart should be. I never really understood how that works. Do vampires have hearts? Clearly, they're no longer human, but what happens to their organs when they turn? I guess I'll leave that in my list of questions I'll ask if I make it out of this thing alive. For the time being, I don't have the luxury of inquiring about such non-life-threatening topics.

"Me neither." He props up onto his elbows and scoots to rest along the headboard. "What are you working on today?"

I sit up and rub at my eyes. "Whatever Charles has in store. That guy is ruthless, but he knows what he's doing."

I sense the shift in Silas's energy. He's finding it difficult to discuss such things.

"We don't have to talk about this."

He reaches out to me and tugs me to him. "Let's not talk at all."

I grin and climb onto his lap. I take his face into my hands and press my lips into his.

Finally, we're on the same page about something, and boy does it feel good.

We stay like this for a while—kissing and holding each other and riding the blissful wave of forgetting all about the world outside of this room.

But, like everything else, it's short-lived.

A heavy knock forms against the door.

I break away from Silas's mouth and roll my eyes at the intrusion.

"It's me," Sydney calls out. "Can I come in?"

"Yeah," Silas responds despite not being fully clothed in the way he normally prefers.

I'm not sure whether to be relieved about his comfort with Sydney or the lack of care he seems to be exuding. I hope this doesn't mean he's accepted his fate of spending eternity in Hell with me.

We may face Hell, but I refuse to let him surrender to it in the way he thinks he will. If I have any say in it, I'll guarantee that never happens.

Sydney comes in and rushes over, completely ignoring how indecent Silas and I both are. His energy is frantic and consumes me in a terrible way.

"What's wrong?" I snatch Silas's grey T-shirt and throw it over my naked torso.

Silas shakes his head and scowls at me.

"Snooze ya lose," I whisper.

"I just got wind of the news." Sydney is a bit out of breath. "The covens, they made a decision. They're moving forward with the angelic calling ceremony."

"When? How long do we have?" My panic starts to match his. They must be moving it up within the next few days if he's reacting this way.

"Tomorrow." Sydney's eyes are wide.

"You're not serious?" I clutch at my chest.

"I wouldn't joke about this."

Although I've tried to steadily prepare myself for this moment, I'm still completely shocked when the calm ends and the storm comes crashing down onto my life.

This is what I have been anxiously waiting for.

The thing that changes everything.

CHAPTER 27

"Okay. We can do this. No big deal." I go into a completely adrenaline-induced management mode. I sense everyone around me panicking, and although I'd love to join in, someone has to be strong for the rest of us. And I guess I naturally fall into that role. "Sydney, you're on research duty for figuring this joining thing out. Lillian, I want you to be his right-hand woman. Walker, you're in charge of finding out specifically when the witches are planning on doing this. Down to the freaking minute if possible. Cam, you need to rest. It is incredibly important that you do absolutely nothing. And, Deghan, you have to guarantee that he does exactly that. I want neither of you to be strenuous. Do you hear me?"

They both silently nod.

"What do you need from me, boss?" Silas stands firmly by my side, awaiting his instruction.

"You get to come with me. I have to spend what time I have left training. If this is going to go down tomorrow, I need to be prepared."

The timeline was already insane, and shaving off more is quite possibly a suicide mission.

If I don't go through with this, though, even if by someone's choice other than my own, I will more than likely lose by default. Balial won't care whether I decide on my own or am forced to not participate, he will collect what he is owed, and I refuse to allow him to win by some fluke.

"Everyone understand what their assignments are?" I glance around at my friends.

A collective murmur lets me know they're in agreement.

I latch on Silas's hand. "We'll be with Charles for the time being. Fill us in if details are found."

Silas stays by my side the entire way through the old and well-built building and to the classroom where the magic happens. His energy seems to neutralize as he matches my now-or-never way of processing the modified agenda.

He stops me right as we cross over the doorway and twirls me into his arms. Silas kisses me intensely for a long moment and lets me go. "Carry on."

"You ready now?" I grin at him.

He nods, and we join hands, reciting the spell to bring Charles to our dimension.

The spinning gust slows to a halt, and he appears. "A bit earlier than usual today? Or do I have my timing miscalculated?"

"No. You're correct. We've had a change of plans, though." I study the sheer older man floating a few feet away.

"Oh? Do tell."

"The calling ceremony has been brought up to tomorrow. We're unsure of the specifics."

"I see." Charles nods gradually. "And you're concerned the

new leadership will disallow the bargain from taking place? So essentially, what you're saying is, the battle needs to begin either tonight or at first light?"

I take in a deep breath then exhale. "That's the gist of it."

"Have you figured out the joining connection yet?" Charles seems unfazed by the change of plans. He's all business, and it's a comfort that he's so well put together still, unlike the rest of my group when they found out.

"It's being taken care of."

Silas stands firmly in place next to me. His presence is such a comfort in these unsettled times.

I will be forever grateful that he didn't choose to walk away. No matter how difficult things become, he stays with me, and for that, I am indebted to him.

Charles comes a little closer. "There's nothing else that can be done. My best advice for you now, Ms. Oliver, is to get your affairs in order. I have no doubt that you'll put up an honorable fight, but in the event things don't go as planned, you should be prepared. You have a matter of hours before showtime. Spend it wisely."

I find myself stumbling for the right thing to say. "You don't think we should train? In the meantime? There has to be something we can do."

Charles holds up his see-through hands to quiet me. "I've put you through the wringer, Willow. You'd be doing the same thing again, and that seems counter-productive, especially if this happens this evening. I'd hate to waste your energy now and risk not recovering in time. If at all possible, I'd preserve every bit of strength you have. You're going to need it."

I hear his words, but I don't want to acknowledge them. I'm supposed to sit back and wait and do nothing in the interim? What if I haven't done everything I could? There has to be some angle we haven't covered. Some stone left unturned.

Charles's tone somehow becomes more serious than it was. "Willow. I'm not one to beat around the bush, I think you know that about me by now. I'm a skeptical man. People often talk a big game but never follow through. You, on the other hand, have continually impressed and proven me wrong. If anything, you think too low of yourself. I'm not so sure you understand how powerful you are. Even without your own magic, you are capable of so much. I'd be lying if I said what lies ahead of you will be easy, because it won't—it quite possibly will be the most fierce challenge known to our kind, but I'd also be lying if I didn't think you were skilled enough to handle your own.

"And maybe that's a good thing. Your lack of confidence in yourself. It disallows you from getting overly cocky and keeps you humble. Grounds you from making the mistakes that fools do. With all of that being said, I want you to understand that in all my experience and lifetimes, I'd still bet on you."

"Charles, I..." I'm truly at a loss for words. I didn't expect a pep talk, not from him at least.

He raises his hands again. "Listen, I'm not a sentimental guy. I said what I felt appropriate. How about you form a response in a few days when I see you again?"

I bite at my lip in an attempt to keep the waterworks display at bay. I'm not sure what I did to deserve this wise man's kindness, but I hope like hell I can make him proud by doing the impossible.

Hell.

The place I'll be sentenced to spend the rest of my life if I lose this battle.

Silas places his hand on my lower back. "You ready?"

I stare at Charles while he smiles at me.

He nods. "I'll see you soon."

Not too long ago I had thought I was training with Charles for the last time, that I would travel to rescue Silas and potentially have to give myself in exchange for Silas's freedom. It seemed so certain then, that I wouldn't make it back. But now, standing here saying goodbye again, the weight of that sureness feels totally different.

I shove the fork around my plate and move bits of the grilled chicken salad around. It's no surprise that I'm finding it difficult to eat in a time like this. I need to—to keep my levels regulated, it's just hard to have an appetite right now.

"Here," Silas says. He holds his hand out toward me with the palm up. A large brownie is resting on top.

I take it from him and break off a piece. I pop it into my mouth and chew the chocolatey thing. If I can manage to get a few bites of the brownie down, I'll have more calories entering my system which equates to more energy.

Fighting the King of Hell on a balanced diet of brownies and caffeine—sounds totally realistic.

I wonder what pre-battle meal Balial is going to have. The flesh and blood of innocents probably. That sick fuck is more than likely not even fazed about the upcoming battle, considering he usually rigs it to where he wins.

I recall some of the simulations I had with Charles and the many talks he gave me about how Balial can be. He mentioned that Balial loves mind games. That he'll trick me, especially with those I care about. Charles told me not to be surprised if there are matches that involve any of my men or close friends. He'll use these moments of weakness to attack and render me defenseless. Charles also mentioned that Balial is a lover of submission, meaning he will put a person in terrible situations and revel in the glory of them begging for reprieve.

No matter what happens, I refuse to give in to his desires. I won't allow him to get the best of me. This may be his game, his territory, but I control how I react to his sadistic ways. I will never surrender to his methods. He'll have to kill me first.

"What are you thinking about?" Silas breaks my train of thought.

I bite off another piece of brownie. "Kicking Balial's ass."

Silas throws his arm around my shoulder. "I'd love to see that."

I lean my head on him and eat the rest of what I can stomach. I'm practically force-feeding myself at this point. Why can't I just get a direct IV of coffee and magic? I wonder if we can work that into the joining connection with Cameron—a direct java supplier from this dimension.

A girl can dream.

Walker bursts through the dining hall entrance. He rubs at his chin, something he often does when he's worked up. Walker would be a horrible poker player. "Okay, so I spoke with some higher-ups about the angelic ceremony. It's rumored to take place at daybreak."

Which is very, very soon.

"What do you mean, rumored?" Silas stiffens in his spot next to me. He's cool and relaxed around me, but the moment anyone else arrives, he's a hardened version of himself.

"Well. We're in cohorts with a LeBlanc—so getting people to want to open up about details to this stuff has been quite a feat. I have close friends on the inside, but between what happened with the breach at the academy and Sydney's parents, this could be false information."

"And hypothetically, if it is?" I look to Walker.

"I don't imagine it is." Walker leans against the table. "From other sources, it's clear that this is happening. And with the state of the witch community, I wouldn't be surprised if it happens sooner rather than later. They're trying to put a stop to any dark magic because of what has transpired. It's safe to say this time-frame is correct, if not expected to happen immediately."

CHAPTER 28

I have to get rid of all of my magic.

Because if I don't, when I call forth to Balial, he'll sense the mixture of sources I have. I can't afford for him to figure that secret out, even if it is a last-minute revelation.

I had expected to wait for Balial's summoning the way we arranged for it to happen, but with the scheduling conflict of the calling ceremony, we have to speed things up. I'm sure he won't mind—to him, that means I'm less prepared than I want to be, and if that's the kind of upper hand he thinks he has, I'll gladly let him have it.

But with this new change, that shifts the timeline on Cameron and I becoming one with the joining connection.

Sydney claims he has all the details nearly figured out, but if we go through with it prior to me contacting Balial, he will feel that change, too.

So, here I am, pushing all of my calming energy into Deghan and Lillian in a quick effort of ridding any remnants of power in my veins that doesn't belong to Silas. Once the well is dry, I try to activate my magic.

Nothing happens.

I attempt it again.

"I'm empty." And it's not just the inability to trigger the influence, it's the shift in the way the world around me is. Colors are a little duller, the lights are dimmer, and there's this sort of... haze. Magic brings everything to life—brightens an otherwise fainter version of everything.

Silas extends his arm. "Here."

I attach on to him firmly and ignite the connection. Within a millisecond, the clarity of my senses is increased, and all is clear once more. I swim in a beautiful pool of Silas and wish for nothing more than to stay this way forever.

But that's not the reality I'm facing. At least not for the time being.

"You'll astral project to Balial, see if he's willing to modify the plans, and once you're back here, we'll initiate the joining between you and Cam." Sydney meets my gaze.

"Yes."

"Okay. We'll be waiting. Do your best to hurry back."

I'll be so fucking relieved once every conversation I have isn't about some life-or-death mission one of us is about to partake in. It's not that I don't enjoy a rigorous challenge, I'm just ready for the day where we can actually be people our age without worrying about Tuesday trips to Hell.

If all goes according to plan, come next week, our life will be exactly that way.

Or...well...we won't think about what will happen if things go awry.

Silas escorts me to the sacred witch cabin behind the academy.

I came more prepared this time with a thick sweatshirt that kept me relatively warm on the journey here.

I cling to Silas's hand and stare blankly at the wooden door to the building.

He doesn't move or speak either, and honestly, it's quite pleasant.

What a beautiful thing it is just to exist.

"I better go," I finally say. We'll never get any closer to waking up from this nightmare if I stand here all day.

"I'll be right here when you're done." Silas slowly lets my fingers unravel from his.

I kiss his cheek and force myself not to look back on my way in. It's hard enough to walk away from him without actually seeing the sadness written across his face.

Immediately, I get to work. I go through the motions of lighting the candles, burning the sage, propping the window open to let out the impurities. I verify the chalk outline is intact and lie flat on the hard surface. I close my eyes and take in a deep breath. I recite the already memorized incantation and brace myself for the shift in the atmosphere.

It's always the smell and the heat that give it away first. That disgusting stench of death that I'm not so sure I will ever grow used to. How does Balial stand the grossness? Maybe it's what he prefers. Weirdo.

I shift my body to glance around the fiery place and settle my sights on him.

He's standing there in the close distance, checking a watchless wrist. "Did I mark the time wrong? I hope you haven't come to cancel on me. I've been rather looking forward to this."

I shake my head. "No. There's been a change in the itinerary. I hope you don't mind me coming here to ask for your permission to alter the timeline."

"Hmm. What were you proposing?" A sly grin crosses his face as he utters the last word. He's trying to unsettle me already, and we haven't even started.

"Sooner rather than later," I say, very matter-of-fact.

"Oh, here I was thinking you wanted an extension. How lovely to begin earlier." He strokes his chin and then points in the thick air like he has an idea. "What about now?"

My heart nearly lurches out of my chest. "I was leaning more toward tonight, if possible."

"Ah, but why wait? This evening is *forever* away." Balial glides within a few feet from me. He towers above me with such arrogance and command.

I haven't prepared, that's why. There is still *so much* to do if I want any chance of beating him. I can't exactly tell him that, though. "I haven't said my goodbyes yet. You're a villain but you have the decency to grant me that, don't you?"

Balial clutches his chest dramatically. "How hurtful!" His demeanor lightens, and he winks at me. "I do rather enjoy being the anti-hero."

His sense of humor is neither funny nor giving me any insight on which direction he intends on making his decision.

"Very well. I will give you until the sun has fully set."

I let out a breath and hope with all my might that it didn't give too much away at the panic that was consuming me.

Balial comes forward and grazes his finger along my chin, directing my face toward his. He lowers his voice. "I'm looking forward to our time together."

A chill creeps up my spine despite the raging heat of Hell around me. I force a smile and take a cautious step back. Thankfully it wasn't my actual skin he touched, considering my body is lying on the floor of a cabin in my home dimension.

"See you soon." I mutter the rest of the spell to send myself home. Everything goes black, and with a sudden jolt, I'm away from Balial. I sit up and caress the spot on my jawline where he touched. It may not have been on this version of me, but it felt real all the same.

Now I can't help but want to put my body through one of those intense drive-thru car washes to erase any residue of him left behind. Don't get me wrong, Balial is a good-looking guy. He's also a complete fucking asshole who happens to be the evil prick who tortured Silas. His actions are unforgivable, and never will I be able to put that aside and see him as anything more than the cruel bastard he is.

A light knock sounds on the still-cracked window.

I turn to see Silas peering inside. I motion for him to enter.

"Are you okay?" Silas rushes to help me from the floor. "Did he hurt you?"

"No." I stand and dust the dirt from my black bottoms. "Just gave me the creeps."

Silas emits a low growl. "What happened?"

"He did this." I repeat his movement on Silas and shake my shoulders in disgust.

"I'd give anything to get my hands on him." Silas clenches his fist. "I'm so sorry."

"I'll be glad when I don't have to deal with him anymore. He's strange." I go around the room and blow out the candles. "He agreed, though, to adjust the time. He said he'd come for me at nightfall. That gives us a few hours to get everything squared away."

And with that limited time, there's one more thing I need to add to the to-do list without letting anyone else know what I'm up to. How I'll manage to pull it off, I'm not sure, but I'll figure it out.

My life depends on it.

CHAPTER 29

Cameron and I sit facing each other with a circle of chalk drawn around our bodies.

Various crystals have been placed along the dusty white line, and candles illuminate our cheeks in the dim room.

We're back in the cabin, but the old curtains are drawn. Aside from us, Walker and Sydney are here, dropping assorted herbs nearby and chanting something under their breath. If I didn't trust the two of them, I'd be concerned we were being sacrificed or something terrible.

Against his wishes, Silas had to stay outside. According to Sydney, Silas's vampire magic would be too much in the room and potentially throw off the balance of the spell. I thought that maybe he was being facetious, but Walker actually backed Sydney up with his rationale, saying that Deghan couldn't join either.

They went so far as to say Lillian shouldn't either since her magic is unstable at this point.

"Join hands," Sydney instructs us. "Keep the connection at all times until I have given you permission to stop. No matter what, do not let go. This may be painful, but you have to remain in constant contact."

We do what he says and link ourselves to one another.

Cam seems uneasy, so I pump a little calming energy into him to settle his nerves.

He shyly smiles, and his baby blue eyes twinkle. "Thanks."

It's been a little while since Cam and I have had some one-on-one time, and regardless of the circumstances, it's really nice to get this level of intimacy with him, even if it is for a situation like this. I hope when this is all said and done, I can see more of all of my guys—not just the instances the world is ending.

Aside from my own drama, Cameron has shit going on in his life that he needs help with, too. His brother is still causing a ruckus and needs to be put in his place. Cam doesn't deserve to be walked all over and treated the way his brother treats him. I aspire to be a part of that problem-solving in the coming weeks once things settle down in the supernatural portion of our lives.

"Stare into each other's eyes and repeat after me." Sydney kneels next to us. "Bronte connecum fina oin nama."

I meet Cameron's heavenly gaze and reiterate the spell with him. We continue this way for minutes, reciting the things that Sydney speaks from his book.

Walker remains pacing around the room with his own text, muttering to himself.

Our skin heats up uncomfortably. It's almost like we're melting and becoming glued to one another.

My immediate reaction is to let go, to break the connection because of the strange pain ripping through my flesh. But I wince through it and keep my sights stuck on Cameron who happens to be experiencing the same thing I am.

He flinches but maintains his grasp on me, not daring to disrupt what we already have started.

There's no way either of us wants to go through this again, so we make sure we get it done in one fell swoop. I knew this would be difficult, but I didn't realize it would be like pouring hot molten lava in between our hands and making us clasp on for dear life.

If this is what it takes to potentially beat the master of Hell, I'll gladly suffer through it. Anything has to be better than the alternative I'll face if I lose. I just wish Cameron didn't have to be involved in this level of discomfort in the process.

Sweat beads on my forehead and rolls down my cheek. It pools in the shallow part of my back and seems to coat nearly every inch of my body.

Cameron's face glistens with the same reaction, he just makes it look a lot sexier than I do. At least the silver lining is getting to stare at this gorgeous man while enduring this torment.

Just when I think I can no longer continue to tolerate this agony, wind swirls around the room, and a glowing rainbow streams onto us, cascading our bodies with a divine cooldown that could only be described as magical.

"You may let go," Sydney says through the chaos of it all.

I glance down at our joined hands.

We were holding on so tightly it seems impossible to release one another. We finally pry ourselves apart and stretch our fingers to release the tension that had built up.

"That was hardcore." I wipe my brow on my shirt sleeve.

"You're telling me." Cameron does the same.

"Well, shall we see if it works?" Sydney stands above us with a serious stare.

Cam and I bring ourselves off the floor.

Sydney latches on to Cameron's wrist. "All you have to do is think about giving Willow the power."

Cameron closes his eyes and concentrates. He takes a deep breath.

Not a moment later, the bubble of fresh life is breathed into me. The sensation is incredibly familiar and welcomed. It's earthy and strong with a touch of gentleness so pure it could only be known as Sydney's power.

I flip my hand over and summon forth the magic. I study the emerald sparkles forming along my skin and smile at the glorious sight.

It worked. It actually fucking worked.

"This is unbelievable." I twist the current around and let it crackle on my fingers.

At the very minimum, I won't be alone in Hell. I'll have my guys with me, even if it is only in magic form. They will be my constants keeping me fueled and ready to take on whatever Balial throws at me. That will be a blessing unlike no other. Something I assume he will never see coming. And hopefully, it will be just the advantage I need.

"I had an idea." Walker joins us.

I put my hand around my mouth to form a little microphone to call out toward the door. "You can come in now," I shout to Silas wherever he may be.

It's not a blink of an eye later that he pops into the cabin.

"You were saying." I focus my attention on the headmaster who is now way more than that. He's one of us. He's family.

"Balial still doesn't know about the conduit source, correct?"

"I don't believe so," I confirm.

"Well then, what if when he comes for you, you still don't have any other additional supplies of power. Prolong him finding out as long as possible. The ultimate element of surprise."

Cameron joins in. "How will we get the timing right then? What if she needs magic but we aren't aware?"

"You'd need a beacon of some sort. Think there's enough daylight to make it happen?" Walker rubs at his chin.

Sydney smiles. "Already done." He turns to me. "You still have that stone linking you and Deghan?"

"Yep." I just haven't used it in what seems like forever. In the chaos of everything, it got put to the side and forgotten about. The clothes I was in when I came back from Hell have been tossed in a corner and sort of disregarded. I hope Deghan doesn't think I've been neglecting him.

"You'll need to empty your reserves again, but otherwise this is a solid plan. You've already tested the stone long distances, so there's no issue there. You would have to make sure you have access to it to contact us, though." Sydney ticks off the requirements from his imaginary checklist.

Silas grabs my attention. "Are you comfortable with this? Going in without full strength?"

I cup his tense face in my hand. "I'm sure your magic will be enough to tide me over."

Cameron has decided to make us dinner and swears that it won't be physically exhausting by any means. He claims that cooking gives him life, and according to his beaming smile, I believe him.

It takes some convincing, but I manage to break off from the group to do a little research in the library. I tell them that I want to check some last-minute things and get a small moment to myself prior to the big battle. I persuade Silas to take the opportunity to feed since he won't exactly have the chance here soon and he needs to be at max power. I coax Lillian and Deghan to assist Cam in the kitchen. And Walker and Sydney need no push to find something to do to occupy themselves. They quickly jump on the chance to fortify the integrity of the protective barrier of the academy.

I stroll down the basement stairs and into the human section of the library. The place smells of dusty old books, and somehow, it calms my anxious soul. I make my way into the supernatural segment and down the long winding hallway that never seems to end. I continue walking but close my eyes to focus on what I'm searching for. I've decided to keep my magic until I complete my task, otherwise, I'd never finish the thing I've set out to do. Safe-guards have to be put in place, and I have to be the one to do it. I'm the only person capable of stopping the worst possible outcome from coming to fruition.

My borrowed magic leads me to the part of the enchanted archive I'm searching for. I go into the unfamiliar room and to the far side. I skim the wall until I've found what I'm looking for. I carefully place the book onto a nearby table and glance at the door to make sure I'm alone. I wipe at the cover to verify the title. I flip it open and scroll through the table of contents to find the specific article I need.

My heart skips a beat when I turn to the page. It's a simple spell, but potent. I'm not sure why such a thing is so easy, but luckily for me, I don't care to ask questions. Not with the clock ticking away the minutes until I'm in a dangerous land far, far away.

I shift my gaze to the entryway again and then do a once-over on the incantation.

I let the words flow from my lips and call forth my power. I do exactly what the page reads, flipping my hand over and putting it out about a foot from my head at eye level.

Green and purple dance together to create a tiny little tornado in my palm, tickling my skin and creating an even smaller capsule in its wake. I grip it between my fingers and examine its mighty yet petite form.

Without wanting to get caught, I tuck the thing into the pocket stitched into the waistband of my bottoms. I've never really had a use for the awkward-sized flap until this very moment.

I slap the book shut and shove it onto the shelf and hope like hell that no one knows I was here. I poke my head outside the room, and when I confirm the coast is clear, I make a beeline straight for the reserved space I've spent so much time in while at Harper Academy.

Once I'm safely where everyone thinks I should be, I calm my breathing and regain my composure. I won't let them find out about what I'm up to—not until it's already said and done.

I rummage through the stacks of stuff near where Sydney usually sits and locate a spiral notebook and pen. I settle into the chair at the far side of the room and turn to the first blank page. I bite at my lip and do my best to come up with the right words to say.

I've never really been good at goodbyes, but for once, I owe it to the ones I love to try.

CHAPTER 30

I channel my strength, but not the magical kind, the kind that's ingrained deep within me.

I put the tip of the pen to paper and speak with my heart.

To my friends and loved ones, if you're reading this, I am no longer with you. I was faced with a decision, a tough one, and ultimately, I felt this was the best option. I don't want to leave you, but the alternative was something I wasn't willing to go through with. I don't expect you to understand, I just hope that one day you'll forgive me. I have cherished every moment with each of you, and wherever I end up, please know that I will hold you in my heart for all of time. Thank you for every single moment, the good and the bad. Always, Willow.

I gently rip the sheet out of the binding and fold it carefully. I set it aside and focus on the blank page staring back at me.

Lillian, you are an incredible friend and a brilliant woman. Nothing will stop you from achieving whatever it is you set out to do. I will never forget the invaluable bond we formed the moment we met. I hope you never give up and continue to fight for what you hold dear to your heart. Tell the girls I love them, and wish them my best. I'm thankful I got to experience the very unique and rare friendships each of you gave me.

I address the note and add it to the slow-building stack to my right. If the clock were on my side, I'd spend an eternity thanking all of them for the precious moments we've shared, but I don't have that privilege anymore.

Mom, I'm sorry we didn't get more time together. Part of me hates how many years were wasted in the in-between, but that was what shaped me into the woman I am today. And I guess, in a weird way, I'm grateful for the chain of events that lead me here. I wish the outcome would have been different, but I think you'd be proud of me for all that I've done, for all the moments where I've faced my fears and overcome the impossible. I am an Oliver witch, and that is some-thing I am honored to call myself. Love is our ultimate, and essentially, that's what has brought me to this fateful outcome. And if I've learned anything from you, it's that there is no greater sacrifice than those in the name of love. So, if anyone would understand why I chose this path, it's you. Thank you for teaching me the importance of life and showing me that those tender feelings are the most powerful of all. Give Dad a hug for me. Maybe we'll get a second chance in another life.

I add the letter to the pile and regain my composure. I'm running out of time, and I have to make sure I include everyone and get these hidden so no one finds them until the right moment.

Headmaster Walker, I'm not sure I've ever properly thanked you for graciously welcoming me into your world. In a matter of months, you became more of a father figure to me than I've known my entire life, and for that, I owe you more than you know. Your guidance and forgiveness have been such a vital role in who I have become. Thank you for never giving up on me and for constantly believing in my potential. Please let Abigail know that her kindness will never be forgotten.

I bite my lip and concentrate on the task at hand. I've saved the most difficult for last, and for once, the impossible seems to be something I'm not sure I can handle. Suffering through the depths of Hell is nothing compared to finding the words to say goodbye to the four men I love more than humanly possible.

But, they deserve *something* from me, so I swallow my fears and cut myself open to bleed onto the pages for them as best I can.

Cameron, you are one of the kindest souls I have ever had the pleasure of knowing. My time spent with you was full of love and happiness, and I can't believe I was ever lucky enough to call you mine. From the very first moment when I came barreling into the academy that rainy day and nearly knocked you down, I knew there was something special about you. Those topaz eyes radiated through me and spoke directly to my heart. If I may ask one thing of you, please don't ever doubt yourself. You are more talented than you realize, and with a gentle push, I am confident you will see great success. Don't ever let anyone dim that light burning bright within you. Hug Deghan for me, he's going to need it. Yours, Willow.

I wipe at the tears streaming down my face and put Cam's page with the rest.

Deghan, I will never ever, ever forget the way your arms feel wrapped around me. You are the epitome of warmth, and I mean that in the best way possible. Your heart is pure, and although I know you've been broken before, your ability to love fiercely regardless of what you've been through is something I love the most about you. Bumping into you on orientation day was one of the greatest moments of my life. As was every other second spent with you. Continue being strong, the world needs more people with a spirit like yours. Maybe one day when you're looking to the sky, I'll find a way to paint it with a shade of pink, so you'll know you're not alone, that

I'm there by your side. Cameron needs you, don't forget that. Affectionately, your cuddle princess.

I blink through the waterworks and glance at the door. I'm running out of time, and I have to hurry if I'm going to get this done.

Sydney, what an honor it is to have known you. You helped me in more ways than I ever expected. You showed me the true meaning of sacrifice, and you were quite literally my rock when I felt the world slipping out from under me. I'll never understand what I did to deserve such a noble and brilliant man in my life. Continue to strive for excellence and overcome the many challenges you are set to face. No matter what, remember that you are the light in this dark universe. You are not what your parents tried and failed to make you out to be—you are so much more. Your future has endless possibilities, and I put faith in your continuous perseverance. My battle may have ended, but I trust that you'll carry on the torch of my legacy in your humble acts of humanity. Keep an eye on Silas for me, and don't let him wander too far into the abyss. You might be the only one left who truly understands him. Until we meet again.

My heart aches like it's being torn in a million different directions.

Silas, I never wanted to say goodbye. Not now, not ever. I thought we had an eternity together, or at least a lifetime. Sometimes things don't always go as planned, and this is one of those instances. I hope you know that I didn't do this to punish you, or because I didn't love you. In fact, my love for you is what forced my hand and sealed this fate. I regret nothing. Not a moment of us or the cost of this outcome. I promised myself that I'd never let you experience the torment that Balial put you through ever again and the only way I could guarantee that was to take the option of you serving him in Hell off the table. You are the other half of my soul, and as much as it pains me to depart from you, I will hold on to the memories we shared and the many impossibilities that we overcame together. Please don't blame yourself. This was my choice. And I will constantly choose love. An infinity wouldn't have been long enough with you, but I'm grateful for our tiny always. Forever, okay?

"And ever," I whisper through the tears that rain down.

I carefully fold Silas's page and put it with the others. There's only one left, and even if I had all the time in the world, I would still only use one line to express what I want to say. I pour every ounce of rage I have into my very last goodbye.

Balial, I'd rather die than be yours.

CHAPTER 31

"**D**id you find everything you needed?" Walker eyes me from overtop the book in his hands.

I pray that my voice doesn't crack despite the overflow of emotions I left in the library. "For the most part. You?" I put on my game face and do my best to not show anyone how badly I'm freaking out inside. I cannot afford to show any weakness, not even to my loved ones.

"Yep. Fine-tuned the calibrations. Didn't take long."

I glance out the large windows overlooking the patio and note the shifting hue of the sky. The sun will set soon, and before too long, Balial will come for me. I reach into my pocket and grip the smooth stone into my palm. It's not two seconds later that a warming sensation coats my body entirely.

I smile at the thought of Deghan's warm hug.

He pops his head out of the kitchen doorway. "Princess!"

"Hey, Degs." I walk over, closer, and the aroma of something delicious caresses my nostrils. "That smells great."

"I call it..." Deghan thrusts his hands in the air to enunciate the words. "Pasta ala Cam."

I laugh and continue toward him. "Yeah? Sounds very exquisite."

"Oh, it is." Deghan gently seizes my arm and twirls me toward him. "How about a real one?" He folds me into his smothering embrace, and if this is the last memory I have of him, I will die a content woman.

I squeeze him back and allow my body to dissolve into his.

"I wasn't sure if you still had it." Deghan plants kisses along my forehead. "I've been wanting to use it to see if it still worked but I didn't want to accidentally give that devil dude a hug if he had it."

I let out a chuckle. "It only works for me and you. Plus, didn't anyone tell you we needed it for the battle?"

"Must have slipped their mind."

"I should have told you." I stand on my tiptoes and press my lips to his cheek. "I'm glad you didn't toss it."

Deghan's eyes go wide. "Are you serious? It's my favorite gift ever. Even if it lost its power, I'd keep it. Hands down the most thoughtful thing in the world." He leans down and gently puts his mouth onto mine. "I'll always keep it with me."

I hope even after I'm gone it will still bring him comfort when I can no longer.

"Dinner is served," Cameron calls out from across the way. He takes off his apron and tosses it onto the counter where me, him, and Deghan got freaky not too long ago.

The memory brings a blush to my cheeks, and he seems to pick up on my train of thought.

He winks at me and grins.

"I'm starving," Deghan exclaims.

Cam shakes his head. "Aren't you always dying of hunger?"

He carefully takes the massive serving dish full of noodley stuff and carries it into the dining hall.

Deghan follows behind with a large salad and a tray full of dressings.

Lillian shadows him with a basket brimming to the top with bread. "I hope you brought your appetite."

And although the idea of eating at a time like this is a bit difficult, I pretend for a moment that life is normal. That I'm not about to be summoned to Hell to risk my life for a chance at redemption. That this is just another day at Harper Academy surrounded by those I love while we wait for the transition to the next school term to begin.

Because if I focus on the reality of it all, I might possibly break down in front of everyone who is counting on me to keep it together.

Sydney and Silas stroll into the room at the same time, but from opposite ends. They claim their spot next to me at the large round table where all of us fit.

Cam dollops food onto the plates and passes them down the line until each one of us has a hefty serving in front of us.

Deghan fills up all of our glasses and then takes his into his hand. He raises it into the air. "I'd like to make a toast." He observes the waiting faces. "To friends. To this meal. To little moments that lead us to big ones. And to Willow, who I have no doubt will kick some major Devil ass."

"To Willow," the group cheers.

I smile and take a nervous sip of my tea. Will this be the last time I ever drink dirty sock water ever again? Is this my last supper?

I can't think that way, otherwise, I've already let Balial win.

"This is really good, Cam." Lillian shoves another bite in her mouth.

"Couldn't have done it without you," he tells her.

Walker points his fork at Cam. "You're going to go places with this kind of cooking."

It brings my heart a calming comfort to hear other people confirm Cam's abilities to him. Without me here I worry he'll push his talents to the side and not follow through with his dream of being a chef. He has so much potential, and I would hate for that to be wasted.

Silas puts his hand on my knee and whispers. "You okay?"

I force the corner of my lips to turn up. "Yeah."

In reality, there is a war brewing on the horizon, and it's everything I can do to stay present in the moment.

"You still need to get rid of your magic." Sydney nudges his plate forward and turns to me.

I stand from the table and put my arms up in the air. "Who wants some calm?"

"Anyone but Silas." Sydney joins me in getting up from our seats. "You don't want to risk cross-contaminating sources when he replenishes you."

I place my palm on Sydney and push some of my energy into him. I tap into the pool, and it's relatively filled. "I'm fuller than I thought."

Walker comes over. "Here."

The rest of the bunch come closer, too, waiting for their turn to get a little mood booster to help me clear out my magical reserves. It takes pumping myself into every single one of them for my supply to dry up. The feeling is strange, going from vivid colors and crisp senses, to the dullness of the mundane world. No wonder humans are often miserable, they're living in a world with much more to offer than they actually receive.

"Have you put any thought into what you'll be wearing?" Sydney skims the outfit I'm currently in.

"Not entirely." What a very stupid thing for me to have overlooked.

Sydney reaches out to graze my hair out of my face. "I have something in mind if you're open to suggestions."

Leave it to Syd to have thought of everything.

"Of course."

I follow him out of the dining hall and around the corner, up the stairs, and down the hallway to his dorm.

Silas shadows closely behind, regardless of not being formally invited by Sydney.

I think at this point they have an unspoken understanding by now.

Sydney opens the door for us to enter. He latches it shut and motions for me to go to the center of the room. "I did a little research on combat clothing and tailoring it specifically to the person. I found a way to incorporate things exclusively to you."

"That sounds helpful." I wait for him to show me what he's talking about.

"Stand still."

Silas leans against the wall and watches us with a careful eye.

Sydney mutters and raises his fingertips like he's playing the piano mid-air. Radiant green magic flows from his digits and gushes toward my body.

I squint for a long moment to block out the bright light that comes from his spell. I open fully and settle my gaze on my altered clothes.

My normal leggings have transformed into a pair of skintight thick but movable pants. My thighs have straps around them with various daggers and crystals tucked accordingly. My sweater is now a black three-quarter-sleeved shirt. It's shiny and stretchy, and even with its tautness, it's incredibly comfortable. The new garments are fitted perfectly to my body and provide the appropriate coverage and support.

"Both fire and water-resistant, they also deliver compression in case of injury. Worst case scenario, obviously, but if you get hurt, it could come in handy. The knives respond to your touch only, meaning the second you grab them, you'll infuse them with whatever magic you have access to which will increase their effectiveness. They also respond to your location, so you can summon them back to you. The stones are all tailored to you, too, for protection, health, stamina, all that jazz." Sydney appears like a lightbulb went off in his head. "Oh, I almost forgot." He offers a small pill to me. "This will repel your glitch. The effectiveness varies from witch to witch, but it won't hurt to try."

I run my hands along the slick exterior of my new wardrobe. A sudden panic assaults me. What happened to Deghan's stone and the thing I had tucked in my waistband?

I frantically feel at my upper thigh and let out a huge breath as I skim the round rock protruding from my pocket. I don't check for the other item, but I assume if the one is there, the other is, too. At least I hope so, or I'm fucking screwed if I lose this war.

"It's only modified, so anything you had in your possession will still be on you." Sydney confirms my frantic thoughts.

"It's perfect, Syd. Thank you."

Sydney nods to Silas. "He helped, too."

I turn to Silas and take in the beauty of his existence. "You two are a great team when you want to be."

Silas rolls his stunning eyes. "Don't push it."

CHAPTER 32

I spend my remaining moments hugging the ones I love and watching them walk away to their respective areas in an attempt to prolong my ruse that they have no idea what I'm about to do. It's not entirely a lie, considering the backup plan I have in place in the event Balial actually defeats me.

I don't want them to leave, but it has to be this way. Instead of having them near, I cling to the lingering memory of their bittersweet embraces. Deghan's—warm and strong. Cameron's—gentle and kind. Sydney's—reassuring and comforting. I recall Lillian's hopeful expression, and Walker's supportive yet concerned final nod.

Silas stays by my side, though, until the very last minute. He grips my face in the palm of his strong hands and stares into my eyes. "No matter what happens, I'll be there when this is all said and done. I won't lose you again, not like this."

Little does he know, he has no choice in the matter. I've already made my decision, and unless I win, our journey ends here.

"Forever, okay?" Silas kisses the spot just between my eyebrows, then my nose, and lastly my lips.

"And ever." I tug him toward me and hold on for dear life. I don't want this to be our last moment together, but I may have no other option. Getting back to him, to the rest of my men, to my friends and family—that will be the drive I take with me to fuel my fight against Balial.

Silas weaves his fingers through mine. "Take it all."

I close my eyes and breathe him in. I ignite the connection and summon his strength. With every bit of it drained from him, I gain more power. My entire being awakens with each drop of his magic. I fill myself to a capacity I've never experienced second-hand. I slow down as I feel his well becoming empty.

"No, keep going," Silas urges me to continue despite his weakened state.

I take a little more but refuse to dry him out completely. "I have enough, for now. Go recharge. I'm going to need you soon."

It's not until his vampire senses pick up on the shift in the atmosphere that he goes to leave. "This isn't goodbye, it's see you later." He kisses me one last time.

I back away slowly and ache at the tether that pulls between us. If I thought walking away from him was difficult before, boy was I wrong.

I move away from the patio and into the forest behind the school. I don't go far until I find the portal that Balial arranged for me. It's dark and reddish with a murky haze around it. I haven't even stepped into Hell and the gross odor oozes out and into this air. I take one last breath of the cool and undiluted oxygen and step into the spiraling vortex that sucks me into the abyss.

I spin and spin and spin for what seems like entirely too long.

Is this part of the challenge? Whirl me around and make me walk a straight line without falling over or puking up my pasta?

"Sorry about that," the thick voice calls out. "All these years and I haven't quite perfected the transportation part of this process."

The darkness fades away, and I find myself standing in a much more temperature-regulated part of Hell than I've ever encountered. The cave-like room is vast, and when I turn around, I spot a bulky throne at the top of a set of three large stairs. I take a step closer, and my eyes adjust to what is in front of me. The chair is made up of skulls and bones and large black and grey rocks. A smaller, similar one is placed to its side.

"What do you think?" Balial tips his head toward it. "We can redecorate if you'd like."

I scowl at him. "You haven't won yet."

He points his long gangly finger at me. "That last word... that's the key there." Balial strides down the steps toward me. "Although, if you'd like to save yourself the trouble, you can forfeit now."

I narrow my gaze. "Over my dead body."

"Now, now. Don't be so rash." He motions around the expansive area. "You will grow to like it here."

"Doubtful." I cross my arms over my chest. "Have we started already or is this just your way of taunting me?"

"Well, as a matter of fact, I thought we could exchange pleasantries first. But if you're so eager to begin." Balial straightens his black dress shirt and fixes the cuffs on his designer suit.

Does he outsource his fancy clothes or have some minion make them for him? Either way, they fit him perfectly.

With my heightened supply of magic, I can actually sense Balial's mood in the slightest. If my reading is correct, he's truly nervous. The origin of that feeling is entirely lost on me.

Is he worried he might lose? Or that I'll refuse to be his queen if he wins? Maybe he ate some bad sushi for dinner?

I continue to watch him come closer. "What better time than now."

Balial approaches and stops a few feet from me.

I keep my body rigid and ready in case he decides to attack. I have no idea what to expect from him, but I choose to be prepared for anything.

Balial frowns. "It bothers me that you think I'll hurt you."

I blink up at him. Fuck, can he read my mind?

"Your body language." He signals to my arms to answer the confused look that must be on my face. "You're guarding yourself."

"I think it would be foolish of me not to assume the worst at this point." Especially considering I came here to battle him. Is this another attempt of getting in my head? Weakening me and making me think he means no harm so he can strike when I'm most vulnerable? "I'm not going to fall for your mind games."

"If I wanted to cause you pain, I would. And trust me, you'll know if it's going to happen. Right now, though, we're simply two people having a conversation." Balial takes another step forward.

I take one back and cock my head to the side. "I think that's close enough."

Balial stares at me with those dark onyx orbs of his.

I should be intimidated but all I see is a man I can't wait to destroy.

"Very well. How about I offer you a friendly inside scoop?" Balial mimics my stance.

"And why would you do that?" My heart races at the uncertainty of his intentions. They seem genuine, but I could be wrong. This could be part of his façade.

Balial's expression softens. "You really don't get it, do you?"

"I guess not." I truly don't understand the way this man's brain operates, and if it doesn't pertain to the task at hand, I don't care to find out.

"Never mind, then." He seems to wave off that train of thought. "There will be three stages of the battle. I don't typically divulge this information to all contestants, but...you're different." He puts a sort of emphasis on the last word. "I want to give you a fighting chance. That seems a fair thing to do. You won't come into contact with me until the last phase. No one ever makes it past the second round, so I wish you the best of luck." Balial meets my gaze again. "If you choose to give in, all you have to say is *mara em.*"

"What does that mean?" I maintain eye contact with him. The phrase sounds familiar, but I can't quite place it.

He smirks. "I'll tell you once you've finished."

"Whatever." I shouldn't mouth off to him, but his arrogance irks me.

"I'm going to snap my fingers, and the second I do, everything will be set into motion." Balial moves toward me.

This time I don't back away.

His eyes narrow, and he sniffs the air. "You performed a joining connection."

Fuck. He figured it out. He's discovered my one advantage, and now I have *nothing* to work with. He'll adjust the difficulty level to ensure that there is no way I can make it out of this alive.

A smile breaks across his villainous face. "That's clever. I mean, you'd be foolish to come here with a limited supply. Hopefully, that vampire boy knows what he's doing if he's going to keep replenishing you."

I nearly choke on my own saliva. Balial thinks I linked myself to Silas, not Cameron.

And if that's the case, he still has no clue about my secret weapon.

I put on my best *you got me* performance in an attempt to keep up my charade.

He gently nudges my shoulder with his fist in a playful manner. "That's my girl."

Anger boils inside me and rids any carefree attitude I once was putting on. I'm going to make him pay for calling me that. And thanks to him, I now know that I have to get to round three to make that happen.

CHAPTER 33

Balial was right.

The moment his fingers graze each other, I'm pulled from the confines of that strange chamber and dropped out onto the ground of a wooded area. It strangely resembles the one from Charles's simulation with its tall lanky trees and sporadic growth.

My sights settle on a small placard near the spot I landed.

Make it through the forest and you shall pass onto the next level.

I rise to my feet and unsheathe one of the daggers from its tucked away spot. A bubble of purple flows through my skin and onto the handle, illuminating the shiny metal. If I were in a movie, this is where they would add some random sound effect that makes no sense at all but causes people to think something exciting is about to happen. Like a clanking or clanging of knives, or whatever arbitrary weapon noise they could come up with.

I study my environment. The very obvious path would be the one that leads me straight along to the finish line of the forest challenge. It seems easy, right? Just make a beeline through. But Balial would never allow something so trivial to happen. The trail is probably laced with explosives or booby traps that render a person incapable of completing the mission. On the other hand, though, he could have also anticipated the contestant realizing he wouldn't permit a walkthrough, when in reality, there are no traps at all.

My first instinct is to summon forth my floral magic, but considering it's Silas's that's running through my veins, I don't have access to all of my abilities like I used to. They're there but not prominent.

"Which direction," I ask myself.

I study my surroundings again and listen intently for any inclination of what's to come.

I'm deep in a standoff with myself when a loud crunch sounds in the distance. I look toward it and spot the trees swaying and being thrown apart while a giant creature barrels through them toward me.

I can't stay here out in the open anymore, I have to move. I go with my gut and take a sharp left and follow the tree line parallel with the path. I take three solid steps and fall flat on my face. I brace myself with my free hand and end up scraping a long section of my forearm in the process. I waste no time assessing the burning wound—whatever this beastly thing is, it's after me.

The thought crosses my mind that I'm in over my head, but I quickly push it aside. Regardless of what I think, I'm in this and I have to do everything I can to make it out alive. I've come too far to succumb to the very first of Balial's challenges.

He's probably sneering and laughing while he watches me panic from his big screen or wherever the fuck he is.

My anger burns bright, and if I'm being honest, it snaps me

out of my doubtful stupor. Balial doesn't get to make a fool out of me, not if I have anything to say about it.

I stop in my tracks. There's no sense in outrunning this thing given I have no idea what I'm soon to face on my journey to the end of this trial. I will take this one move at a time, and right now, I need to destroy this thing that's pursuing me.

Balial would never see that coming.

I brace myself and plant my feet firmly while maintaining a loose fighting stance. Blood trickles down my arm, and I ignore the raging pain that zips through me. I steady my thoughts, clearing my head completely of anything except my ability to channel my strength. I could easily grab on to the stone in my pocket and request backup, but I'm hoping I can save that for round three when Balial least expects it. The longer I can keep this secret from him, the better.

Although, if I don't defeat this gigantic three-headed dog that's the size of a fucking house that's coming straight for me, I might never get to pull out my secret weapon.

I narrow my gaze and focus. The magic in my veins flickers to life and quite literally shoots out of my eyes like laser beams at the demon running toward me.

It yelps and cries as the purple current cuts into its flesh.

I take another breath and concentrate harder. I maintain my foothold and a low guttural growl rumbles. I realize a moment later that the sound came from me.

With one more deliberate lungful, I send a rapid blast of razor-sharp magic toward the beast, slicing the thing completely in half. It tumbles onto the ground and rattles the earth upon impact. I blink to sever the magical rays coming from my skull and tuck Silas's power just under the surface of my skin for safe-keeping. I assess the well and find it's still decently full despite using an abundance on this very dead demon in front of me. I have to be careful with my usage if I'm going to delay calling in for back up.

I wait a cautious second prior to turning my back on the lifeless thing.

Once I'm almost certain it is no longer, I continue on my previous path along the trees.

I'm more thoughtful with where I place each foot, not wanting to trip and fall again. The wound on my arm is searing, but I refuse to look at it. If I push away the pain, maybe I'll forget it's there at all. That's how avoidance works, right?

A rather loud galloping brings me to reality in full force. I swivel around until I locate the source of it. The silky black horse-like creature is running straight down the already carved-out path in the direction I'm headed. The thing is massive, easily triple the size of an earth-bound mare. It's bewildered and afraid. It doesn't seem to notice me hiding behind a large tree—it just continues on its trek, whipping around to look behind it every so often. A second sound fills my ears. It's much fainter than the first. Buzzing maybe. A steady humming of winged creatures perhaps. I steady my gaze until a thick cloud heads in my direction at a rapid speed.

It's not just the large quad-animal that's retreating from it that startles me, it's the remaining greenery on every single plant, shrub, and tree that the haze touches being seared off upon its briefest touch. Whatever this floating wave is, it's deadly. And I'm in its direct route.

I rally my rational brain to help me process what the fuck I'm going to do.

I size up the finish line—it's entirely too far considering the rate at which this death mist is traveling and how fast I can run, not to mention anything that might slow my journey along the way. I could try to exit its lane and let it continue its pursuit of the stallion thing, but what if it decides to come after me next? I can't afford to lose myself any deeper into this Hell forest, otherwise, I'll never make it out.

I'm going to have to exterminate the pesky swarm of demon insects.

How? I've never dealt with these types of creatures in the past. But I've also never encountered a gigantic demon dog, either. I'll have to get creative and figure it out.

That's what I do—improvise.

The horde moves closer and closer, demolishing everything living in its wake. It doesn't seem to deter from its already intended lane. I've already come to the conclusion that I can't outrun it, but what if I can outlast it? If I can survive the surge hitting, maybe I can jump up and follow it to the end once it passes. I'll use it as a buffer to kill anything else that may attack me.

It's a solid plan, pending it actually works.

I watch the tree line and calculate the speed at which they're traveling. It's semi-consistent, and if my math is right, I have about sixty seconds to brace for impact. I need to wait until almost the last instant if I want to ensure maximum efficiency and the least amount of magic used. I still have to reserve enough to get through the rest of this challenge and the second stage if I want to blow Balial's mind with my surprise.

I count down until the buzzing becomes so loud it rattles my eardrums. The cloud becomes thicker and denser and darker and kills the greenery only twenty feet away.

I inhale deeply and close my eyes. If this doesn't work, if death is nearby, I'd rather not watch it come and swallow me whole.

I channel forth my borrowed power, letting it rumble around and mix into the correct ratio. I push it outward and hope with all my might the protective barrier will shield me from this assault.

The humming grows rowdier, and I cover my ears to meagerly protect them. The bugs rattle my defensive wall and nearly throw me off-balance. I hold tight to the purple power flowing around me and pray it will be enough.

A secondary noise source emerges, kind of like zapping. A snap, crackle, pop type of sound.

I peer through my squinted lids to see the throng of jet-black death things being parted by the radiant orb around my form. I blink fully to life while maintaining my reign on the magic pouring out of me. The cloud is halfway past me, and I'm still here, I'm not dead.

My plan actually fucking worked—I just have to put faith that the magic will endure while they go by.

I gawk at the tiny creatures flying past, eating everything in their path, and thank the angels that I didn't fall to the same demise. I let out a breath of relief when the darkness passes and continues on its journey toward the frantic stallion in the near distance.

I allow the barrier to drop and tuck Silas's magic away again. I dig my hands into the warm dirt and find myself thankful that I'm not bug dinner. I rise to my feet, and the moment I turn my head to look behind me, a lone winged creature staggers behind its group, zooming right past my face. It clips my cheek and continues on without a care in the world, leaving me with a gaping cut that burns worse than the one on my arm.

"Fuck," I call out. I bring my hand up and apply pressure to the cut. I pull away and my palm is covered in bright-red blood. I grunt and bite at my lip.

It's then that I recall the magical daggers on my person. I slide one out and allow only the smallest of power to flow out of me. I don't want to use any at all, but if I die to some fucking technicality like bleeding out, I will never forgive myself.

I think fire, and the blade roars to life with a blooming flame. I let it heat up until it glows and then extinguish it with my mind. I have an inclination that what I'm about to do next will hurt worse than the initial injury itself.

Not letting myself ponder on it too much, I press the flat side of the ruby knife on my cheek and grit my teeth as my flesh sears in response. Tears well in my eyes without my approval, but I refuse to acknowledge them. Once I've finished with my face, I ignite the dagger one last time. Without another thought, I raise my wrist to my body to expose the section of my forearm that's sliced open. I lay the thing longways along the wound and wince upon impact.

I breathe deeply and allow no other emotion, not wanting to give Balial the show he is probably expecting. I wipe the knife onto the leg of my pants and tuck it back into its home.

I stare ahead at the cloud paving the way to the end of this angel-forsaken place. I vaguely spot the enormous horse still trying to get away.

A strange sort of remaining steam lingers in the trail of the demon insects.

I glance all around and decide to take the direct route straight to the end. The bugs have already killed everything else on their way, so why should I waste any more time perusing the outskirts?

I walk at a brisk pace, carefully eyeing the black fog ahead of me. It gains a heavy lead on me so I break into a run. There's no sense in being out here any longer than I have to be, and if this thing is scaring off everything else, why not use that added benefit?

I stumble over a random root growing through the path but quickly regain my composure. I cover a decent amount of ground in a matter of a few minutes but am still far away from where I need to be to get out of here. This stage is like a strange optical illusion, making you think you're almost there when in reality you're nowhere close.

My ears alert me to a painful yelp, followed by loud squealing.

I steady my gaze ahead and bring my hand to my mouth when the horde finally catches up to the stallion. Regardless of the horse's large and intimidating size, it's no match to the death bugs and their insistent pursuit of consuming everything they come into contact with.

A few seconds later, the wailing stops, and bulky bones fall to the ground, showing the only thing left of the horse-like animal.

I come to an abrupt halt the moment the pack changes its path and starts its killing voyage in my direction. I thought I had outlasted them and used them to my advantage, but it appears they will stop at nothing to make sure I don't make it to the end.

CHAPTER 34

I'm not going to make it out of here alive.

That's what the insane amount of fear racing through my body tells me.

I recall Balial's words, *"No one makes it past the second stage."*

Meaning others have made it past the first. There's no way I'm not going to be one of those poor saps who can't even win round one.

I am an Oliver witch. Descended from the angels. My journey can't end here. Not if I have anything to do with it.

I tap into my reserves and sigh at the capacity. I run my palm along the rock still tucked into the pocket of my specially tailored pants. Calling in for help is my last resort, and right now, there are still other options on the table. I have to keep thinking—come up with *something* to save my ass. There's no way I'll make it past round three if I don't maintain the element of surprise. Although, if I can't live past this death brigade, I'll never get the chance of facing Balial.

The buzzing grows louder the closer the flying things get.

I play the memory of moments prior. It took them nearly three minutes to pass me once before. And that took a huge toll on my supply of Silas. If I want to make this work, I can't stay stationary. I have to move, and I have to do it quick.

I've never projected my protective barrier and maintained it while under attack, at least not in this capacity. I'm not even sure if it will withstand their assault.

I don't have the luxury of coming up with another plan, though, so this one will have to work. My life and my revenge scheme depend upon it.

I do the only thing left to do—I run.

I break out into a sprint toward the deadly creatures and at the last possible second, I flip my wrists and throw the purple shield around myself and barrel into the dark and lethal cloud. I push against the current and struggle to gain footing to power through. I grit my teeth and shove my body forward, digging the toes of my shoes into the dirt and grinding further. With each brutal step, I get closer to the end, and closer to running out of magic.

I squint ahead and spot the line which I have to cross.

My power flickers, and a scream leaves my throat upon contact from the bugs that touch my bare skin. I don't allow myself to concentrate on the pain. This is nothing compared to what Silas went through.

Balial's voice rings into my head again, reminding me that I can give up at any time, all I have to do is say the words, *mara em.*

I'd rather die than quit fighting.

So, I do exactly that. I plow through the haze of incessant buzzing and heave my weakened body toward the stripe on the ground that means I did it, I progress to the next stage. My magic flickers out upon impact to the hard land, and I close my eyes as the angry and hungry bugs flap their tiny wings inches from my face. Like a quarterback on the bottom of a pile of football players, I hold on firmly and wait for the referee of this Hell to tell me whether or not I've scored a touchdown.

The fluttering disappears and is replaced with a slow clapping of hands.

"Well, well, well," Balial says cheerfully.

I peek through my lids and spot him standing a few feet away in the chamber we were in not too long ago. I'm lying in a heap on the floor of the cave-like structure, clutching my knees to my chest. I pry my hands free and go to rise to my feet. I refuse to look weak in front of him.

"That was rather impressive." Balial tries to help me up. "You took a different approach than most. I wasn't so sure it would work, but you surprised me. I was actually worried at one point; I had thought I would have to intervene to save your life. Can't have my new bride being torn to shreds, now can we?"

I cringe at his words and swat away his assistance. "Don't touch me." My shoulder stings from the new burn marks left by the destructive bugs. "What were those things?"

Balial lets out a little laugh. "My little creation. Clever, you think?"

I clench my jaw in an attempt to soak up the pain in my body. "You're sick."

"Now, Willow, don't be quite so harsh. It gets rather boring here, I have to mix things up." Balial points to my wounds. "Would you like me to have that looked at before your next match?"

"No," I bark at him. I drop my hands to the sides so I'm not holding on to my injured self. I need to appear stronger than I am. I hate the way he looks at me like I'm this fragile and weak being in need of his help.

"Fine." Balial takes a short glass from the tray and pushes it into my hand. "You must be parched."

I narrow my gaze at him and bring the thing to my nose. I

sniff the clear liquid. "You're a fucking monster, you know that, right?" I throw the contents in his face like an angry woman does when she finds her man cheating. I toss the glass across the room and stare him dead in the eyes while it shatters into endless pieces.

Balial sucks in a breath and pulls a black handkerchief from the front pocket of his jacket. He dramatically wipes at his alcohol-soaked cheeks. "That was a bit uncalled for. I take it you're not much of a drinker? I shouldn't be so astounded; you're not like the rest of them."

"No, as a matter of fact, I'm not. But you already knew that, didn't you?"

With what little magic I have left, I sense Balial is sincerely confused.

"I didn't. Had I, though, I would have offered you something else." He blots his collar. "This was my favorite suit, too."

"Oh." A strange bit of embarrassment registers through me. In any other situation, I'd apologize. This one, though, he deserves none of my remorse.

"Usually contestants desire to take the edge off, hence the liquor." Balial tosses the moist hankie onto the silver platter he retrieved the drink from. "Would you fancy I fetch you another beverage? What do you prefer? Water? Coffee? Perhaps a fruit punch."

"I'm not a child, stop treating me like one." I motion between us. "Whatever this is, these pleasantries, they're not necessary. Is this part of your twisted game, the ruse you put on to get your rocks off? I won't be a part of it. You don't have to pretend to be nice to me." I reach forward and boldly grab on to his hand. "Snap your fingers already, send me into the second stage."

Balial doesn't pull away. Instead, he stares at our joined embrace like it's a fascinating and foreign thing to him.

I break free. "Come on. What are you waiting for?" Each moment that passes is another that I become more exhausted and lose any ounce of adrenaline-induced power to drive me toward victory. Unless there's a bed where I can rest and Silas to replenish my magic, there's no need for me to waste any time between one challenge and the next.

He comes out of his trance and slowly meets my gaze. "Okay." His voice is low and saddened. "As you wish."

The last thing I see is Balial's distressed face, and then everything goes black.

I spiral into the abyss and wonder for the briefest instant whether Balial became so fed up with me that he ended it all. It's not until I land on my butt on the hard ground that I recognize he sent me where I asked him.

Near my right hand is another placard. In red bold letters, it says: *Ring the bell.*

Such a simple task, and yet no one has been proficient enough to pull it off.

I scan my surroundings. This time, I'm in an old village encircled by stone buildings with moss-covered roofs. It reminds me of the pictures I had seen in my mom's travel magazines of England. Only my actual setting seems much more medieval than that of the pretty settlements deemed worthy of those fancy publications.

I rise to my feet and cautiously search for any incoming threats. I anticipate the worst, considering the success rate we're dealing with. Once I'm on solid footing, I spot the large metal shape dangling from a wooden setup. It hangs higher than I can reach, but there is a ladder along the side of it for access.

What could be so difficult about this seemingly meek assignment?

It's then that my gaze lowers and settles upon the bulbous wart-covered ogre-looking thing lying at the base of the entire structure. That's where the trouble must be—getting past that beast.

Instead of attacking it head-on, I choose another route. I am a witch after all. I have to ring the bell, but it didn't specify *how.*

I summon forth a little bit of Silas's magic and focus on creating a wind strong enough to clang my victory. I send a wave inconspicuously flying up and over to the bell. Just when I think I have this thing in the bag, the greenish creature grumbles and swats away the flow of power I sent toward it.

Shit. Maybe this won't be so simple.

I tiptoe closer and hide behind a stone wall, not wanting to bring attention to myself. I peep through a hole from a fallen rock and study the guard.

The large thing stirs and pulls itself onto its behind. It yawns loudly, exposing its long, sharp yellow teeth, and stretches its thick and meaty arms. The curly horns on its head remind me of a goat. If I'm not mistaken, this being might be a troll.

For the sake of not going back and forth on what it is, I'm going to name it Jerry.

Jerry, the keeper of the bell.

The warden of my fate.

Jerry seems grumpy and annoyed by my waking him up.

I conjure a sleeping potion and let it bubble up into my palm. I blow it through the crack in the wall and toward him. Here's to hoping I can put him back in a trance and sneak by. All I have to do is climb to the top and then the rest is history. If he wakes up at that point, Balial will have already brought me to his chambers, right?

But it doesn't matter, because Jerry swats away the light-purple magic floating his way. He grunts and stands on his big heavy feet. His stance is easily higher than the ladder itself.

I crane my neck to take in his vastness.

It's then that he lands his sights on me through the wall. He groans and picks up a nearby boulder and tosses it carelessly in my direction, completely disintegrating my covering.

So much for being inconspicuous.

Balial is probably thoroughly enjoying watching me fail. He's more than likely giggling to himself and poking fun at my inability to figure out this easy task. But Balial isn't the smartest man in existence, and this challenge has to have some angle that I'm not considering. There has to be *some* way to defeat Jerry and ring the bell.

Am I supposed to kill him? Wouldn't everyone else have tried that, though?

If others have been capable of beating the first stage, they're clearly skillful enough to take out a troll. But maybe that isn't the best approach.

Every time I've tried to outsmart Jerry, his anger has risen. And since I have a very limited source of magic, I have to be thoughtful with what other options I try.

I boldly step out into the open and confront Jerry.

He growls and slams his fist into the ground, throwing debris flying in the process.

I raise my hands into the air in front of me. My heart pounds feverishly, and I wonder whether or not I'm being brave or foolish. It's definitely one or the other.

Jerry snaps his mouth shut and curls his lips, letting out a snarl that sends a chill down my spine. He must be letting me know I need to back off or he's going to attack.

I disregard his warning and continue forward slowly with my arms still raised. I don't want him to see me as a threat. If he's spent his entire existence guarding this bell, he's only ever known people who wanted to hurt him. People who have been desperate to defeat the beast and advance to the next level.

If Balial was ever right about anything, it's that I am not like the rest. And I decline the predestined path that I have to use violence to overcome this challenge.

It may be the death of me, but, if anything, I went out nobly.

Jerry puts one foot forward and bangs it with force into the paved patio he's chained to.

I lower my gaze to the thick clanging metal clasp around his ankle. For some reason, when I look at him, I don't see a big scary ogre, I see a creature who's been tied up their entire life to serve others. To sacrifice themselves for the good of nothing. Someone who is hurting inside from never being shown an ounce of kindness. Sometimes people aren't as scary as they seem. Sometimes they just need a little love and compassion instead of harsh judgments.

I do what any insane person would do in this situation. I invoke a blip of my remaining magic and send it flying. Somehow it does the trick, unlocking the bangle and flinging it onto the ground with a crash.

Jerry lets out a grumble and turns his attention to his now free leg.

I swallow the uncertainty that rises in the back of my throat. I either did a great thing, or quite possibly the dumbest thing ever.

I suddenly realize it was probably the latter. I frantically search within me for any remaining magic and find myself nearly dry.

Jerry takes a hesitant step toward me. He snarls and exposes his teeth.

A strange shift happens when I pick up on his energy, something I wasn't in tune with before.

Jerry is mad—really, really mad. But it's a familiar feeling I've had myself. Something I'm actually very acquainted with.

I almost laugh at the realization. This is a rage like no other, and if I don't act fast, I'm going to be pummeled to smithereens.

I channel the last fragment of Silas left inside me and do the only thing I can think of. I raise my palm in the air and kneel to the ground. I lower my head and wait for whatever outcome to come to fruition.

Jerry's warm and foul breath consumes me with each passing second.

I can't help but wonder what kind of death will greet me. Will it be fast and painless, or will Jerry take his time dismantling my body parts to devour one by one?

But my untimely demise never comes. At least not from Jerry.

I gander up at him in anticipation of his move.

Instead of ending me, he carefully picks the ruby red apple from my outstretched hand and pops it into his mouth. Jerry isn't a violent being, he was simply hangry.

I expect him to do something, but what he does next completely throws me for a loop.

Jerry extends his own monstrous paw and nods toward it, calling me forth to climb aboard.

In an effort not to piss him off, especially considering I used up the rest of my magic on his snack, I scale his fingers and hang on tight. If I weren't living through this myself, I would never believe my own story.

Jerry elevates me into the sky and plants me firmly next to the giant bell.

I carefully gain my footing and grab the rope hanging from the headstock. Not wanting to leave anything else to chance, I give it a solid tug and swing the heavy metal thing back and forth. The sound is sweet and heavenly to my ears, and honestly, I can't help but feel like this is some kind of dream.

Jerry manages to let out a smile as he lowers me gently to the safety of the ground.

I smile back. "Thank you." I have no idea whether or not he can understand me.

He doesn't get a chance to respond when I'm sucked from the old village and thrown back into oblivion. A few seconds later, I land in Balial's throne room.

CHAPTER 35

"Y ou never fail to astonish me." Balial saunters over with a different suit on than earlier. This one is similar, but not covered in the alcohol I threw on him.

"Is that supposed to be a compliment?" I glance around the room.

Balial is my third and final challenge—does that mean it's already begun?

I drop my hands to my sides and casually graze the rock in my pocket to confirm it's still there. I'm fresh out of magic and I'm going to have to call in for backup soon.

"I feel rather foolish, really. This seems like taking candy from a baby at this point." Balial motions toward my pathetic and powerless body.

I'm injured, and he's very aware of that. I'm also bone dry on power. He's probably picked up on that, too.

"I thought I made it clear to you that I'm not a child." I glare at him with an overconfidence that could only be provoked from a near-death experience. I've been through so much, what's mouthing off to the Devil?

Balial nods. "On the contrary, I assume nothing of that nature. You are very much a woman, Ms. Oliver. And I am eagerly awaiting making you mine." He raises his palm and lets my pink magic flow to the surface. "This will soon be yours again. Win or lose."

I suppress the anger building within me. "On with it then."

"Always in such a rush." Balial strolls closer. "What are you thinking? A spring or fall wedding? I assume you want to stay true to your human customs and formalities."

How can he be so arrogant in a time like this? I guess when you know you have your opponent beat, that superiority comes naturally.

"You can wear white, too. If it pleases you." Balial dusts the imaginary dirt off his sleeve. "I'll be the one in black, obviously."

Is he stalling or is he always this egotistical?

I ignore his snide questioning. "Are you ready or not?"

"I'm nervous, can you tell?" He circles around me. "Or perhaps I'm excited. I haven't done hand-to-hand combat in millennia. This ought to be fun." Balial tugs on his ear. "Oh, shall we go over the rules?"

Finally, getting down to brass tacks. I wait for him to continue.

"There is only one. Everything else is fair game. First person to put the other into submission wins." Balial grins with such over-confidence. He thinks he has this in the bag, but he has no idea that I plan on putting up a fight.

If he thinks for a second that I'm going to submit to him, he's so fucking wrong.

"I'll go easy on you. I mean, you are to be my wife and all." Balial winks at me.

I loathe how attractive he is despite being such a shitty person. Even those unendingly black eyes and effortless beauty don't erase the desire I have to rip him to shreds.

"Don't do me any favors." I ready my hand near my thigh in anticipation that our match is to begin. I do my best to make it seem like nothing out of the ordinary.

Balial hovers toward me and leans down close. His cool breath caresses my face. "I'll give you a few moments to prepare."

All I really hear is that he enjoys the thrill of the chase. He wants me to run in terror of what he'll do to me, but he's going to be in for a rude awakening when I don't give in to his twisted desires.

He snaps his fingers and tosses me into the same familiar darkness I've encountered in the past.

I wait for the black to fade into whatever setting he has arranged for us.

The dust of my vision resolves, and I take in the serene backdrop to this final battle. I'm surprised to discover myself surrounded by a lush forest, beaming with life. Nothing at all like the drab one from my first challenge.

I breathe in the scent of something floral and earthy and listen to the calming sound of a nearby waterfall.

I shake my head to rid myself of the unexpected distractions and shove my hand into my pocket to give Deghan a hug. I grip the stone firmly and squeeze it tight. I clear my mind and allow myself to be open to a response.

A minute goes by and nothing happens.

Panic consumes me. What if I'm too far away? What if the connection is no longer? What if more time has passed in the real world than I anticipated and the expiration on the joining is done? What if the angelic ceremony has commenced and they've already shut down demonic activity? Or worst of all, what if something terrible has happened to those I love, and they're unable to help me right now?

I've made it this far and now I'm going to lose from a lack of power.

How hilarious, considering I was once an influential witch.

I trail my finger along the seam of my waistband until I stumble upon my backup plan. If Balial puts me in a position I cannot escape from, I will follow through with making sure I am never his. I have no other choice—I could never allow myself to be claimed by that sick man.

A large black portal opens about ten feet from me. Balial gracefully walks out and onto the grassy area. He cocks his head to the side. "You waited for me?"

"Something like that." I go within myself and frantically look for any remaining power. Not a drop is left in my system. I guess I'm going to have to face him the old-fashioned way. I slide my hand down and latch on to one of the daggers. Typically, it would spark to life with my touch, but nothing happens. The knife is mundane in my grasp.

A grin spreads across Balial's face. "Ladies first." He bows.

I waste no time and throw the blade straight toward his head.

Somehow, he moves elegantly and swiftly enough to catch it the second it flies close to him. "Going straight for the kill. I like it." He tosses my weapon to the ground. "Here. How about we fight fair." Balial flicks his wrists toward the ground, and two opposing yet identical swords appear. One is lined with black, the other with pink. He strolls toward me.

I take a few guarded steps back.

"Oh, please. I'm more of a gentleman than that." Balial drops the thing into the dirt and retreats. "I assure you, there are no tricks."

I glare at him and then at the discarded sword, and for some unknown reason, I choose to believe him. I grip the handle and let the weight of it settle into my body. I adjust my stance to accompany the shift in mass. If I weren't mistaken, the thing was tailored specifically to fit my exact hand.

"Did I get the measurements correct?" There's a strange sort of gleam in his onyx eyes. "What do you think?"

"I think you should stop talking and get on with it." I wait for him to charge.

"Do we really have to do this?" Balial holds his sword nonchalantly in his hand. "Can't you just give in so we can go home?"

I've had enough with him thinking I would ever follow through with being his. Over my dead body. I've let the rage simmer long enough. It's now or never.

I take off in a sprint toward him and strike his blade. A loud clank sounds, and my forearms tremble from the reverberations. I spin around to the left and circle his back, slicing toward his ankles.

Balial jumps to avoid the blow and whirls to block another of my cracks. He smiles, and for the slightest second, he seems younger. I'd go so far as to say happy even. What a strange sight on the Devil himself.

I push away the intrusive thoughts and match my blade to his. I take the lead, playing offense with every swing of the perfectly crafted weapon in my grasp. I continue moving forward, walking Balial back into a nearby tree. The second I think I have some kind of control over what's going on, he throws me for a curveball and advances on me.

I hate that he so easily switched gears and now I'm blocking his blows.

He forces me farther away from the clearing and into the area with the flowing water.

I catch the sight of a bountiful waterfall in my peripheral vision.

He's taking me farther than I had hoped for, and I'm quickly losing any sense of confidence I had going into this.

That is, until the slightest tickle of power slowly drips into my body.

A devious grin spreads across my face, and somehow, it's the very thing I need to throw *him* off his game.

All at once, magic flows into me, igniting my senses and bringing forth a renewed sense of life that I wasn't so sure I'd ever had the pleasure of feeling again. It's warm and comforting and vibrant. It's Silas and Deghan all at one beautiful moment, coursing through my veins simultaneously. I only let it simmer for a split second before calling it forward, enriching the blade that Balial had made for me and using it against him.

I take authority over the swordfight and regain my advance on him.

"I'm not going to lie," Balial says through the clanking of metal on metal. "I did not see that one coming." He dodges my blow. "Got you a conduit back home, do ya? Those are rarer than a Malachi. And you have both."

I answer him with a magically infused crack of my sword. I nick his shoulder and draw the faintest first blood.

"You're really going to have to stop ruining my best clothes." Balial jumps out of the way and rubs the spot where I got him. He sighs and launches himself back into battle.

Just by the manner he goes to and fro shows me that he has way more control over this situation than he's letting on. If I'm going to win this, I'm going to have to play dirty.

CHAPTER 36

I summon my purple-and-gold magic, and upon my next slam, I toss a ball of power at him with my left hand. I latch on to the handle and grip it tightly, infusing it with whatever strength is within me. Sydney's mighty aura gives me a gentle comfort as it joins my reserves. A trickle of emerald sparkles across the blade.

"I didn't realize you were so loved. Although..." Balial spins around and dodges my next blow. "I'm not at all surprised." He slices the air when I escape from his attack.

"You talk a lot." I run up a small boulder and leap off of it toward him.

He narrowly misses the assault. "What can I say, you bring it out in me." Balial winks at me despite the roaring sword fight we're engaged in.

He's barely winded, and that alone pisses me off.

I may have three sources of magic flowing through my veins, but I'm still injured and weak from my previous battles. And I'm sure as shit out of breath. If I had spent more time training with Charles, I should have worked on my endurance. I wasn't aware I'd have to partake in a marathon combat.

I plant my feet firmly on the hard ground and channel my men into my every move. I blast my sword down onto Balial's and somehow slice the very tip of it off. Sparks go flying, and sincere surprise crosses his face.

"Wow." Balial strengthens his grasp and pushes his black magic into the thing, renewing the severed edge. "I may have met my match."

He easily towers over me and he's clearly more powerful. Why is he taking his sweet time in finishing me off? Why doesn't he attack at full strength and end this here? Why prolong the inevitable? To allow me to think I stood a chance? To lessen my embarrassment of having the king of the underworld defeat me?

If anything, it's been an honor to make it this far. I'd rather not have charity be the reason why I'm still standing.

"Why are you holding back?" I duck to avoid his blow and slice at his legs.

He jumps out of the way and laughs. "Who said I was?"

Our weapons clang together, and we maintain that stance, inches apart with our swords pressed firmly into each other, neither of us wanting to give in.

I narrow my gaze and focus on melting him with my eyes. A purple current flows from my pupils and onto his cheek.

He thrusts me forward and away from him. "That was a low blow."

I do my best attempt at winking. "All is fair in love and war."

Balial smirks. "Actually, it's *the rules of fair play do not apply in love and war.*"

I take a deep breath and pull more of my magic to the surface and into my blade. "Never would have pegged you as a fan of poetry." I hit him with all my might and slice off another section of his sword.

He quickly replenishes it. "You'd be pleasantly surprised if you took the chance to get to know me."

"I know all I need to." The thought of Silas being tortured is enough to knock me out of this playful stupor. The rage within pours out onto my blade, and with my next blow, I knock Balial's out of his hands. I steady my gaze on it and send it flying out of his reach.

I point my sharp edge at him, but he doesn't seem bothered.

Balial takes a bold move toward it, resting the tip against his throat. "I can make another." He flicks his wrist and removes the weapon from my grasp, throwing it somewhere near where his went.

A low growl leaves my chest as I muster my power into my hands. My skin glows a radiant shade of green and purple and gold. I throw both of my fists into the air toward the horrible man standing in front of me.

He stumbles backward but regains his composure and blocks my power with his black current.

Our magic meets in the middle, playing a dangerous game of tug of war with each other. Whoever's stronger will be the one that wins, and I know with certainty that it's only a matter of time before mine gives out completely.

I'm no match to Balial. I never was, and I never will be. He'll always be one step ahead. Everyone was right, this was a losing battle. And I was the biggest fool of them all to think I ever stood a chance at defeating him.

I won't give up, though, not yet. I pour everything I have into standing my ground and quite literally giving him my all. I have never been a quitter, and now will not be the time I start.

"I don't want to hurt you," Balial says overtop the blaring noise of our powers fighting each other. "Just say the words and this will all be over."

"Never," I yell back at him.

He strengthens his stream and pushes me down onto my knees. He has the upper hand and he knows it. He has me beat.

A tear rolls down my cheek. All I wanted to do was make him pay for what he put Silas through. To take back my magic and force him to suffer the same wrath Silas did. I was disillusioned to think that the many times I did the impossible, this would be another one of them. A difficult challenge that I would somehow overcome. Because that's what I do.

My entire life has been one giant shit show after the next, but I have never not powered through and come out on top. I put too much confidence in my ability to persevere. And now I will finally meet my end.

I cower on the ground but continue pulsing every single ounce of magic I have left in me. I don't focus on the pain scorching my skin, my eyes, my head. I disregard the warm trickle coming from my nose and the ringing in my ears. I will die here, one way or another, before I submit to him.

But instead of death, a faint shimmer of Lillian passes through my veins, giving me just a little more strength. I smile alongside the tears flowing down my cheeks. She's with me when I meet my end and there's a sort of comfort in knowing that.

Headmaster Walker isn't too far behind, joining in with his crisp and bountiful strength.

Balial tilts his head and narrows his gaze. "That's impossible."

I cough up blood and spit it onto the cold hard dirt. I wipe my mouth on my shoulder and keep pressing on. I am not a coward and I refuse to die like one.

Balial shoves his arms forward, suppressing even the new magic I have in my supply.

Nothing I do could possibly match his sheer depth of muscle.

"Give in, Willow." Balial grits his teeth. "I'm hurting you."

I shake my head. "You were hurting me long before we started."

Balial acts dumbfounded. "Is this about that vampire boy?"

I slam my magic into him and barely make him budge.

"You think you love him. And that's okay. But you will learn to love me. After all, we have eternity." Balial maintains his flow steady against me.

A fresh magic enters my system. It's familiar and foreign all at the same time. It's bright and chipper and a level of relief only one person could offer.

Mom.

I choke on a sob that bubbles out of me. I don't know how she's here, but she is, and for that I am grateful.

"Just give it time." Balial stares at me through our glaring magical forces shattering into each other.

I dig my footing into the ground and somehow find the strength to regain my purchase on this land. I grit my teeth and scream the words at him one at a time. "I. Will. Never. Love. You."

I straighten my posture and thrust my hands toward him, pushing back the heavy advantage he had on me with my rainbow-colored magic.

Another burst of light enters my system, followed by another. Soon, there are more unrecognizable sources of magic than those I am accustomed to. I use the advantage to take one step at a time closer and closer until we are neck and neck in this blistering final battle.

Dozens of currents of power surge through my veins, threatening to explode them. I call upon them to unleash at my fingertips and take control of this once seemingly impossible situation.

Balial grunts and pushes with all his might, but his magic is showing weakness against mine. Concern pours out of him in heaps as I continue to inch farther on his side of the battlefield.

A glaring angelic light appears from my palms, strengthening the lead I have on him. It's blinding and glorious, and I refuse to let up. I had thought the angels left me the instant Silas vanished with Sydney's parents, but maybe they were holding out for this very moment.

It's not long until I'm the one pushing Balial to the ground and towering atop this pathetic excuse of a man. I surge forward and continue on and on, taking every single millimeter I can.

Finally, just as I'm about to break the last remaining bit of his black magic and completely annihilate him, he calls out, "Mara em. Mara em!"

I back off from ending him, but only slightly. "You give up?"

Blood trickles down my chin and onto his petrified face.

"Yes. I give in."

"You swear it? This isn't some trick?" I stare at him intensely and desperately try to read his intentions.

"I promise. You have defeated me."

Relief flashes over my entire being, and I fight the urge to vomit and pass out.

A laugh finds its way out of my mouth, and the next thing I know, my entire world fades away.

CHAPTER 37

I'm either dead or dreaming. Neither of them really matters to me at this point.

All I know is that I won.

I beat Balial. And even if I died in the process and I dreamt up his submission, the satisfaction of watching and sensing the fear pass through him was enough to make everything absolutely fucking worth it.

But, if this is death, why does it hurt so bad?

I try to pry my eyes open, but I can't. Or maybe they are, and I'm blind.

The last thing I recall was the blasting light seeping from my palms and Balial admitting I had bested him.

Oh, what sweet reprieve at hearing him concede.

My head is pounding, so much that there might be a second

heart beating inside of it. Is that my brain thumping against my skull?

I taste blood, which makes sense considering it was oozing out of all the holes on my face. Which, speaking of, has a pretty gnarly gash that has dulled down to a mild throb.

Voices appear, and feet shuffle against the ground.

I suddenly realize it's cold here and I'm shivering. At least I have some kind of control over my body, even if it's not totally on purpose. It's probably a good thing I'm reacting to the frigid temperature, right?

Wind whips by.

"Angels," Silas's sweet voice rings clear. "Willow, can you hear me?"

I mumble something in return but fail at forming anything coherent. Why am I struggling to maintain function?

"She's over here," Silas calls out into the rustling of leaves headed our way. "Will, love. I'm going to pick you up." He slides his hands under my frail form and winces.

I have a feeling it's because of me, not him.

I must look like shit. My bad.

Silas raises me off the ground and into his arms.

Regardless of how careful he tries to be, the shift in weight still sends shockwaves of pain coursing through me.

No one ever said that battling the Devil would be easy.

"I'm here," Silas mutters into my hair on our trek to wherever he's taking me. "I'm not going to leave you. You're safe now. You did it. Willow, you did it."

His voice pacifies me and lulls me back into the darkness. I'm safe now, in his arms, and that's all that matters.

"Take her to the infirmary," Walker's voice wakes me from my dreamless slumber.

More shuffling and muffled sounds follow.

"Is she okay?" someone whispers.

"She's in pretty bad shape," another person answers.

I don't recognize them at all. If I'm at the academy, shouldn't it only be Walker, Lillian, and the guys? Who are these other mysterious beings?

A large gasp is followed by thumping footsteps. "Willow." That one is undeniably my mother. "Oh, my sweet girl." Her voice fades. "What can I do?"

I recall her magic flowing through me during the final moments of the battle.

Someone else chimes in. A man this time. "She's lost a lot of blood. She might need a transfusion. Are you a compatible donor?" This guy touches me with something cold. "Her heart rate is low. Get her onto the table."

Silas gently lowers me onto the cold metal bench. "Stay with me, please." He doesn't let go of my hand.

"I'm going to need to remove her shirt."

Silas growls and stops the man in his tracks.

"Silas, you have let him do his job." Sydney steps forward and takes my other hand. "Come on Will, you're going to make it."

"The room is too crowded," the doctor figure says.

"Let them in," Silas demands.

More shuffling and soothing presences.

"We're here, Willow." Deghan grazes my cheek.

"We're not going anywhere," Cameron confirms.

I finally gain the strength to open my eyes again. I find myself in my own bed in my dorm, except it's been modified. I'm hooked to various beeping machines, and oxygen tubes are up my nose holes.

I clear my parched throat.

Silas nearly jumps out of his chair and rushes over at vamp speed. "You're awake."

"Are you..." I reach up and cup his face in my palm. "Real?"

He smiles and melts into my embrace. "Yeah. I'm your Silas."

I soak up his warmth and take in the rest of the room.

Silas weaves his thumb around mine and kisses my knuckles.

"What happened?" I try to scoot and sit up, but I wince when I put pressure on my arms.

"Let me help." Silas guides me back and props me up with two fluffy pillows.

I glance out the window and see that it's pitch-black outside. It must be sometime in the middle of the night. I'm guessing I passed out for a few hours while they patched me up and hooked me to all this medical equipment.

I pat the spot next to me. "Sit. Tell me."

Silas exhales. "Where do I begin?"

"How long have I been out?" My voice is crackly, and I hate how weak it makes me sound. It probably matches my appearance.

"Two days." Silas rubs his neck. "A brutal two days." He nods to my body. "You sustained pretty serious injuries. Broken ribs. Severe burns to your face, shoulder, and arm. A fractured wrist. Bruised spleen. Severe dehydration and overexertion. Not to mention all the other bumps and cuts. I did what I could with our Malachi bond, but some things are out of my scope of expertise."

I place my fingers on top of his. "I didn't mean to worry you." Without thinking about it, I push a little calming energy into him. I pull away when I realize it wasn't borrowed magic this time —it was mine. I turn my wrist and allow the pink to seep to the surface.

I can barely believe my own eyes.

"You did it." Silas tucks my hair behind my ear. "You did the impossible."

I laugh and don't care that it sends a shock of discomfort through me. Tears flow down my cheeks, but this time it's not from anything other than pure fucking happiness.

Silas's mood shifts to something else, much more serious. "I, um…"

"What is it?" I force him to look at me.

"Remember that whole angelic calling ceremony that was going to happen?" Silas swallows like he's nervous about this topic.

"Yeah..." I anxiously wait for him to continue.

"It happened."

"And?" What isn't he telling me?

"They chose you."

I blink twice and try to process what he's saying. "Me?"

He nods his head. "Yep. I'm sure you felt it, but that's what all that extra magic was from. Once they crowned you the leader, they could recognize you were in danger. All of the coven leaders came along with numerous other powerful witches. They joined in to deliver every ounce of strength they could to assist you. It was incredible, really."

"Wow." No wonder I felt magic from so many unknown sources.

"You have such a big heart. It was only natural that they would love you so easily in return." He pauses. "You're *Queen Willow of the Witches* now, according to all of the supernatural world."

I have no clue what that entails, but it sure sounds a heck of a lot better than *Queen Willow of the Underworld*. And for that, I am grateful.

I don't know what life will look like from here on out, and for once I'm okay with that.

No matter what the universe or any other supernatural creature throws at me, I'll do everything I can to overcome each challenge. I didn't sign up to be an Oliver witch, yet I was blessed into this bloodline. I will never take that for granted. I will continue to overcome adversity and always focus on persevering, no matter the hurdle. Because what kind of woman would I be if I didn't choose to fight for what I believe in—for what's right? And at the end of each day, I will know with certainty that above all else, love conquers. That alone is something worth going to war over.

And the best part? I don't have to do it alone. My friends and loved ones have proven that they will always be there when I need them the most. With them and the four completely wonderful guys at my side, we will stand together and face each new enemy who threatens to bring darkness to this world.

EPILOGUE

"We need a bigger vehicle," Silas whines. "This is going to take all day."

"Aw, don't be a baby. Aren't you having fun?" Deghan punches Silas in the shoulder.

Silas rolls his eyes and crosses his arms.

I laugh at his clearly childish behavior and look out the back window of Sydney's car.

Today is moving day, and according to Silas, it's taking entirely too long.

"We could borrow my brother's truck," Cameron adds.

"See, why didn't we go with that?" Silas glances at me for a little backup.

I shrug and smile. There's no other place I'd rather be than shoved in here like sardines with the men I'm so incredibly in love with, driving around and picking up load by load of our stuff to move into our very own house together.

The five of us. Living under one roof.

We were doing that when we were at the academy, but with totally different circumstances. Now it's *our* place. Where we will share meals and make memories and grow as one unit.

A happy supernatural family of misfits.

I don't get much free time anymore, given I have an endless list of responsibilities now that I'm considered royalty and all. But with that came a few perks. Like the massive house that has been passed down from angelic generations to the next. Only, it's been a while since the mansion has been occupied, so we have a little work cut out for ourselves to get it up and running. It's on a large estate with plenty of land, allowing each one of us the freedom we need while supplying a level of intimacy our relationship deserves after all it's been through.

I'm looking forward to getting settled and finally making my plans to travel back to Hell to initiate Balial's torture sentence he agreed on. I didn't anticipate it taking this long to make my journey back there, but with recovering from my injuries, maintaining my cover story of falling down the stairs, and finishing up school, I figured I would hold off until the timing was right. My newfound position in the supernatural world has kept me busy enough. I didn't want to miss a precious moment of his torment because I was rushed by other things.

"Which way?" Sydney points to the grassy area ahead.

"Through those trees." Silas shows him the path.

A few bumpy minutes later, we pull up to Silas's tucked-away cabin in the woods.

He told us he didn't need to get anything, but we insisted that he take *something* to our new home.

All of us funnel out of the small but reliable car and walk up to the front door.

Dust fills the space as we walk inside. I'm assuming the last person here was me when I broke in during Silas's stint in Hell. I had missed him bad enough that I resorted to breaking and entering. Although, the key I found made it less of a criminal offense.

Silas flips the light on and goes straight to his bookshelf.

I skim through a stack of scattered papers on the table. I find one labeled *translations* and browse through until I catch sight of those two words that have been haunting me—*mara em.*

Next to them in parenthesis, *marry me.*

Balial would have been arrogant enough to make *me* ask *him* such a thing in my final moments. What an absolute coward, forcing a woman to plead with her life in such a fashion. I thank the angels every day that I was given the strength to overcome him.

I push the thought away. I refuse to allow him to take any more of my time and energy now that I defeated his stupid game.

"You've got some super old stuff in here," Cameron says while looking through a few trinkets on the stand near the door.

A sudden memory hits me from that moment I was rummaging through his space. I turn to Silas. "I can't believe you knew James Dean."

"No way," Deghan calls out.

Silas laughs, and there's something about it that lightens the mood of everyone else in the room. It's beautiful and simple and lets my heart know that everything will be all right.

We're all going to be okay.

And for me, that's enough.

Want more from this magical universe? Dive into Stolen by Monsters (Book One) of the Falling for the Enemy series!

Acknowledgments

What a wild ride this has been. This series tore my heart apart and challenged me in ways I never imagined. It was an unbelievable honor to tell Willow's and her mate's story. What was supposed to be a three-book series that turned into five, became a rollercoaster ride I never wanted to get off of. All of these characters will live on forever in my heart and I hope you enjoyed coming along on their wondrous journey.

I wrote this series during one of the most challenging times of my life. Willow and I shared heartbreak and grew together on these pages. I've had readers come to me and tell me how raw and real some things felt while reading this series and I owe that to my own experiences with love and loss. Granted, I'm not a supernatural creature, but, we all bleed the same. We all ache and hurt and grieve and have complex emotions. Allowing Willow to transform herself in the way that she did, was a tribute to who I am shaping myself to be. No matter what brokenness we face, we can be whole again.

We owe it to ourselves to fight like hell to overcome any impossible thing that comes our way. Just like Willow has done time and time again.

To my daughter—you give me the courage to be a woman you will forever look up to, even if you're going to be taller than me soon.

To my parents—for everything you've done for me, especially the last year.

Victoria—my bestie. *something mushy*

Kelsey & Kate—I am grateful this career has brought you both into my life.

My Patrons—Clayton, James, Tyler, and Victoria. Thank you for continuing to support my journey as an author.

My amazing PA—Niki Trento. And my immense support team—Kyliegh, Elizabeth, Sam, Michelle, Jo, Erin, Shannon, Dianne, Mindy, Raveen, Grace, Blt, and many, many more.

A few of my fellow authors who I admire tremendously— Yumoyori Wilson, M. Sinclair, Cassia Briar, Elle Lincoln, and Zoe Ashwood.

My editor, Emmy, and my cover design team, Mibl Art. I would not have such well-received books if it weren't for both of you!

And to you, my reader. Thank you for taking a chance on me. **Until we meet again. Forever, okay?**

Also by Luna Pierce

The Harper Shadow Academy Series

(Paranormal academy reverse harem)

Hidden Magic

Cursed Magic

Wicked Magic

Ancient Magic

Sacred Magic

Harper Shadow Academy: Complete Box Set

Falling for the Enemy Series

(Paranormal reverse harem)

Stolen by Monsters

Fighting for Monsters

Fated to Monsters

Sinners and Angels Universe

Broken Like You (Standalone)

Untamed Vixen (Part One)

Villain Era (Part Two)

Wings of a Devil (Standalone novella)

Ruin My Life (Standalone)

London & Archer's Story (Standalone)

About the Author

Luna Pierce is a paranormal and contemporary romance author who loves getting lost in her stories. She brings you tough characters that love fiercely and fight for what's right. Luna loves all things gritty, and even supernatural, especially: witches, vampires, and werewolves.

Join Luna's newsletter to receive updates at:
www.lunapierce.com/subscribe

If you enjoy my books, please consider leaving a review on Amazon, Goodreads, or BookBub.

Want to chat about the book and tell me the things you liked and disliked about **Sacred Magic**? I'd love to hear from you!

Join the exclusive reader group — Luna Pierce's Gritty Romance Squad